wrong FOR YOU

USA TODAY BESTSELLING AUTHOR
HARLOE RAE

Editor: Infinite Well
Cover designer: Harloe Rae
Photographer: Wander Aguiar
Model: Chris
Interior design: Champagne Book Design

novels by
HARLOE RAE

Reclusive Standalones
Redefining Us
Forget You Not

#BitterSweetHeat Standalones
Gent
Miss
Lass

Silo Springs Standalones
Breaker
Keeper
Loner

Quad Pod Babe Squad Standalones
Leave Him Loved
Something Like Hate
There's Always Someday
Doing It Right

Complete Standalones
Watch Me Follow
Ask Me Why
Left for Wild
Lost in Him
Mine For Yours
Wrong For You

Screwed Up (part of the Bayside Heroes standalones)

This book is dedicated to the backward hat flip, and to the fierce individuals who melt into a properly swooned mush puddle in sight of it.

For Niki too. You're a warrior. Stay strong always.

wrong FOR YOU

I used to believe Jacob Evans could be mine.
That was before he delivered unforgivable news rather
than sweeping me off my feet.
Not that I can fault his choice.
He got the sweetest little girl out of the deal.

I took the heartbreak as a learning experience and
moved on for the better.
Jake did the opposite—allowing
bitterness to fill the void.
Only his daughter can pull him from
the broody gloom.
Those moments are my favorite.

Not that it matters.
Jake isn't anything to me other than a reminder of
what almost was.

Besides, we couldn't be more wrong for each other.
I've come to accept that.
But as it turns out, Jake hasn't.

the jake & harper playlist

"Long Trip Alone" | Dierks Bentley
"Last Night" | Morgan Wallen
"It Must Have Been Love" | Roxette
"One Life" | Ed Sheeran
"The Climb" | Miley Cyrus
"The Kind Of Love We Make" | Luke Combs
"Hold Me While You Wait" | Lewis Capaldi
"Can't Help Falling In Love" | Samantha Harvey
"H.O.L.Y" | Florida Georgia Line
"You Are The Reason" | Calum Scott
"Tell Me That You Love Me" | James Smith
"Say You Won't Let Go" | Samantha Harvey
"I Feel Like I'm Drowning" | Two Feet
"Please Notice" | Christian Leave
"Fix You" | Coldplay
"Biblical" | Calum Scott

Wait.
Wait and you will see.
What I have waiting for you beneath.
It's beautiful and deep.
A sea without a beach.

—Harloe Rae

wrong

FOR YOU

prologue

Harper

GOSSIP IN A SMALL TOWN SHOULD BE IGNORED MORE often than not. I learned that lesson after my fifth-grade teacher almost quit her job based solely on spiteful hearsay. That doesn't stop the rumor I heard earlier from playing on repeat.

I whirl on my heel and pace to the tall oak that marks the hiking trail's entrance. Dust kicks up from my frantic stride as I turn to retrace my path for the ninth time. My skin is slick and balmy, which has little to do with the nerves eating at me. The July heat hasn't relented even as dusk casts shadows across the woods.

A twig snaps to my left and I pivot to see Jacob Evans—the one I've been waiting for in more ways than one. I rush forward to fling myself at him. Fresh pine blended with lingering traces of motor oil and fraying patience welcomes me.

My arms struggle to encircle his torso as I soak in his sturdy warmth. Jake is already broad and muscular, far larger than the boys I just graduated with. His steady pulse drums beneath my ear and soothes me. I breathe him in again while trying to silence the doubt pestering me. Everything is going to be okay.

"You came." Stark relief raises my voice to an embarrassing pitch.

"Said I would." Meanwhile, his tone is flat and stiff.

The brittle response sets off an alarm in my brain. Denial and desperation have me clinging tighter to him. It's only then I realize he isn't returning my embrace. Toned arms that rarely hesitate to haul me in stay glued to his sides.

I step back from the false comfort of his presence to do a quick assessment. Only three years separate us, but Jake appears older than twenty-one right now. There's an underlying tension thrumming from him. His rigid posture matches the stony expression avoiding my gaze. The dark features I could trace from memory are purposely guarded.

Only his eyes reveal emotion. A barely contained storm swirls in those blue depths. Jake must feel my imploring scrutiny and bites off a curse from his clenched jaw.

"Please tell me it's not true." I lift trembling fingers to my lips.

He averts his stare further from mine. "Afraid I can't do that."

Fire blasts under my skin as understanding dawns. I lunge at him, bunching his shirt in my fist. "You cheated on me?"

No wonder he was willing to wait until I was ready to lose my virginity. The good guy act was just for show. He's really an asshole in disguise, getting action elsewhere.

"Didn't fucking cheat." The icy retort might as well be frozen shards stabbing at my flesh.

I scoff to hide the pain. "How else do you explain getting Morgan pregnant when you're dating me?"

Jake pins me with a glare, but his face remains an impassive mask otherwise. "It happened before we started seeing each other."

"And she just found out about the baby?" Disbelief drips from my snarky reply.

"Guess so," he drawls.

"That would make her four or five months along. She should've noticed her missing period much sooner."

He shrugs. The motion is jerky, much like the rest of him. "Don't ask me."

My fingers clench the fabric still in my hold. "Are you sure the baby is yours?"

"I'll get the test done, but there's no reason for me to assume she's lying."

None of this makes sense. Heat begins to collect in my eyes. His indifference is worse than this unpleasant detour. He's already shutting me out, minutes after confirming what I swore was fake news. Too many thoughts and emotions pummel me at once. I'm more confused than anything. Answers would be appreciated.

"But when…? How…?" It seems that I can't form a proper sentence. "You told me this is exclusive between us. That you'd wait until I was ready."

Jake dips his head in acknowledgment. "Already

said we are, or were. I slept with her in March. It was just once. Hadn't talked to her since until she texted yesterday."

That's a lot to digest, but my mind snags on a single word. "Were? As in, past tense?"

The defeated grimace pinching his expression is telling. Then he's withdrawing further behind the blank walls he thinks I can't see through. "This is over between us, Harper. I have to do what's right for Morgan and the baby."

It feels like my chest is caving in with that declaration. I could gasp or scream or wail, but that won't accomplish a damn thing. It's not as if I expected him to stay with me while another woman has his child. I did think he'd be more upset about it, though. For my benefit if nothing else.

That's precisely why I pound my fist against his sternum. If only I could break through and shatter his hardened resolve. Just for a moment to prove he gives a shit about me. A sob rips from my tight throat and I thump him again. It's silly to be this upset over something I never had. That doesn't stop a lone tear from escaping, though.

"Knock it off, Pitchy. What's done is done." He pries my fingers from his shirt, releasing me without care.

I let my hand drop with the weight of his rejection. His use of my nickname is a hammer to my crumbling heart. I turn away from him to shield the hurt streaming down my cheeks.

"I thought we had something special," I whisper into the dark. Our chance at happiness goes up into thin air with my foolish dreams.

"It's better this way. You and I weren't meant to last."

My eyes squeeze shut, sending more sorrow down my face. "Don't be cruel."

He kicks the dirt and a rock rolls toward me. "Nah, I'm being honest."

Which delivers the parting blow. There's nothing left to discuss. If he wants to pretend our relationship is that disposable, I can play along.

I give myself two more seconds to mourn what could've been. The ache in my chest doesn't cease, but I don't reveal the cracks splintering through me. My heart pumps and air continues to flow into my lungs. On the grand scale of shitty situations, this bump in the road doesn't deserve mention.

My sandals grind into the ground as I spin to face him. I ignore the burn spreading from behind my breastbone. The grin I force to appear might as well be made from plastic. But I'm the picture of acceptance.

I swipe at my wet cheeks to erase the leftover evidence. "You're right. It's for the best."

Jake rocks backward. His lips part and press together to a disjointed tempo. For the first time, he seems to flounder for a response. "Yeah?"

My head bobs in agreement. "I'm leaving for college at the end of August. There's a dorm room on campus with my name on it."

And I couldn't get there fast enough after this relationship demolition.

"Thought you were commuting?"

"Plans change," I clip.

Something painful flickers over his features before he smothers it. Then he's the mask of indifference. "Right."

"So, I guess this is goodbye." My voice cracks, but I ignore the stumble.

Jake squints at me. "You're good with this?"

"Absolutely." I laugh, but the tone is humorless. "And congratulations. You're gonna be a dad."

His eyes blow wide, and he drags a hand through his dark hair. "Shit, that's weird to hear."

"You'll get used to it."

"Not much of an alternative, huh?"

"Good luck." My smile wobbles with the farewell.

He pauses to study me again. "Why are you acting so chill?"

"My pity party came to an abrupt end. You told me to knock it off, remember?"

A breeze stirs at that moment. He glances at the swaying branches above. I allow my gaze to follow his lead. What little brightness still exists on this day shines through the leaves. It offers us much-needed peace.

His stare is unfocused when he looks at me next, but determination squares his shoulders. "I'm sorry, Harper."

"Don't be."

"But—"

"You're starting a family. There's nothing sorry about that." Or that's what I'll trick myself to believe.

Jake's sigh sounds heavier than the elephant crushing my chest. My throat clogs as conflict pinches his somber appearance. He fidgets, curling his fingers into white-knuckle fists. Muscles bunch and twitch beneath his shirt. It almost looks like he wants to reach out to me. But then, just as before, his features return to their stoic state.

The sight is almost too much for me to balance on

this teetering farce. I gulp to trap the hiccupped sob ready to betray me.

After a single nod, Jake turns away. His retreating footsteps threaten to weaken my willpower. I want to chase him. Beg him to choose me. But that would be selfish. His path is heading in a different direction. One I can't follow.

I can only watch him leave our love behind.

chapter one

Jake

TIGHTEN THE FINAL BOLT ON THE FORD'S LATEST REPAIR under its rusty hood. The wrench drops from my grip, landing in the box at my feet with a satisfying clank. That signals the end of a packed week at the garage.

A glance out the front window warns me that a celebration is premature. Snow is just beginning to fall. Streams of white flakes are visible in the glow of the nearest floodlight. It might be late February, but winter in Minnesota isn't ready to quit. We're predicted to get no less than six inches. And that's not all.

After a day above freezing and the temperature plunging after dark, the roads are bound to be slick. Countless calls for a tow will begin soon after. Maybe Penn or Kade will join me for a few extra hours on the clock. But that's a worry for later. First, I'm going to close up shop and take a load off at Roosters.

Several joints crack when I stretch my back. The persistent ache in my muscles makes me feel old and weary, yet I'm still two years short of thirty. It's my spirit that's tired—a fact that's highlighted as I stare straight ahead at a night alone with nothing but an empty house to keep me company. I scoff at the downward direction of my thoughts. No sense in wallowing when there's still work to be done.

I hop in the truck, slide the key into the ignition, and crank hard for good measure. Another job done right is revealed when the newly fixed engine roars to life without a single sputter. That smooth rumble is a mechanic's greatest prize. It almost eases the strain in my shoulders until the tires spin on wet slush that's already layering the lot. The reminder kicks me into higher gear.

Once I get the pickup parked out front, I jog to the lobby where the owner is waiting. The bell jingles to announce my entrance. A blast of heat welcomes me, chasing off the bitter chill. Pete is next to greet me with a sharp nod. I offer him one in return, brush the melting snow from my shirt, and switch off the neon sign that proclaims the shop is open.

He stands from his seat while I move to lock the door that connects to the shop. His hitched gait matches the deep wrinkles lining his face.

"How's the new hip treating you?" I walk behind the desk, jutting my chin at his noticeable limp.

He leans heavily on the counter. "Better than the old one."

"It's good to see you upright again."

"Bet it is. Must've been hard to get by without your best customer."

I snort. "Sure was. Speaking of, here's the recent damage."

Pete barely spares a glance at the itemized invoice I set in front of him. "Appreciate you stayin' late to fix her for me."

"Got nowhere else to be." Other than the bar, which is calling my name.

"Is Sydney with her mom this weekend?"

I glare at the old man who knows better than to ask. It's not a secret I try to hide. The entire town is all too aware of the drama surrounding our dysfunctional family unit. News is bound to spread in a community the size of Knox Creek. Small population aside, Morgan Jones carries the reputation of being unreliable like a designer purse. Unfortunately, that toxic trait spills over to her involvement with our daughter.

Morgan is lacking at best where Sydney is concerned. The urge to spout uglier—though accurate—terms claws at my throat. Her presence in our little girl's life has declined with each passing year. If it were my choice, I'd cut our losses and gain full custody. We'll be signing the paperwork by summer if her flakey habits are any indicator. I doubt Morgan would hesitate to surrender her parental rights. Her last visit was over three months ago, for deadbeat's sake. It's gotten to the point where I assume she's done with us.

If only it could be so simple.

Her extended absence suits me fine. But Sydney

still asks about her. She loves her mother, as she should. Too bad Morgan has a shitty way of returning the affection. It almost pains me to think it's because she doesn't care. I just can't fathom how else she could leave Syd behind, not to mention break every promise since. My hands curl into fists as I recall the crushing disappointment that crosses my little girl's face too often.

The last time her mother didn't follow through, I made a vow to protect Sydney from feeling abandoned. That's why I don't tell her Morgan is coming until I see the woman on my doorstep. Eventually, something has to give. I'll do everything in my power to ensure that isn't Sydney. She's sacrificed more than I care to admit. But I refuse to influence Syd's opinion, regardless of the innate instinct that demands I should. It's a battle I fight with each breath.

Rather than feed the hate festering in my gut, I gulp and give Pete curt honesty. "Syd is staying with a friend."

"Glitzy too?"

My lips twitch at the mention of my daughter's beloved Pomeranian. "Another question you don't need to ask."

"Doesn't hurt to check on you."

I grunt at the transparent excuse. "For no reason other than to satisfy your curiosity."

The old man stoops lower, as if we aren't alone in the small room. "Listen, kid. You're the only one that sweet princess needs. Don't let anyone tell you different."

Warmth spreads through me at his high praise.

I cough to cover the rising emotion. "Kissing my ass after trying to dig for dirt?"

Pete's wrinkles deepen with a crooked smirk. "Can you blame me when my better half is the self-proclaimed driver of Knox Creek's gossip train? If I came home with a juicy bite for her to chew on, I'd be handsomely rewarded."

"Give Claudia my best, yeah?" I tap the invoice in a silent reminder.

He squints at the total, a thick sigh pushing past his lips. "Trying to get rid of me?"

I watch the snow fall faster. "The roads are gonna be shit soon."

Pete turns to follow my gaze. "Suppose I better get home. It'd be real unfortunate if I'm one of those you're hauling from the ditch later. You've taken enough of my money already."

"Wouldn't be an issue if you'd get a new truck rather than insisting on fixing this beater." My chin juts in the general direction of his rusty Ford.

"Why would I bother with all that when you keep her in such pristine condition?"

"Just looking out for you and your wallet."

"That's awful considerate," he drawls while pulling out his credit card.

"Sometimes I surprise myself." I get his bill paid, passing over the receipt. "Guess I shouldn't complain about the business."

"Probably not." He pats my shoulder. "You followin' me out?"

"Yep, I'll be right behind you. Gonna grab a beer while I still can."

"Wise man." Pete seems to consider his options.

I round the desk and usher him toward the door. My jacket is waiting for me on a hook. "Don't make Claudia worry about you."

"Yeah, yeah," he grumbles.

"Drive safe, okay?" I watch as he gingerly steps up into the cab of his pickup.

"Same to you, kid." With that parting remark, Pete pulls from the lot and disappears from sight.

I'd be more concerned if his house wasn't two miles down the road. Knox Creek isn't large by any stretch of the imagination. Even in a blizzard, it wouldn't take more than thirty minutes to cross from one end to the other on a snowmobile.

When the icy wind smacks my cheeks, I lock the deadbolt and tread carefully toward the three vehicles parked in a row. My boots crunch in the fresh snow with each step. In an attempt to be proactive, I choose one of the tow trucks. I slide behind the wheel, blast the heat, and turn onto Main Street.

The windshield wipers squeak in a lazy cycle as I drive the three blocks to Roosters. My favorite watering hole glows brightly like a damn beacon reaching out to haul me in. There just so happens to be a spot out front along the curb with my name on it.

A vicious chill attacks me as I hurry to the entrance. The temperature is dropping by the second. Calls might start streaming in before I can even park my ass on a stool. I yank the door open and squint against the brightness. My eyes are quick to adjust thanks to the dim setting.

It only takes a single breath to spot the blonde

bombshell attempting to blend in with the sports memorabilia and rustic wood décor. The clench in my gut bellows that she doesn't belong, especially not slinging drinks behind the bar.

But the logo stamped on her shirt and the apron tied around her curvy waist suggests otherwise.

chapter two

Harper

"YOU BETTER BE FUCKING JOKING."

I wince at Jake's bellowed outrage that can be heard across the entire bar. From my section a few paces away, the battle cry almost topples me sideways. The counter keeps me upright as I study his furious expression.

Reflections from the overhead bank of televisions flicker in his glare. Beneath the scruff coating his jaw, a muscle pops and twitches. Veins bulge in his inked forearms while he stands too still. Steam is going to spew from his ears at any second. The reaction sends a giddy thrill through me. I'm easy to please like that.

Garrett Foster is the first to intercept the new arrival's hostility. Roosters' cocky—pun intended—owner doesn't look flustered in the least as he props an elbow on the wood counter separating them. "Hey, Evans. What's got your panties in a twist?"

"You hired Harper?" His tone could slice through rock.

My boss tosses me a wink before answering. "Sure did."

From where I stand, I can hear Jake's molars grind. "Why?"

"Not that it's any of your concern, but she asked. My sister would have my ass if I turned her best friend away. I'm not gonna be the target of a pregnant woman's hormones."

The grumpy asshole still hasn't sat down. He just looms like a thunderous cloud waiting to strike. "That's all it takes to get a job in this place?"

"Are you unhappy about my methods?"

"Yes."

Garrett rolls his eyes. "Too damn bad."

"You're choosing her over me?" Jake cringes as if the words taste bad.

"If you're stooping to that petulant level, I'll choose me over you. I don't question how you run your garage. If you need to be in control, feel free to mosey on back to where you just came from."

"It's gonna be like that?"

"Apparently," my boss retorts. "You seem to have an issue with a member of my staff, which concerns me. Harper is a model employee. The compliments from customers are already flooding in. I'm not sure what your problem is with her, but keep it away from my business."

I preen under the praise but choose to remain silent. For now.

Jake's fierce glare slides to me. Tension crackles as our eyes collide. There's a promise of retaliation in his gaze, as if my employment status at his beloved bar is offensive.

"This is bullshit," he spits.

"Matches your temper tantrum," Garrett scoffs. "Can I get back to work without you causing another scene?"

The grumbling brute slides onto an empty stool. "Yeah, yeah. Fuck off."

The bar owner just laughs in the face of Jake's shitty attitude. "That's the spirit."

Before Garrett leaves the scene, he glances at me and signals that he'll just be on the other side of the room. I smile and wave him off. The supportive gesture is appreciated but unnecessary. Bickering with Jacob Evans has become somewhat of a standard affair. This is just another opportunity to sharpen my skills.

While a thrum surges under my skin, I shift my attention to the man responsible for unnecessary turmoil. Jake's startling blue eyes are already pinned on me. That icy stare is cold enough to freeze a lake in July. I wiggle my fingers at him in return. There's not a chance in this century that I'll let him see me crumble. Been there, done that, and moved on.

Although, that last point isn't one hundred percent solid.

Curiosity hooks into me like an addiction I can't kick. I don't have the foggiest clue what I've done to trigger his wrath. It's almost as if he has a personal vendetta against me. That's why I can't seem to stay away, even though he's wrong for me.

I square my shoulders and strut toward him. My

pulse drums against my sternum, pounding faster as I near his broody presence. The air grows thicker as he watches my approach. His steady focus is predatory, and I'm the prey willingly crossing into dangerous territory.

My shoes squeak on the rubber mat when I stop in front of him. I can't get too close without wanting to erase the space between us entirely. That's a slippery slope I have no intention of sliding down. But even from a safe distance, his spicy cologne teases me. Just one more reason to slam my guard down.

"Why the sour face, Jerky Jacob?"

If possible, his scowl stoops lower. "Real cute."

"At your service." I fluff my hair in a theatrical fashion.

Jake rips his gaze off me with a foul curse. "And here I thought the week was going well."

"Aww, shucks. You say the sweetest things." I cross one hand over the other and lift them to rest under my chin, blinking with mock adoration. Then I drop the act and pop out a hip. "Are you going to order something or continue loitering?"

"Tall Coors," he mutters.

I grab a glass and pour his beer from the tap. It's encouraging that my hands don't shake under his watchful stare. "Would you like to start a tab?"

He's silent as I set his drink down on a fresh coaster. Thick fingers curl around the chilled glass, lifting until he's glaring at me over the frothy rim. A bit of foam sticks to his full upper lip when he's done taunting me with that slow sip. "You had to choose Roosters?"

It doesn't go unnoticed that he ignored my question. That prompts me to do the same. "Is Syd at Polly's house? Susan is the sleepover hostess with the mostest. She probably deserves an award."

Jake sneers at my choice of topic. It's not a secret that his daughter is his soft spot. She's also the only— and safest—subject we can agree on. "Why do you care?"

"Sydney is my student." A fact that grates on his nerves and brings me pure delight. His little girl is proof that one piece of him isn't completely rotten, small as that sliver might be.

"You teach her to twirl and point her toes for an hour twice a week. That's not vital for her education."

The dig is a brutal strike, but my smile doesn't falter. "She loves to dance. That's why you're stuck paying me for classes."

"Wouldn't hear the end of it otherwise."

The victory is slight and feels petty. My skin crawls in the lull that follows. Some days, it's difficult to remember what I ever saw in this man. Then there are others where I struggle to reinforce our boundaries. Maybe there was an unflattering motive behind asking Garrett to hire me. Pressure lodges in my chest and I gulp for a decent breath.

"Excuse me," I mutter.

A break from the tension is required if I'm going to survive this shift. I trot off to check on my other customers. The crowd isn't too thick thanks to the falling snow.

After closing a check and grabbing two refills, I circle round to the one I can't stray too far from. I tell myself the magnetic pull is just an instinct to hold my ground. Jake doesn't intimidate me. This is my turf too. Besides, I have a job to do.

"Can I get you anything else?" Such as a swift kick off the stool he insists on occupying.

Before Jake can answer, his phone buzzes on the counter. I'd heard the thing rattle against the wood on and off for several minutes. He ignores it, keeping his gaze firmly trained on me. There's a brief pause where I tap my foot in time with the country song that's blasting from the speakers. Then the vibrations begin again.

"Aren't you gonna get that?" I point at the lit screen of his phone on the counter. It doesn't seem to be stopping anytime soon.

He still doesn't drop his stare. "I got Kade handling it."

"Oh? I figured you'd be taking the lead on towing this evening." My eyes shift to the front window, where I can see his garage's truck parked along the curb.

Jake takes a swig from his beer. "Gonna tell me why you felt the need to get a job at this bar in particular?"

"If you tell me why it bothers you so much," I quip.

"This is where I come to unwind and relax. I can't do that with you"—his large hand flings in my direction—"hovering nearby."

I laugh to cover my sputtered exhale. "Careful, or you'll make me feel special."

"Wouldn't dream of it."

The force from his unwavering focus shifts away from me. His gaze roams over the other people in my section along the rail. I follow his drifting attention to three guys who aren't shy about ogling my ass. The trio appears to be near my age, mid-twenties or so. Cute enough to consider. Not stingy with tipping either, which is a bonus in this new gig. They notice me looking and raise their drinks in a synchronized motion. I reciprocate with a wave, which earns me triple grins.

Roosters has a no-frills vibe that appeals to a certain crowd of the male variety. The painted brick walls are cluttered with sports memorabilia and beer signs. Oversized booths frame the sides while an assortment of tables are scattered across the wide room. The bar section is monopolizing, staged front and center. There isn't a fancy cocktail menu or excessive food options. But we're popular with the locals.

A wistful grin blooms as my attention sweeps to the dining area nestled in the far corner. On busy weekends when the crowd gets restless, if Garrett and the other owners are in a good mood, a portion of that space gets cleared for a makeshift dance floor. Those nights are my favorite. Other than that, it's pretty basic.

"Bent Pedal is better suited for you," Jake cuts in.

I huff and tack on an eye roll at his suggestion. Not that there's anything wrong with the posh establishment farther down Main Street. Rhodes and Rylee Walsh are lovely, as are their adorable kids. But Roosters is closer to home—in more ways than one.

There's no doubt my smile is smug. "I'm here to stay. Deal with it or feel free to leave."

Jake's glare manages to find another level of intensity and I nearly shiver. "You're doing this on purpose."

"Doing what? This bar and town are big enough for both of us."

Although, I can silently admit it isn't easy seeing him daily. There are a handful of happy memories between us. That was before he ripped my heart apart and stomped on the remains, of course. I cringe at the pain

I'm still harboring in my dampened spirits. That was years ago.

He reads my pinched expression like a picture book. A smirk dipped in malice tilts his mouth. "Sure about that, Pitch?"

"Nice try," I chirp. With added effort, I smooth my features into an impassive mask. It's not like I'm going to reveal what that old nickname does to me. "I'm not stooping to your level. There's nothing for us to fight about."

"Oh, fuck that. You're not making me out to be the only bad guy."

"I wouldn't dream of it." My lashes flutter at him as I recite his earlier phrase. "Besides, you do that all on your own."

Every muscle in Jake's body coils tight. That's when his cell begins buzzing for the sixth time in as many minutes. He releases a muffled curse and stands. "That's my cue."

"It takes six to get you off your ass? How fitting. I'll be sure to remember that." Shouldn't be hard seeing as that's how long he's been brewing this animosity toward me.

He tosses cash on the bar to cover his tab. "Don't expect me to answer your call."

"That shouldn't be a problem, seeing as I'd never bother."

Jake takes a final glance around Roosters. "Unbelievable."

"You're too kind. Better hurry to the door before I fall in love with you."

Most would miss his reaction, but I'm not most. His

eyes are always the ones to betray him. For a brief flicker, the angry clouds part to display a different blue emotion. There's an unspoken hurt swirling within. He almost appears wounded.

While I attempt to trap a gasp, the stony indifference reclaims his handsome face. The shield is thicker than a chisel could break. Jake turns on his heel, stalks toward the exit, and storms away.

I offer him a farewell salute with his empty glass, not that he sees it. "Tootles, Jerky Jacob. Until next time."

chapter three

Jake

STARE AT THE COLORFUL PILE IN FRONT OF ME. DISBELIEF once again worms through logic. In one hand, I clutch four single socks. The other is used as a scoop to dig in the seemingly bottomless basket for a match. My hunt proves unsuccessful, only serving to taunt me with three more for the solo mound. There are several choice words tickling my tongue. It never ceases to amaze me how these damn things vanish.

Sydney giggles, breaking me from the pointless search. "You're doing it again, Daddy."

"Stumped over how the washer eats socks? Or maybe it's the dryer. Either way, it's a nonstop cycle. Put a matching pair in and only one comes out. It doesn't make sense, Boop. A real mystery."

"No!" Her squeal is ripe with amusement. "You're

grumbling to someone I can't see. Do you have an imaginary friend?"

"That would be preferable," I mutter.

Her freckled face screws up. "Pref-a-what?"

"It means I wish there was a person to sort this puzzler out rather than just myself." Even if that individual is a product of my imagination.

Syd's wide smile slips into an exaggerated pout. "Are you lonely? Is it 'cause Mommy left?"

It takes heroic effort I don't possess to contain a grimace. "Nah, Boop. I'm used to her being gone."

And good fucking riddance. That woman is nothing but trouble. Chicago isn't far enough away for my personal preference.

The relief Morgan's absence brings vanishes when my little girl hunches her shoulders. "Me too."

Her disappointment is a sucker punch I can't prepare for. The secondhand sorrow is crippling, making me feel helpless even as I sit here trying my best. I silently curse her mother for putting us in this position. It would be easier for everyone if she stayed away permanently. But that tough option won't help right now.

"Hey," I say softly. "She'll come to visit you soon."

Sydney sniffs and drops her gaze. "Whatever. I don't care."

"C'mere, Boop." I lift my arms, beckoning her in for a hug. Nobody would accuse me of being the warm and fuzzy type. But for this precious princess, I'll be a gooey marshmallow.

My little girl doesn't hesitate to launch herself at me. We're silent for a beat as she soaks in the paternal affection I offer in abundance. It seems only fair, seeing as she taught me how to give freely. She won't be lacking unconditional love so long as I'm near. I rest my chin against her crooked ponytail while focusing on a framed photo of us from this past Christmas. Warmth spreads through my chest, happiness only she provides.

She loops her skinny arms around me, holding on with a strength that shocks me. "Promise you won't leave too."

The quiet demand is a sledgehammer to my composure. Tension coils in my gut, set to strike a very specific target. I want to rage in my daughter's defense. Bellow at the selfish choices and injustice I can't control. Then drag Morgan's ass back to Knox Creek so she can see the impact of her absence. Our child is suffering, and she couldn't care less.

My blood could boil in seconds just considering the long-term repercussions of Morgan's careless habits. It's one thing to chase dreams. To abandon who should be her main priority is another entirely. I couldn't make sense of it when she moved three summers ago. Understanding has yet to dawn on me.

Rather than stew in fury, I concentrate on staying calm. One forced exhale after the other and my wrath fizzles into a dull roar. My palm rubs Syd's back while I soothe the fear no child should know.

"I'm not going anywhere, Boop. You're stuck with me forever."

"M'kay, good. You're the bestest daddy ever," she whispers.

My heart squeezes. "You're the bestest, kiddo. A miracle. My greatest gift."

She pulls away until her misty eyes meet mine. "I'm a present?"

"With a big bow." I tug on the one that's managed to stay in her hair. A miraculous feat I take full credit for.

Sydney blinks wet lashes at me, her smile returning. "You made my hurt better."

I boop her nose, then wipe my brow. "Phew. That's why they pay me the big bucks."

She mulls that over for a beat. "I don't need Mommy."

My attempt to lighten the mood falls flat. I don't mask my wince. "You do. She's always gonna be your mom. That's important."

"Doesn't feel important," she grumbles.

The urge to agree parts my lips. As the product of a single-parent home, I'm well aware of how it feels to wonder if I wasn't good enough for my mom to stick around. My dad didn't bother to fill the gap she left. I refuse to make those same mistakes. Sydney will never question if she's cherished.

That includes nurturing her sensitive heart while also protecting her from additional pain. It's a damn slippery slope and getting harder to navigate by the day. "Don't give up on her yet. She'll do better."

Or I'll force the issue I've avoided for too long already.

Her sniffles crack through my jaded heart. "That's what you always say. I don't know how to feel about Mommy anymore."

"Wise beyond your years, Boop." Which is a sliding scale. She's advanced for her age, but I don't want her to grow up faster than she already is. Especially when it can be avoided. "It's okay to be sad that your mom isn't here more often, but don't stop missing her."

Syd slides off my lap to slump on the floor in front of me. "But why doesn't she miss me?"

"I'm sure she does, but her job keeps her extra busy. It's hard for her to leave." The excuses taste bitter. If Morgan wanted to be involved, she would be. Doesn't get more cut and dry than that. Not as if I can tell my daughter that.

"But you always make time for me." Her observation fills me with pride.

"My job is…easier."

She huffs. "Nuh-uh. You told me fixing cars isn't easy. That's why I can only help with certain stuff."

"Not letting me get away with much today, huh?" I match her grin with one of my own. "What I meant was that I'm the boss and set my own hours. It's easier for me to be home more."

Her brow knits as she thinks over my reasoning. "Nope. You work super hard while I'm at school. That's a really long time, Daddy. But even when you're tired, we still play lots. You're like a superhero."

Emotion swells until it's difficult to breathe. "Thanks, Boop. I love you. Don't ever forget, okay?"

"Love you too!" She flings herself at me for another hug. Then, like the resilient kid Sydney is, she hops to her feet while grinning wide. "Can we go for a snow-mobile ride?"

My gaze returns to the overflowing basket. "Right after I get these clothes sorted and folded."

"But I'm borrrrreeeeed," she wails. "Even Glitzy is tired of chores. She's pouting."

I follow her gaze to the ball of fluff snoozing on the floor. The sprawled position is typical for Sydney's pampered Pomeranian, but I won't be the one to announce that fact. "You two could play tag while I finish."

My daughter scrunches her face in consideration. "Nope, Glitzy doesn't wanna do that."

"Oh, she talks to you?"

"Uh-huh. She's taking a break after chasing me earlier."

"I guess that's fair. How about you color a picture then? Or maybe you could finish the popsicle stick house? It's still on the table." I hitch a thumb over my shoulder in the general direction of the kitchen.

"But we're making that together. It's a group project. You hafta follow the rules." Her insistence is admirable. She's only in kindergarten, but there are moments when she acts much older.

"All right, what if your dolls have a pageant or something? You can be the judge."

"Sally Sue already won."

"Wow, that was quick."

Syd wiggles in place. "I like to do stuff fast. When can we play?"

"It's almost time," I offer while reaching for a pair of jeans.

"You've been saying that forevvvvver."

"Sorry, Boop. This stuff has to get done." But ditching the mundane task is tempting.

"You need a helper," Sydney chirps.

"Are you offering?"

There's a desperate plea in her eyes. "But I already cleaned my room."

"How about trying to find a pair for me?" I hold up two different socks.

"They don't need to match, Daddy. I'll wear those just like that." She wiggles her toes into the carpet.

My head hangs low. "You could've told me that much sooner. This mission has been my Everest since you were born."

"What's an Everest?"

I blow the air from my cheeks with a grunt. "Mount Everest has the highest peak in the world. It's a big deal when someone reaches the top."

She blinks at me. "Have you climbed the mountain?"

I chuckle. "Uh, no."

Syd rubs her forehead. "I don't get it."

"It's just an expression. When something is really hard, people might say it's their Everest. Much safer than climbing a mountain."

Amusement brightens her expression. A shrill sound escapes her gaping mouth, and she slaps a palm over the noise. "You think finding matching socks is really hard?"

I narrow my eyes at her clever snark. "It's harder than it looks, but someone's gotta do it."

That makes her lips squish to one side. "I think we need a nanny."

I drop my jaw in offense. "For what? I've got this handled."

She bounces on the balls of her feet. "But you take a super long time. If you had an assistant or something, we could do more fun stuff together. Laundry is realllllllly boring."

And these are the moments where she definitely acts her age.

"We have plenty of time for fun stuff," I mutter.

Sydney giggles. "It's silly when you're grumpy, just like Miss Harper said."

The mention of the pesky blonde raises my guard against an enemy invasion. Not only does she intrude on my thoughts, but also the one spot in town that offers a semblance of peace. Next thing I know, she'll be dropping by the shop to get her car repaired. My fist clenches an innocent shirt from the heap as her potential destruction rains down. That woman gets under my skin like no other.

I shake off the irritation, forcing a smile for my daughter's benefit. "Harper talks about me?"

She raises her arms and turns in a circle. "Only sometimes."

I wait for her to elaborate, which she doesn't. Grilling my daughter for more information is going too far, even for me. Or maybe I just don't want to reveal more feelings. I'm raw enough as it is. Those musings break apart when Syd expels a loud sigh.

"Daddy, you aren't watching."

I blink to regain focus. "Huh?"

"Miss Harper taught me how to pirouette." She lifts her arms in preparation to repeat the motion.

I stare as she bends her leg to rest a foot on the opposite knee, wobbling slightly before doing a slow spin. She almost topples sideways halfway through the action. That doesn't stop pride from lifting my lips. "You look like a ballerina."

Sydney beams at the praise. "Miss Harper says I'm the best in my class."

"I bet she did," I grumble under my breath.

"What'd you say?"

"You're the best, Boop. Just like I said earlier."

"It's 'cause I never miss a class. Miss Harper tells us practice is very important."

"Sure is," I mutter.

That encourages my daughter to prattle off a list of why *Miss Harper* is the greatest teacher ever. Fuck, the woman is officially haunting me. In addition, the recent altercation with Roosters' new bartender streams through my mental speakers like a solo track playlist. I'm not sure why she bothers me so much, but I need to get the fuck over it. As she flippantly mentioned yesterday, Knox Creek is big enough for both of us.

A decision arrives with startling urgency. If I simmer in her compliment stew for another moment, I'm bound to ask questions that are better left unsaid. The strain between my shoulders immediately relaxes.

I stand with an exaggerated groan, tossing in a stretch for bonus points. "My old bones are ready to move."

Sydney gasps, abandoning the Harper topic with ease. "Does this mean we're finally going outside?"

"Get your suit on, kiddo. The snow is calling." And leaving other distractions behind.

chapter four

Harper

INHALE THE STRONG AROMA OF HAZELNUT COFFEE BREWED to caffeinated perfection. A small sip further proves that theory. Rich and sweet flavors burst on my tongue. The moan I release is too illicit for a public space.

A quick glance at my fellow java junkies in Bean Me Up shows them occupied with their own beverages. The late-morning crowd is thin, leaving most of the tables open. There's no shame in complimenting the light roast. Not that a full house would stop me. With my next taste, I don't stifle the satisfaction from spilling free.

"Careful, or you'll turn me on." Joy smiles at me from across the small table.

"It's just too good." I treat myself to another generous mouthful. My swallow is smoother than the caffeine.

"Rub it in a little harder." She glares at her decaf like

it's personally offended her. Maybe it has, seeing as she's in a very delicate state.

My gaze lowers to her rounded belly that's even more pronounced in her seated position. "Thanks for meeting me, bestie."

Joy huffs, sending stray hairs flying off her forehead. "As if I'd miss the chance to get a secondhand buzz off you. I gotta get my kicks wherever I can these days."

I laugh while she rubs her bump. "Your little girl gives you plenty."

"That she does. I can hardly go five minutes without needing to pee."

"Bladder aerobics," I giggle.

She wiggles in her chair for emphasis. "Ah, yes. It's great for getting off my butt. Not so stellar for productivity. Thanks for picking up my slack."

My eyes roll on their own. "Puh-lease. As if you wouldn't do the same for me. That's what we do. We're partners, and always will be."

The reminder sparks a not-so-distant memory of how we used to sit in this very spot planning routines. We'd spend hours collaborating before introducing the steps to our students. Lately, most of the work falls on me while Joy waits for her little one to arrive. The arrangement gives me full control, but it's lonely. I miss bouncing ideas off my best friend.

Barre Twirl began as a dream between two college freshmen. It felt like fate when a space became available in our hometown. Our business sprouted, grew, and blossomed in the years since graduation. I believe the best is yet to come.

"Just don't get too comfortable running the show without me," she says.

"You're still present."

"Not where I want to be." Joy pouts in the direction of her ankles that are no doubt swollen.

"There's no better excuse for taking a desk job. Besides, you make a wonderful receptionist."

Her lips purse to one side. "Let's be honest, pregnancy brain makes me forgetful at best."

"Nobody's sent any formal complaints. They must appreciate your efforts behind the scenes."

She nods, but there's a frown holding her smile hostage. "I miss teaching the kiddos."

My heart clenches on her behalf. "Don't fret, babes. You'll be back on your twinkle toes soon enough. Until then, Ginger is more than willing to assist when needed."

Joy's lips curve upward. "I think you went into the wrong field. Look into becoming a motivational coach. Just imagine setting up a booth to offer pep talks. You're top-notch."

"Could be a decent side hustle. But only for women who are about to give birth, yet are more concerned about their job rather than what's about to happen to their vagina." I lean forward to stage whisper, "It's gonna be messy."

She snorts, which morphs into a throaty cackle. "You're ridiculous."

"And you're welcome. Take the hint, yeah?"

Joy shudders. "I prefer not to think about being torn to shreds."

"Can't say I blame you. It's going to be just fine, though. You're a trooper. Always have been."

"There you go again," she chirps.

"Moral support." I dust off my shoulders. "Tell me how you're feeling."

"Like I ate a school bus packed with toddlers on a sugar craze." She gives her stomach another loving pat.

"That's...oddly specific."

"Seems appropriate under my current circumstances."

"Well, you don't have much longer to wait." I prop my elbows on the table and tap my fingers together in a giddy motion.

"Two weeks if she's precise. Even sooner if she's eager and cooperates. I'm not willing to entertain the idea that she'll be tardy to the party."

I hum in agreement. "As you shouldn't. That little cupcake won't keep us waiting."

"Fingers crossed. Our doctor said it could be anytime now. I'm already dilated one centimeter and eighty percent effaced. But that doesn't mean much yet. Those measurements can stay stagnant until contractions begin, as we learned from Bossy Barb." She winks while mentioning the strict instructor.

Since Joy's baby's daddy was nowhere to be found for the first six months of her pregnancy—by no fault of his own—I attended the classes with her. Cole studied his butt off to make up for his absence. He might be better prepared than Joy at this point.

I squeak, adding a silent clap for extra enthusiasm. "Oh my gosh, it's almost time! This is so exciting. How's your stocking stuffer handling the countdown?"

She grins at her fiancé's nickname. "He gives an excellent foot massage."

"Hard and fast or slow and gentle, depending on your mood?"

"Exactly," she sighs.

"You trained him well." I lift my coffee mug in a salute.

"Damn straight." A telltale sparkle enters Joy's gaze. "In all seriousness, Cole is more than I could've imagined. A true fairy tale prince."

A pang echoes in my chest. Not in envy, but hollow absence. I've never had what she's describing. Well, that's not entirely true. Jake held promise during those four measly months we dated way back when. Too bad it turned out to be a trick. That horrible tease has stuck with me.

Joy notices my silence. "How's your dating life?"

The topic is a gray abyss that I've been treading water in. "You ask that as if you don't already know."

She laughs. "I had to get that sad look off your face. It's bumming me out."

I wipe the gloom away, forcing a grin. "Just caught in the moment. I'm fine. Totally fine."

Her eyes narrow. "Don't lie."

"Why would I? Everything is how it's meant to be. You're living the romantic dream. No one deserves it more. I'm happy for you." Heat stings my eyes. I fan the burn, which does little to dry to moisture.

Joy flails her arms. "Oh, no. You can't cry. That'll get me started and you know I can't stop."

I blink at the lingering pressure. "Crisis averted. Only a momentary emotional burst."

"Just wait until you're raging with hormones."

"If that ever happens," I mutter.

"Harper," my friend scolds in a tone that will serve her fast-approaching role in motherhood well. "You're only twenty-four."

"Twenty-five."

She quirks a brow. "Seriously?"

The gasp I let loose is purposefully loud. "Were you so whacked out on pregnancy hormones that you forgot my birthday?"

"You're ridiculous."

"And you're repeating yourself."

Her exhale is thick, matching the shrewd squint aimed at me. "No prospective candidates?"

"You'll be the first to know."

"I better be," she gripes. "We don't see each other as often these days."

"If you hadn't moved out, that wouldn't be an issue." I stick my tongue out.

"As if I don't feel bad enough."

"I'm joking, obviously. It's actually nice having the apartment to myself."

She tosses her hands into the air. "That's even worse."

"Jeez, you're hard to please. I'm trying to ease your guilt after abandoning me."

Joy tips her head toward the ceiling and groans. "We gotta find a man to keep you occupied. Once this baby arrives, I won't be able to pamper your fragile ego."

"Very funny. I'm doing great on my own, but thanks for the concern."

I allow my gaze to drift in a subtle hint that this topic is a steep decline I'm not interested in pursuing. The rich scent of freshly brewed coffee wafts toward me. Steam spews from a machine as the barista whips up a fresh cappuccino. The sputter reminds me of my heart's reaction to a certain grumpy mechanic, but I refuse to travel down that rocky road.

Instead, I focus on my best friend, who's glowing like an advertisement for getting accidentally knocked up after a no-strings bang with a guy she only knew by first name. Repeat that five times fast. I laugh to myself after a failed attempt.

That's when I realize Joy is studying me too closely. Her unwavering attention almost makes me squirm. "How's Roosters?"

I glance through the window at the bar across the street that won't be open for a few more hours. "Um, I think it's okay."

"That's all I get?"

"Well, it's kinda hard to tell when the lights are off."

She huffs. "Are you being obtuse on purpose? I'm talking about your new job."

My amusement trickles out in a deceptively smooth tune. "Obviously, I'm trying to avoid the subject."

Her chair squeaks as she leans forward. "Why? Is my brother being a jerk? Garrett promised to behave himself."

I wave her concern away. "Yeah, he's a great boss. He actually defended my honor against... an especially disgruntled customer."

Joy makes a strangled sound. "Please don't tell me you have a crush on my brother."

I choke on my spit. "Absolutely not."

She wipes fake sweat from her forehead. "What a relief. That would be weird."

"You're telling me," I mumble.

"But it's going well?

"So far. I've only had three shifts."

She nods, but doesn't appear appeased in the slightest. "I'm still curious why you wanted to work there to begin with. Other than having an easy in thanks to yours truly."

My shoulders droop under the pressure. "I need the extra money. My rent doubled with you gone. The other bills aren't cheap either. Besides, it keeps me busy. What else am I going to do on the weekends with my bestie tied down?"

"You have other friends," she mutters.

"Who I have plans to go out with on Saturday." I flutter my lashes.

She sighs with longing, adding a pout to get the message across. In the next second, she recovers to swerve back on track. "But why Roosters? It's a total sausage factory."

"Which is excellent for tips." I rub my fingers together to represent the influx of cash.

"How many numbers got shoved into your bra?" She wiggles her brows.

I inspect my manicure, which is in dire need of a color change. "A lady doesn't flirt and tell."

Joy snorts. "Liar."

"There's nothing juicy to report. I've turned several heads, but none that are memorable." That's mostly due to my concentration being derailed by the resident grump at every turn.

My best friend has an uncanny talent for teasing apart my train of thought. "Have you seen the one who shall not be named?"

There goes the hope that Jake could stay kicked to the curb. My stomach clenches at the savage glare he shot me. The flames in his blue eyes have kept me hot and bothered in the days since. Not that I'll ever admit such a weakness.

"The purpose of not mentioning his name is defeated if we talk about him."

She slumps in her seat, as low as her belly will allow. "Oh, come on. I've been biting my tongue since I sat down. Feed me some scraps. I'm about to pop and need to live vicariously. Give me the dirt, pour it straight down my throat. Take pity on me, Harps."

I widen my eyes to comical proportions. "Is that how you talk to Cole? No wonder you're preggers."

"Quit trying to distract me. Fess up," she prods.

"You know I saw him. He was a jerk, as usual." And I got a thrill from verbally sparring with him.

Joy rests her cheek on an open palm. "I'm just waiting for the day he pulls his head outta his ass."

"Don't hold your breath."

"You could be good together."

"Pass," I scoff. "I'm not interested in a repeat performance."

"Uh-huh, that's almost believable after you got a job at his favorite bar. We'll see how he appreciates you serving him."

I dry heave, strictly for her benefit and my pride. "Maybe Roosters was a bad idea."

"Too late," she croons. "You can't leave my brother high and dry. He's depending on you."

"Nice guilt trip." I swat at the air. "It doesn't matter. I'll treat Jacob like any other customer."

"Jacob," Joy echoes. "Good luck with that."

A wince pinches my features. I have a sneaking suspicion I'll need all the luck I can get. "Thanks, I think."

I sip from my mug for a much-needed boost. The coffee is cold, similar to this unpleasant topic. A chill creeps in and pebbles my skin. Maybe the bar really was the wrong choice. But letting him scare me off is even worse. The bitter taste lingers in my mouth as determination rallies.

Joy must recognize the stress seeping from my pores. "Okay, what's next?"

"Figured you'd find a comfy couch and take a load off."

"It's too early for that. How about we go shopping?"

My eyebrows fling upward. "Is that wise in your condition?"

Her scowl is humorous. "I'm pregnant, not fatally ill."

"Heavily pregnant," I correct.

"Whatever. I can stand for an hour at Creak & Barrel. They have a robe that's essential for my hospital grab bag."

The mention of my favorite boutique piques my interest. "Are you sure?"

She begins collecting her stuff from the table. "Yes, please. This might be my last opportunity to be out and about for a while."

"Who am I to argue with that?" I stand and grab my purse.

She loops her arm through mine. "On the way, you can tell me more about your admirers."

"Ah, there's the catch."

Joy's cackle would make any B-list villain jealous. "As if you'd assume otherwise. Spill. Now."

"Directly down your throat?"

Joy smacks her lips. "Just the way I love it."

After a genuine laugh, I recall one or two guys that are honorable mentions. Jacob Evans gets left behind where he belongs.

chapter five

Jake

A COLD GUST SNEAKS BENEATH MY JACKET AS I LINGER on the sidewalk. The icy blast reinforces my guard against what's to come, yet I remain frozen on the spot. It's going to take more than wind to push me faster. I'd rather freeze my ass off than go inside.

Large lightbulbs frame the front window, drawing attention to the studio within. The bright interior promises warmth. White walls display frilly tutus and leotards. Ballet shoes hang on metal racks. A couch and two chairs are arranged around a low table. It appears welcoming, but I know better. There are ulterior motives hidden in the glow.

My next exhale streams out in a foggy cloud. I search for restraint and patience. Both rest dormant beneath the surface, just out of reach.

"Daddy! Why're you just standing there? Let's gooooo." Enter the reason I put myself through this bi-weekly torture.

Sydney had been practicing her twirls. I was just fine hanging tight while she delayed the inevitable. Then she had to go and realize I wasn't moving.

"After you, kiddo." I motion toward the entrance.

My daughter doesn't hesitate to rush toward the door in a blur of excitement wrapped in tulle. I hang my head. The fact that tulle is in my vocabulary is telling. This little girl has me wrapped around her finger tighter than dental floss.

A pitchy tune announces our arrival. I steel myself against the seduction lurking behind the desk. A set of blinders should've been included in my earlier list. Only this woman gets a rise out of me. She plucks a hidden chord, otherwise long forgotten, that demands I surrender. It takes monumental effort to keep my attention trained straight ahead.

"Hey, Syd. You look adorable." Harper's melodic voice should grate on my nerves. Instead, it has the opposite effect.

I fight the urge to glance at her while striding forward like I belong. As if I'm not an imposter. As if I could fit into her world. My worn boots scuff across the polished wood floor, calling bullshit within seconds. This is her domain and I'm the intruder. That doesn't mean I'll cower.

Meanwhile, my daughter preens under Harper's praise. Her jacket gets cast aside without a care. Then she hops in a circle to show off the entire mismatched ensemble. "Thanks. Daddy let me dress myself."

A snort gets lodged in my throat. There's not a chance in hell I'd take credit for pairing neon leopard with purple stripes, green polka dots, and a pink tutu.

"And your bun is almost smooth." Harper motions to her own hair that's pulled back in a similar style.

"Daddy's been practicing. We bought more pins and a new comb."

"I'm surprised you hold still long enough," the blonde temptress teases.

Sydney huffs. "I try my bestest. It takes him foreverrrrrr."

They continue chatting while ignoring my presence, which suits me fine. It gives me the opportunity to peek without getting caught. A quick glimpse doesn't satisfy the gnawing hunger. This wouldn't be an issue if I didn't deprive my physical needs. It's been too long, and I'm weak against the lure. I shift my stare to appreciate the full view of my fantasies. The error in my ogling—as usual—sets my blood ablaze the instant my eyes feast on Harper.

Once again, I'm tormented by the total package she flaunts. Stretchy material clings to her generous curves. Black and sleek and too fucking appealing. Flames burn under my skin while my muscles flex. I have the means to prepare myself but it's never enough. She's too fucking sexy.

It's a testament to my willpower that I haven't made a scene. I'm convinced Harper's dance attire is created to tempt me. I want to peel those tight layers off to reveal—

Nope, not going there. The fire in my veins is horribly inappropriate. This is the worst place to get aroused. Talk about creeper status. I widen my stance and think about Glitzy acting tough at the dog park. Her growl couldn't scare a mouse. That visual does the trick, all traces of heat fizzling out with a grunt.

"Problem?"

I snap out of the distraction method to find Harper arching a brow at me. "Nope, just waiting for time to pass."

Sydney begins bouncing on her feet. "That's what I do when you're busy folding clothes. It's so boring."

"That builds anticipation for the fun," I reason.

My daughter blinks at me. Something gleams in her blue eyes, which instantly puts me on alert. Alarm bells clang against my skull when she pins those concerning intentions on Harper.

"Are you good at laundry?"

The vixen shrugs as if she's innocent. "Probably as good as the next gal."

Sydney's smile curls with devious plotting not fit for a six-year-old. "Can you find—?"

"Why don't we discuss this later? Your class is about to start," I cut in. "Let's not waste precious moments asking your… teacher about chores."

"But why not, Daddy?" My daughter stamps her foot, betraying her true age. "Maybe Miss Harper can help us."

"With what?" The woman in question glances between us.

"It's nothing—"

But Sydney's blurt overpowers my brush-off. "My daddy has trouble finding matching socks after washing them. They always gets lost, and it takes him a super long time to sort through the piles when we should be playing, and I get really tired of waiting. Glitzy docs too. He needs a helper."

Harper hums in acknowledgment. "There's a mesh pouch that goes in the washer and dryer for that exact purpose."

My daughter's eyes expand into saucers. "Really?"

"I bought it as a baby shower gift for Joy, mostly as a joke. It's actually useful since the dryer can eat socks. They get stuck in the vent or something. Not often, but it's possible. Especially ones meant for little feet." The woman sent to test me wiggles her fingers for emphasis.

"Like mine!" Syd kicks her leg in the air to show off her small shoe.

"Yep, look at those cute tootsies. No wonder the dryer gobbles up your socks." Harper pretends to chew with extra smacks from her lips.

My daughter giggles. "Maybe you can show my dad where to get one of those pouch thingies."

The blonde bombshell looks at me. There's a knowing twinkle in her eyes. "Sure, if he's interested."

I avert my gaze as if she didn't catch me leering moments ago. "I'll figure it out on my own."

Sydney whirls to face me. "Miss Harper is super smart, Daddy. You should listen to her. She can help you with all the boring stuff."

"I'm positive she has her own boring stuff to do," I mutter.

Harper rolls her eyes but doesn't respond.

My little girl grins, appearing pleased with her meddling. "I'm gonna go dance now."

It's about damn time I get an out from this pressure cooker. "I'll be here when you're done, Boop."

She lunges at me to wrap her arms around my legs. "Love you."

I kneel to return her hug. "Love you more."

"Nuh-uh." Sydney struggles to get free. "I love you the mostest."

"If you insist, but I love you the most of the mostest." I tap her nose before rising to stand straight.

She parks her tiny hands on her hips. "Ugh, you never let me win."

"But me loving you that much is a win for you," I insist.

Her face scrunches while she considers that. "Okay."

Then she spins on her heel and takes off down the hallway. Her positive energy is infectious, erasing more stress I'd been carrying. I almost chuckle at the dust cloud she could create with that speed.

"Be right in," Harper calls to her retreating form. "Listen to Ginger, okay? She's in charge until I get there."

Sydney tosses a thumbs-up over her shoulder before disappearing around the corner. That's when I realize who I'm alone with. Harper's decision to lag behind feels purposeful, and personal. The strain returns to my posture as she studies me.

"You're a really good dad," she whispers.

Warmth instantly spreads through my chest, which immediately irritates me. I scowl to offset the sensation she has no business stoking. "That means so much coming from you."

She glances at the ceiling while mouthing a few choice words. "Still can't play nice, huh?"

"Nah, Syd gets the best of me."

Harper tilts her head to the side, watching me. "And there's nothing left for anyone else."

"No." Simple as that.

"Got it," she mutters. "I won't keep you long. Just wanted to mention the partner dance since you didn't respond to my email. Has Syd told you about it?"

"The fuck? They're in kindergarten and first grade. You shouldn't be partnering them up." My little girl dancing with a boy didn't sit well with me, harmless twirling or not.

"Um, wow. You certainly have a secret talent for jumping to conclusions." She reaches for a flier and slides the paper across the desk. "The child's partner is a trusted adult that they choose. Not every dancer has a parent, so we avoid referring to the routine as something more specific. This option doesn't exclude anyone and gives me more creative freedom."

Guilt is a well-deserved punch to my gut. Even an insensitive asshole like me remembers that her father passed away when she was little. "That's actually…really considerate."

Harper's smile is kind, lacking the mockery I've earned. "It's shocking that I'm not a dating service for children, huh? Maybe you'll let me prove that I'm not trying to make your life miserable."

"Unlikely, but solid effort."

She shakes her head. A long-winded sigh breezes from her lush mouth. "Too bad. I think we'd be better off as allies than enemies."

The idea is laughable. "That's even less likely."

Her shrug is weak, just like her fading tolerance for my bullshit. "Are you going to stick around and watch for a change? You stopped once Sydney switched from Joy's class."

My attention veers to where she points. There's a television switched on, already streaming a live feed from inside the studio. Syd bounces on and off the screen in a chaotic whirlwind. From this safe distance, I won't cause a distraction as she learns new steps. But that's not my main concern.

I return my gaze to the one responsible for dismantling my sanity. As if connected to my mental upset, Harper leans on the counter while waiting for my verdict. The position further accentuates her form-fitting outfit that leaves little to the imagination. Suffering through an hour of her bending and stretching would put me over the edge.

"Pass." My legs shift in reverse to make a hasty exit.

She crosses her arms, effectively shoving her tits together. "Should I be offended?"

"Whatever blows your tulle up."

"Aww, come on. I won't bite... hard." Harper gnashes her teeth.

The depraved part of me wishes she would, which is sure to haunt my nightmares.

chapter six

Jake

"ARE YOU SURE WE GRABBED EVERYTHING?" I DROP the oversized backpack on the floor mat. Even with the bag stuffed to the seams, there's foot room to spare.

"Uh-huh, you checked like a bazillion times."

"Just want to be sure. You can always call if I forgot something." That option is probably more for my sake than hers.

Sydney giggles and rolls her eyes, as if proving that theory. "Okay, Daddy. You gotta relax and take a chill pill."

"A chill pill? Where'd you hear that?"

"At school. Mrs. Johnson told Mr. Burns that he's stressed from the job. She gave him a chill pill. I think you work too much. Should I get you a chill pill?"

"Nah, I'm good. We're done for the day thanks to

your help with that last oil change." I blindly wave at the shop behind me.

"I'm gonna work here someday, right?" The hope in her gaze is a sight to behold.

Pride fills my chest that she'd even consider following in my footsteps, regardless of the premature career planning at age six. "Sure, kiddo. If that's what you want."

Sydney beams at me from the spare booster seat in the luxury minivan. Glitzy is buckled in a harness beside her like the loyal sidekick she is. There are already two different movies playing from the screens in the headrests. A control panel displays too many options for me to count. The smell of expensive leather wafts out with a breeze. This kid hauler has more bells and whistles than a cruise ship.

I straighten from my stooped position to address the gracious owner. "Thanks again for coming to get her. Can't say it's easy for me to let her go, but I know she's in excellent care with you. She loves spending the night at your house."

Susan's palm flutters to her chest while she laughs. "Oh, heavens. It's our pleasure. Sydney is a delight. You're doing a wonderful job raising her."

Heat prickles the back of my neck. "Appreciate you saying that. She makes it easy for me."

"No doubt about that. She's extremely polite and considerate of others. Our little Polly loves her to pieces. She'd be devastated if she didn't get frequent slumber parties with her best friend. I'm glad you're willing to let her stay the entire weekend."

My spirits tank at the reminder of two full days

alone. FaceTime is a small blessing. "I'm happy to take a turn—"

"You already do plenty. Enjoy the time to yourself, or share it with someone." She winks.

I'd balk at the action if I wasn't positive that she's a happily married woman. A discount on repairs goes a long way. Pity plays a role too. People in Knox Creek aren't shy about their knowledge where Morgan's absence is concerned. They're aware that I might as well be flying solo in this parenting gig.

It's better for everyone if I don't take their kindness for granted. I tell myself it's important for Syd to witness a fully functioning family unit. Fuck, that makes me feel like shit. I hate doubting my ability to provide my baby girl with everything she needs. My reputation doesn't require more tarnish. On cue, I glance at the grease smeared onto my hands. Scrub at the grime all I want, but it never truly comes off.

The last thing I need to do is wallow, especially with an audience. "I'll stay occupied. There's plenty to keep me busy."

Susan hums agreeably. "I can only imagine."

Syd tugs on my shirt to get my attention. "Are you gonna have dinner at Roosters?"

"Maybe." But my reliable routine deceives me.

"Tell Miss Harper I say hi, m'kay? She's gonna be there too."

My gut clenches. I retract my earlier comment. Sydney mentioning Harper while we have an audience is very last on the list of things to do. The answering glint in Susan's eyes reveals as much. That sparkle might as well be a town-wide announcement.

Her smile only grows as the potential for gossip sinks in. "Oh, that's right. I heard she got a job at your favorite bar. She also teaches our girls dance twice a week. You must be bumping into each other quite often as of late."

And this is how an innocent comment from my daughter turns into gasoline on a fire.

I tug at my hat, turning it backward. "On second thought, I'll probably stop by Bent Pedal."

Not that it matters, seeing as the damage is done. If I change my predictable course, everyone will assume I'm avoiding Harper on purpose. I can't dig myself from this hole, but Susan is too polite to point it out. Not blatantly at least.

"Rhodes and Rylee snatching a loyal customer from Garrett? That might raise a few brows." Her expertise in this game is admirable.

My lips remain firmly sealed to trap the expletives that would traumatize listening ears.

Sydney glances from her to me. "Huh?"

"Don't worry about it, Boop. Have fun."

"I will. You too, Daddy." She lifts her arms for a hug that I'm eager to grant.

"Love you," I murmur into the embrace.

"Love you the moster of the mostest most."

I chuckle and pull away. "Okay, I can't top that. You beat me."

"Yay!" Her small fist pumps up and down.

"Just precious," Susan coos before sliding behind the wheel. "Take care now, Jake. See you Sunday."

I watch them drive from the lot while my brain reboots. It's moronic that I even need a second to consider the options. The choice is simple, and allows me to repay the favors tossed my way. It's only fair to give the good folks in Knox Creek something to talk about. Amusement tips my mouth into a crooked slant. Look at me, acting for others.

The ease of that decision gives me pause halfway to my truck. I breathe deeply while tipping my face to the dark sky. There's a slight chill in the air, but it's not cold enough to stop me from walking the three blocks. That'll give me a chance to clear my mind before a certain blonde fills it with nonsense.

I flip the collar on my jacket and tuck my chin against the wintery elements. My boots crunch over salted ice while I stride to the road. March has arrived, but the foot traffic is still minimal. I only cross paths with a few others willing to take a chance against the unpredictable climate.

Cars crawl at a lazy speed. Main Street becomes an illuminated blur to cast shadows across the brick buildings. I keep my head down and trudge forward. Before I recognize how far I've gone, the glow from Roosters' neon sign shines down on me.

I step inside like usual. The stiffness in my stride can be blamed on the cold. As predicted, Harper is front and center behind the bar. Everything else fades until she's all I see. I curse at the weakness she spreads inside of me.

My approach is measured, but not cautious. This is just a bumpy patch in the long haul. We've been seeing too much of each other. She belongs at the dance studio. Roosters is mine, dammit.

Her grin almost suggests that she's pleased to see

me. "Well, look what the creature of habit dragged in. Didn't think I'd be seeing you in this fine establishment tonight."

I check my watch while sliding onto an open stool. It's barely seven o'clock. "Feel free to pretend you didn't."

"Aww, there's the grumpy asshole I've grown to adore. I would've missed out on these warm fuzzies if the tabloids were true." Her upbeat attitude grates on my composure.

Flames lick at my chilled cheeks while I pin her with a glare. "What the fuck are you going on about?"

Harper wipes at a smudge on the counter, then flings the towel over her shoulder. "A well-informed tattletale told me you were going to Bent Pedal."

"You've got to be kidding me," I spit. "Word traveled that fast?"

She snorts. "You sound surprised."

More like impressed. The purpose of my waltzing into Roosters was to appease the masses. It usually takes longer to spread. Apparently, the juice is extra rich when it comes to us.

I smooth my features into a neutral scowl. "Susan left my shop ten minutes ago."

"And you walked here. That was a mistake." Her observation is too keen after the gossip train already blew through town.

Tense alertness straightens my posture. "Keeping tabs on me?"

A blush rushes up her delicate throat. She rips her gaze off mine and digs in the cooler. "Uh, you look... parched."

A Coors Light appears on a coaster in front of me. I grab the bottle and guzzle a generous swig. "What if I wanted something different?"

A careless shrug is her initial response. "Too late. You already drank from that one. Better luck next round."

"Shitty customer service," I grumble.

"Would you like to speak to my manager?" Her grin is smug as she nods toward Garrett across the room.

"Hey, sugar! Don't forget about me." A guy whistles from a few spots down the rail. His arms wave in frantic motion, as if his prized possession might disappear.

"Duty calls," Harper chirps.

I seethe as she skips off to dote on the rude interruption. The eager beaver isn't shy or quiet with his affections. Every smarmy compliment is a gong in a silent temple. My knuckles tighten into a furious white around my drink. His attention on her resembles a slobbering golden retriever. A puddle of drool is about to form on the wood separating them.

Harper smiles and laughs, even twirls her hair, but the actions seem forced. That's what I tell myself to stop the deafening roar from stabbing my eardrums. In reality, she's about to grab a fork to eat up the bullshit he's feeding her.

To drown the fire in my veins, I lift the beer to my lips and chug. The contents get drained at an alarming rate. It's not to call her back to me faster. I'm just thirsty, and too damn warm. Heat pumps under my flesh like a fog machine. I strip off my jacket that's suddenly suffocating.

"Another?"

I damn near startle at the gravelly timbre. Ridge Carter is casting a shadow over my personal space like a broad building. The former professional hockey player is tough to miss. That makes this delayed reaction caused by my singular focus even more embarrassing. Not that he needs more ammunition against me.

"Need something?" I square off against his towering form.

"Do you?"

"The fuck?"

"You're empty." He juts his chin at my bottle. "Want me to fix that?"

"Nah, I'll wait a bit."

His chuckle cracks through my pathetic excuse. "How about you do me a favor then."

"Doesn't sound like a question," I drawl.

Ridge skewers me with the fierce determination that made him famous on the ice. "Calm the storm, eh? Your mean mug is gonna scare off my customers."

My nod is automatic, but there's nothing I can do about it. I can't fault him for giving a shit about morale. He owns Roosters along with Garrett and Drake.

"Glad we have an understanding." He knocks on the counter. "Cheers."

Once Ridge ambles off to harass another unsuspecting regular, I'm free to let my gaze wander. Harper is dumping cocktail ingredients into a shaker several feet away. Even from this distance, I can hear her singing along with the popular country song blasting through the speakers. Her sharp notes hit me below the belt. I'm hard in an instant listening to that pitchy melody. It's how she earned the nickname from me. Memories from our months together assault me on a reckless wheel. Those days are long over, but I find myself captivated again as she belts out the lyrics without restraint.

It takes more effort than I'll willingly admit to stay in my seat. The slipping control makes me feel unhinged. When she begins swiveling her hips, my brain gets fuzzy. Her song and dance combination is even more intoxicating than the booze. I grip the counter for some semblance of balance. She fills my vision with smoke and temptation and lust. My eyes clench shut against the onslaught. At this rate, I'll be tripping to the door with a pitched tent in my jeans.

A sideways glance proves that I'm not the only sucker caught in her trap. Harper's performance catches the eye of many admirers. She shakes her ass faster for the grand finale.

On cue, the guy from earlier releases a douchey howl. "Damn, blondie. You're trying to steal my heart with those moves."

Harper peers over at him, the picture of coy innocence. "Why would I need to steal what you're willing to give me?"

He hoots. "And you're sassy? We're soulmates."

I gag on the idiotic sap's cheesy lines. If Ridge circles back, I'll order a glass of wine to choke it down.

"Not sure I believe in that sort of thing," Harper retorts.

"Allow me to sweeten the deal." He wags his brows and whips out a Snickers bar from who knows where.

"Real smooth, dumbass." I'd been biting my tongue hard enough to taste blood.

Candy man swivels on his stool to face me. "Are you talking to me?"

"Do you see anyone else acting like a dumbass?"

He blinks in rapid succession, taking several beats to process my words. "What's your problem?"

Oh, let me count the ways. "First off, who passes out candy bars when it isn't Halloween? You're just carrying that in your pocket, waiting for the right moment? Fucking lame. Second, she's allergic. Two strikes and you're out, buddy."

He snorts. "It's three. Now who's *fucking lame*?"

"Still you."

It's then that the more important factor registers. His eyes blow wide, directed at the Snickers in his grip. "She has a peanut allergy?"

A look at Harper confirms my declaration. Her cringe is aimed right at him. "I do."

"Well, shit." His head hangs low, properly chastised. "I thought that'd be romantic as hell."

Even with a front-row seat, I can't believe anyone would think that's a solid strategy. But good on him for shooting his shot.

"Guess she's all yours," he mutters.

Not even remotely.

Harper's scoff echoes my internal sentiment.

"Try a KitKat next time," I offer in farewell.

"I'll remember that." Leather creaks as he slides off the stool, tucks tail, and makes a wise retreat.

When I flick my gaze toward Harper, her focus is already narrowed on me. She saunters to my corner of the rail in a lithe prowl. I'd be a fool to miss her hips swinging with extra enthusiasm. Most definitely on purpose. A low rumble builds in my chest as another battle crests on the horizon.

"You're something else," she says in greeting.

"Like ready for another?" I tap my lonely coaster.

Harper mumbles under her breath while fetching me a fresh Coors. "Sure we're not allies?"

"Positive."

"Then why not let him give me peanuts?"

"I won't let my daughter's second-favorite human keel over on my guard." Sydney would never forgive me if she heard the truth.

She mulls that over on an extended pause. "Second?"

"I was giving you a boost in rank to be nice."

"Bullshit," she laughs. "You and nice don't belong in the same sentence."

I smirk and lift the bottle to my lips. "For once, we can agree on something."

Harper's silence is alarming. There's a static energy in the air that clogs the lull. Her voice is soft when she says, "I think you care."

Animosity gets sucked between my clenched teeth. "That line of thinking will get you hurt."

"Let me worry about that, huh?" She leans on the counter, getting into my space.

Endless optimism and compassion swirl in her

green eyes. Her presence is intoxicating. Warmth still clings too close. The spike in temperature is paired with attention from other patrons. If I strain my ears, curious whispers drift across the idle chatter. Fuck it. Let them talk.

I roll my sleeves until the fabric rests below my bent elbows. Harper's gaze takes a noticeable dip to the skin I've exposed. Tattoos decorate both arms, the bottom halves on display for her perusal. She isn't shy about her appreciation, staring longer than appropriate. Especially if she doesn't want to get caught.

That doesn't mean I tuck the temptation from sight. "You working tomorrow?"

She spins a bottle opener around her finger. "Who's asking?"

"Just wondering if I have to deal with you two days in a row."

The spell is broken, and her mouth forms a tight line. She straightens from her slouched pose. "Where's Syd?"

"At Polly's house."

"The entire weekend?"

"You sound surprised." I recite her earlier phrase with a sneer.

It's not a secret that she's regularly invited to spend nights at a friend's house. My daughter's social butterfly status began the moment she started talking. Her first birthday party had a guest list longer than Knox Creek's spring festival.

"When is it your turn to host the sleepover?"

"Don't ask me." The parents never expect me to reciprocate, even when I offer. I'm thankful for that, in all honesty. One little girl is already above my pay grade.

"What should I ask then?"

A humorless chuckle rolls off my tongue. "Why you're wasting breath talking to me."

The bitter comment does the trick. Harper's glare could slice a muffler in half. "You're a real jerk, Jacob Evans."

I lift my beer in a solo celebration. "At your service."

chapter seven

Harper

SYDNEY SPINS TOWARD ME IN A CONTINUOUS TWIRL FIT for a mini prima ballerina. What the move lacks in technical form is more than compensated for in fun. Her feet are a blur as she spirals in a relatively upright position. I laugh and clap, cheering on her natural talent. She turns faster with my encouragement.

When Syd comes to an abrupt halt, her eyes are unfocused. "Whoa, I'm dizzy."

The little girl stumbles sideways and I lunge forward to catch her. "Take it easy, superstar."

Her posture is still unsteady in my grip. "Did I do really good?"

"The best," I confirm.

"I love to dance!" She thrusts her arms in the air, wiggling her butt to a giddy beat.

"Which makes me very happy. You're keeping me in business." I give her more applause.

Sydney takes a gracious bow. "And I'm gonna get extra better with more practice."

"Yep, you got an individual lesson for free. How special is that?"

"Like a lucky wish." She throws her arms around me. "You're my favorite teacher ever."

My heart swells while I return her hug. "I'm not supposed to choose favorites, but you make that extremely difficult."

And let's be honest, she steals the top slot.

She breaks our embrace and drops into a bouncy plié. "Is my daddy gonna be done working soon?"

I glance at the clock, not that the time is telling in this case. "He's probably on the way."

There was an accident involving multiple cars in town. Jake got called to the site since Kade and Penn—the only other mechanics at his shop—weren't available. Apparently, tow trucks are few and far between in these parts. Job security at its finest.

I could hear how much it pained him to ask me for a favor. Jake didn't have much choice, which put me in control for a change. That doesn't mean I'd take advantage of his vulnerable position. It just gives me the chance to reap kindness from him in return. The theory is comical, but possible. If only slightly.

In any event, I don't have plans until later. I was happy to oblige for an emergency. It's not like Syd is difficult to entertain.

"What should we do now?" Sydney attempts a pirouette, but falls from position halfway through.

"Try again," I urge.

Her smile doesn't slip as she prepares to do just that. She sets herself straight ahead at the mirror wall. Her right foot notches to her left knee. She holds steady for several counts, only her lips moving with the numbers. The motion is slow and wobbly, but a complete turn.

"Yay! You did it," I praise.

"I did it!"

Our palms meet for a celebratory high-five. She glances around the otherwise empty studio for a wider audience. Her enthusiasm dims with a slouch.

"What's with the frown, cutie?"

She pouts. "When is Joy gonna be back?"

"After her baby is born," I explain.

It's a question I've become very familiar with. My bestie's absence is a noticeable gap. As co-owner, she's been a constant presence since we opened. Well, until she was put on bed rest. The day we went shopping last week was truly her last hurrah before delivery. I've been carrying my phone like a third arm just waiting for a labor alert.

Sydney cuts into the pause as if listening to my thoughts. "When will that be?"

I heave a thick sigh. "Next year at this rate."

Her gasp highlights my error. "But you said she's about to pop!"

Crud, that was a bad joke. "She is. Don't worry. Her baby will arrive really soon. Then she'll be on a short break to stay home with her little girl."

Syd bobs her head too fast. "Okay, is that gonna happen tomorrow?"

"Not quite. Once the snow starts to melt, Joy

should be ready to visit. She'll bring her baby to the studio when it's warmer outside." Which is a vague and unreliable estimate in Minnesota.

The little girl beside me goes quiet while trying to grasp that concept of time. "After Spring Break?"

"Somewhere around there," I hedge.

Her lips squish into a contemplative pucker. "I think that's three weeks away. Daddy marks off the dates on our calendar."

"Now you can keep track of Joy's maternity leave too."

"Her what?"

"Never mind." I swat that off our radar. "First, we have to cross our fingers and toes that Joy's baby is born healthy and strong."

Sydney immediately completes the task. Both hands resemble luck-inducing prongs while her ballet slippers shift with the effort to match. "Done."

"Great job. We make an excellent team." I give her shoulder a gentle squeeze.

The temporary glee fades from her expression. "Is Joy gonna forget about us?"

"What? No way. It's not possible." But my reassurance falls flat.

Tears collect in Syd's eyes. "Are you sure?"

"Of course," I insist. "She could never forget about us. We're too important."

"Promise?"

"Yes, I promise. We're like a family."

Her blue eyes sparkle. "Really? You're my family?"

I'm digging myself an impressive hole with this

conversation. "Um, sort of. We're your dance family. We gather for class and recitals rather than holidays."

Her skinny shoulders hunch forward. "Oh, that's not like a mommy."

My stomach drops at the broken edge in her voice. It doesn't take a detective to crack the code behind her comment. "You have a mom, Syd."

"But she forgets about me."

I find myself wondering how Morgan could willingly put herself in a position to miss these precious moments to begin with. Platitudes bog down my brain. It's easy to say the wrong thing and cause permanent damage. "I'm sure she'll come see you soon."

Her tiny fingers draw invisible hearts on the floor. Meanwhile, mine is splintering. "That's what my dad says, but she isn't coming."

"Maybe she's waiting to surprise you."

"She isn't," she murmurs almost mutely.

I avert my gaze like a coward. There isn't anything I can say to make this better. That has to come from Morgan, or Jake for that matter. I settle for a distraction.

In a fluid maneuver, I sprawl flat on the floor with my arms and legs spread. Then I begin sweeping my limbs across the glossy wood in an arching pattern more suitable for the snow.

"What're you doing?" The amusement in Sydney's voice makes me smile.

I put more effort into the flat jumping jack motion. "Can't you see? I'm making a dust bunny angel."

She giggles. "A what?"

"Usually we make snow angels outside, right? This

works for inside." There better not be any actual dust bunnies on this floor.

Syd copies my movements. Her arms flap fast enough to launch her into the sky. "This is soooooo fun."

"And good exercise," I exhale.

She stops after finishing another cycle. "Yeah, I'm getting tired."

I glance over at her from my relaxed pose. "Feel better?"

"Lots. You took my hurt away, just like Daddy. That's why I love you."

Heat stings my eyes. "W-what?"

Syd continues as if she didn't just blow my world apart. "I don't like getting sad. It's poopy. My heart should be happy. Daddy says it grows super big the more love I have. You make my heart grow bigger."

Emotion crashes over me. I sit upright before the waterworks begin leaking. "You're the sweetest, kiddo. That's why I love you right back."

Her megawatt smile could power the entire studio. "I'm having the bestest time."

"Me too." I'm still caught in her declaration, but I don't want to appear frozen. The fact this tiny human deems me worthy of her love is a gift I'll never take for granted.

"Thanks for letting me stay, Miss Harper."

"You're always welcome. Maybe we can make it a regular thing?"

"Can we? Please, please?" She folds her hands in a pleading gesture.

"We'll see what your dad thinks." Another thought occurs to me. "You're very mature."

"What's mature mean?"

"You act older than your age."

She wrinkles her nose. "Is that good?"

"Yes, of course. You're really polite and have great manners. Those fit into the pockets of your smarty pants. A lot of kiddos are still working on those skills, especially in kindergarten." Not that I'd claim to be an expert. But I work with enough children to have a decent comparison group.

Sydney is quiet for a moment. "Do I talk too much?"

I balk at the question. "Why would you think that?"

She shrugs. "A boy in my class asked me why I'm such a motormouth. He's not super nice."

Protective instincts shoot to the surface. "No, he's not. Did you tell your dad about this?"

"Uh-huh. The mean boy got in trouble and had to apologize." Her cheeky grin is a reward for both of us. That kid can't dull her sparkle.

"As he should. There's nothing wrong with how much you talk. I really enjoy chatting with you. Be proud your vocabulary is loud and large."

"It's just 'cause I've got lots of words in my humongous brain that gotta get out."

"Let them fly free. I'm always willing to listen."

"M'kay." Her happiness rebounds with a wide grin. She truly is the sweetest.

"Should we—?"

"Where do babies come from?" She also has a

knack for changing the subject out of the blue. One of her many talents.

"Oh, um…" My mind goes blank. "You should ask your dad."

"I already did." She springs to her feet. "He told me it's magic, like from a special wand."

"Magicians pull rabbits from hats. Why not babies?" That explanation might come in handy in the future.

"But the baby isn't out yet. Do magicians put bunnies in hats too? Did Joy visit the circus?"

On second thought, the explanation isn't so great after all.

I rest a palm on my forehead. "These are really good questions."

Which prompts her to ask more. "How did the baby get in Joy's belly? Why is her tummy round? Does the baby look like a ball?"

"Uh, maybe Joy will tell us when she visits."

She squeaks and hops in a fast circle. "I super hope she does. Tell her we miss her extra lots, okay? And we wanna know where her baby came from."

"I'll definitely let her know," I laugh.

Sydney appears pleased with that response, slipping into another momentary lull. A glint suddenly enters her gaze. "Do you get lonely?"

Left field just lobbed me a grounder. It's safe for me to say, "Sometimes. Doesn't everybody?"

She nods. "I think my dad is lonely."

"Oh?" This is heading in a direction I'm not prepared to go.

"Uh-huh. But he has me to keep him company.

You don't have anybody. Does that mean you're extra lonely?"

"I don't mind living alone," I defend. As I told Joy, it's peaceful having my own space.

"Do you eat by yourself? The teachers at school tell us we shouldn't eat alone. They make sure we have a friend to sit with." Her care for my well-being is endearing, and a tad presumptuous. But I'm focusing on the former.

"That's very thoughtful of them. I'm actually having dinner with a… friend tonight."

"Where?"

"A restaurant. It's called The Tavern."

Her blank expression suggests she doesn't know of the place. "With Joy?"

"Nope, I'm going with a different friend."

"What's her name?"

"You're being a curious cat." I lean forward and tap her nose. "His name is Daniel."

Sydney gasps. "Is he your boyfriend?"

"Well, he's a boy. And my friend, I guess." It's not the best sign that our first date doesn't send a single flutter in my belly, but I have to put myself out there. I've been stuck on the singles bench for longer than I care to calculate.

"So, he's your boyfriend."

"Sure," I relent. There's no harm in that.

"I don't have one of those," she mutters.

"Which is perfectly fine. You're too young."

"You sound like my dad." Her gaze brightens as she stares at me. "Are you and my daddy friends?"

That's a complicated puzzle to describe. I settle for simple. "Kinda?"

"Does that mean you'd come to our house for dinner?"

"Oh, that's not a good idea."

"Why not? You're gonna have dinner with a friend later. My daddy is your friend."

"You're very smart, Syd." And I'm out of my element.

"I know," she chirps. "Are you gonna come to my house for dinner? Pretty please?"

A heavy fist pounding on the locked door interrupts Sydney's inquisition.

Saved by the knock.

I'm quick to walk backward toward the hallway, beckoning Syd to join me. "That's your daddy. We better let him in."

And leave the dinner discussion in the dark.

Fingers crossed.

chapter eight

Jake

"AND THEN I DID ANOTHER PIROUETTE. IT FLOPPED. I tried again, and made a full turn. Miss Harper was super proud."

"I'm sure she was." My eyes roll at the windshield as I pull out onto Main Street.

Ever since I arrived at Barre Twirl, Sydney has filled the silence with an extremely detailed recap of her dance class. We've reached the halfway point in her bonus hour. I'm not sure my sanity can handle the rest.

Don't get me wrong—I live for my daughter's stories. Just listening to her idle chatter fills my black heart with warmth. But the context is tainted when every other sentence mentions the woman who monopolizes too much mental real estate as of late. I slammed the door on her over six years ago and have kept it sealed shut without a peek. Why I'm tempted to crack open the barrier now is a detriment that haunts me. It's a weakness I can't afford.

"And Miss Harper loves me too," Syd breaks into my musings.

"Of course she does." The urge to bang my head on the steering wheel radiates across my skull.

"Uh-huh. She told me so. And she has a boyfriend."

I damn near slam on the brakes. "She has a boyfriend?"

That's fucking news to me. It was only a matter of time, though. Anyone with functional vision can see how popular she is at Roosters. Men fight to sit in her section. I put myself through the torture as a reminder of what I'll never have. A burning ache chooses that moment to present itself in my chest. Must be acid reflux.

"They're having dinner tonight," my daughter innocently prattles on. "I think it's a date, like Beauty and the Beast."

"At her apartment?" I don't know what possesses me to ask.

"No, she said a tavern or something."

It's a barbecue joint in the neighboring town. Standard sauce. Mediocre prices. Kid-friendly. Twenty minutes and we'd be there.

A rash decision has me driving straight past the shop and our house nestled behind it. "Would you like to eat out tonight, Boop?"

"Yesssssss!" Her enthusiasm screeches at me from the backseat.

"You pick the spot," I offer. The rotten part of me is hoping she'll suggest—

"Where Miss Harper is," Syd blurts almost on command.

Bingo.

"The Tavern?" And I'm officially reaching a new low.

"Yep," she confirms.

"Are you positive? You just spent an extra hour with her." As if we aren't already en route. But maybe my conscience is creeping in. The full blame for this ambush belongs to me either way. It's not her fault nuclear warfare is destroying my common sense.

Sydney and her stubborn streak rise to the occasion. "But I already miss her. She misses me too."

There's no arguing with that. "Then that's where we're going."

"Yay! You're the bestest, Daddy."

More like a despicable shmuck, but I can't find a single fuck to give. Besides, it's not in my nature to deny my daughter simple wishes. Especially one that happens to align with mine.

I turn into the parking lot and find a slot in the front row. Based on the number of cars, the restaurant shouldn't be too full. That suspicion is confirmed as we step through the heavy doors.

A teenage girl is ready to greet and seat us, but I'm already searching for an exact place to sit. My attention doesn't register the rustic scene. Wagon wheels and rodeo trophies aren't the purpose behind my gaze wildly scanning the room. Golden hair shining bright under the overhead lights sure as shit is. The pressure in my gut deflates as the desperate hunt comes to an abrupt end.

Harper is on the direct opposite side from where we stand, lounging on a cushioned bench that's set along the entire length of the far wall. A man sits in a chair across from her. I can't see his face, but my first impression isn't appropriate for young listening ears. The sections in that area can easily be combined if the group size doubles from two to four. Once again, this couldn't have gone better if I had planned it.

"We'd like that table." I lift my chin toward the empty one beside Harper and her so-called boyfriend. That has yet to be confirmed.

The hostess falters over my specific seating request. "Uh, that would double seat a server. There are plenty of other—"

"But I wanna sit by Miss Harper! She's right over there." My daughter stabs at the air with far less subtlety.

I couldn't have asked for a better interruption. "Is there anything you can do? Miss Harper is her favorite."

The teenager glances at Syd, then studies her tablet. "It shouldn't be a problem."

"That's great. You just made this little girl's night."

Sydney nods. "Uh-huh. Can we go now?"

"Sure," the hostess replies while rounding from behind the stand. "Right this—"

Before she can finish, my daughter takes off in a blazing sprint across the restaurant. "Miss Harper! We're gonna sit right next to you."

The scene would be embarrassing if I wasn't proud of her display. Rumors will spread far and wide about why we're here, especially to any guys interested in Harper. It almost brings a skip to my step.

I follow behind at a leisurely stroll to appreciate the shock value. Syd's outburst has everyone turning to stare, including the guy sitting where I want to be. But I'm not looking at him. My focus is latched onto Harper's blinding grin as my daughter races toward her. She scoots over and opens her arms, eagerly accepting the hug Syd launches at her. My traitorous heart trips over the sight of their effortless connection. The evidence has my crumbling resistance prepared to raise a white flag.

After their brief embrace, Sydney wiggles free and flings herself onto the booth beside Harper. That leaves the chair for me, which puts me at an optimal angle from the main attraction. Her date isn't the only one who should get to enjoy the view. He's stiff in his seat, stunned still by the viral-worthy scene that just occurred.

Meanwhile, Harper appears to be gathering clues to solve our random appearance. Her keen sense roams over my daughter who's glued to her side. "Hey, superstar. Long time, no see."

Syd giggles. "You just saw me at dance class. Did you forget?"

She thumps her forehead. "Oh, that's right. You're still wearing your leotard and leggings."

"We didn't go home," my daughter reveals, as if that isn't obvious with our timely arrival.

Harper must've come straight from the studio herself. The only difference I can see from my vantage point is her loose hair and chunky sweater. Both are a quick change. She finally feels the weight of my stare and shifts her focus to me. "Hello, Jacob."

"Howdy, Pitch." I tug at the brim of my hat like it's of the cowboy variety and not baseball. It fits the establishment.

Her eyes narrow into slits at my use of the nickname I rarely spout these days. "This is a surprise."

I rub the stubble on my chin. "A real coincidence."

It's not in the slightest, and the glare Harper pins on me agrees.

She slides her gaze back to Syd. "Whose idea was it to eat dinner at The Tavern?"

"Yours."

She rolls her lips together, stifling a laugh. "Did you tell your dad I was coming here?"

"Uh-huh."

"And now you're here too." There's no question in her tone.

"Yep."

"Like I said, real convenient." I clap and slouch lower in my seat, a sure sign I'm settling in for a long meal.

The dude beside me shifts, which is a shame. I'd almost forgotten he exists. As if requesting acknowledgment of his presence, he clears his throat. He taps the table and lifts his eyebrows when that doesn't gain the desired response. Fucking douche can introduce himself if he cares that much.

Harper jolts at the reminder that he's in attendance. Unfortunately. Her laugh is tight and awkward. "Oh, whoops. This is Daniel. My… friend."

"Her boyfriend," Syd corrects.

Daniel sits straighter at my daughter's generous—and inaccurate—assumption. "And who might you be?"

"Sydney Grace Evans. I'm Miss Harper's most favorite student." Her smile is pure sugar and sprinkles.

"It's very nice to meet one of Harper's dancers." He extends an open palm to me. "And you are…?"

"Her father." I squeeze harder than necessary, but Dad forgot to teach me proper etiquette.

Daniel yelps and yanks his hand from my crushing grip. "Jesus, man. Be careful with the money maker."

I give him a blank stare. "Huh?"

"Daniel is a dentist," Harper explains.

"A dentist," I echo. My tone holds disdain rather than respect. He'll have to earn that from me without hiding behind a fancy degree.

"Dr. Daniel Pumper." He whips out a business card from his suit jacket. "I'll give you a free cleaning."

"Look at my teeth!" Syd opens wide and sticks out her tongue, hiding her pearly whites from view.

"Very sparkly. You must brush twice a day."

"Yep!" She beams at him like the extremely friendly kid she is.

"And you have a great smile."

"Thanks," she chirps. Then Syd turns to Harper and repeats the process.

That's when Daniel's full name smacks me like a bad joke.

"Wait a second. You're Dr. Pumper?" I chuckle, there's no stopping it. "That's incredible."

He brightens. "You've heard of me?"

Amusement shakes my entire frame. "Yeah, there are a few risqué videos on the internet. I always pass them by, but I'm sure they're a hit and very tasteful. Do you do your own scenes?"

His misplaced glee collapses into a sneer. "How original. Like I haven't heard that before."

"Ah, lighten up. I'm just messing with you." My palm thwacks the center of his scrawny chest.

Daniel winces and rubs at the inflicted spot. "I'd appreciate if you didn't."

"Sore subject," I drawl. "Noted."

Harper is scowling. She mouths something that looks an awful lot like, *Behave.*

Little does she realize that just encourages me.

"So, Pumper," I begin the tedious task of engaging him in meaningless conversation.

"You can call me Daniel."

"I'd rather not. We're better off on a last-name basis. Mine is Evans, by the way. Thanks for asking."

His mouth opens and shuts like a gasping fish out of water. "I thought I did…?"

Guilt tries to worm its way beneath my sullied layers, but the mud is just too damn tainted. "Don't worry about it. All is forgiven. Now, as I was saying, how did you meet Harper?"

"Online," Daniel responds.

"That's… interesting." Which is a far tamer word than I'd prefer to use. Mostly due to Harper dating in general.

"Then he stopped into Roosters over the weekend and we kinda hit it off. One of the rare moments you weren't darkening a stool," Harper supplies.

Which means I need to be more vigilant. "Didn't realize you were in the market for a relationship."

"If the right guy comes along," she trails off after dropping that crumb.

Bile rises in my throat when Daniel winks at her.

"Hey, y'all." A frazzled server slams to a halt at our mismatched dynamic.

It's only then I realize we haven't ordered. The menu remains untouched in front of me. My mind is on more important matters.

"I'm on a date with my daddy," Sydney broadcasts in a loud announcement.

The entire restaurant erupts in a unified, "Awww."

Even Harper's eyes look a tad misty. She taps Syd on the nose, stealing my signature move. "Just the sweetest."

My daughter cuddles against her. "You can be our date too."

I almost offer her a high-five for leaving Dr. Pumper out of the equation.

"Good grief, my ovaries are exploding." The server fans her face. "Anywho, sorry about the wait. There's an eight top over there and each order is modified, plus you were sat at the same time. Not your problem. Apologies again. Feel free to holler if you need me between stops. Should we get these tables pushed together?"

"No," Daniel blurts. "We're separate."

"Oh," the server rears back. "My mistake. I figured you knew each other."

"You don't wanna sit with us?" Sydney's bottom lip wobbles.

"It's not that, but…" Apparently, Dr. Pumper can't say the words that will break a little girl's heart.

Maybe I should give him more credit. A snort rips from me at the audacity. Sometimes I crack myself up.

"Miss Harper, can we eat with you?" Syd blinks adoring eyes at Harper, playing a part I'd never ask her to. But damn. She puts on an irresistible performance.

The woman under my daughter's spell glances at her so-called date, a silent plea in her gaze.

Daniel sighs, the fight leaving him with that heavy exhale. "Fine, you can push the tables together."

I pat him on the shoulder, a satisfied smirk painting my lips. "You're definitely going to regret this."

chapter nine

Harper

THERE'S A DISTINCT THRUM UNDER MY SKIN AS I SHIFT my car into park at Evans Auto Repair. This is my first visit to Jake's shop since he took the business over from his dad several years ago. There hadn't been a reason for me to drop by until now.

I'm still rattled after my failed date featuring Jake's one-sided pissing match. His insufferable commentary chased off Dr. Daniel Pumper—which is a name meant for crude jokes, if I'm being honest. That's beside the point.

No matter which way I flip the scene, it always comes out upside down. I've thought of little else since we parted ways last night. Almost twenty-four hours later and my brain is the consistency of confused mush. There's no logical explanation for Jake's possessive behavior. I'd blame it on Sydney wanting to see me, but her father isn't the type to blindly agree to share a meal with a person he loathes. There's no sense to be made without answers.

His bold logo plastered on the glass door taunts me. He's not the only one who can drop by unannounced. So, here I am, prepared to deliver a taste of his own medicine. If nothing else, I'll leave him guessing.

The lobby is empty when I walk in, only a basic chime welcomes me. My stride doesn't falter as my boots squeak across the linoleum. I show myself into the garage from the door behind the desk. There's not a chance I'm trading shock and awe for hesitation.

Hinges creak in protest at my determined entrance. I've barely stepped two feet inside the concrete fortress when I'm spotted.

"Miss Harper!" Sydney zips toward me at breakneck speed, crashing into my legs for a hug.

I loop my arms around her small frame to return the embrace. "Hey, cutie pie."

Her chin rests on my thigh as she stares up at me. "Hi."

A rhythmic pawing on my shin draws my attention farther down. Glitzy refuses to be neglected and begs without shame. The pampered Pomeranian is more fluff than body with two pink bows near her barely visible ears to show for it.

I lower into a crouch, giving the pooch a scratch under the chin. "And hello to you too."

"We're super excited to see you." Syd bounces on the soles of her sparkly shoes. Her dark hair is wild and quirky, much like her personality. Her infectious energy radiates from the inside out. I tug on an untamed curl while a smile spreads across my lips.

"How was school today?"

"Great! I colored a picture. Wanna see?" She whips out a piece of folded paper from her dress pocket and thrusts it into my hands.

I open the creases with care. My next breath whooshes out in an unexpected rush. "Oh, my goodness."

The sight blurs my vision. Three misshapen figures are drawn in a crooked line. There's a ball of brown under the largest one's arm. Neat handwriting tags the identity of each individual.

"Miss Tiffany helped me write the names. See? There's my daddy holding Glitzy 'cause she *loooooves* to be carried. I'm the one dancing in the middle. My tutu has lotsa colors like a rainbow. And there's you, cheering for me like always!"

I lift my watery gaze to find Jake staring at me from in front of an elevated truck. It doesn't feel right that Sydney left her mom out of the picture. Morgan should be included, not me. But I'm not sure it's my place to mention that detail.

Regardless, my role in Syd's life doesn't deserve a front-row seat. Maybe I'm getting too involved. The pang that immediately smacks my chest demands that I retract the comment.

"This is very special. I love it," I manage to whisper. "The resemblance is uncanny."

Sydney's smile could illuminate the sky. "I tried my very bestest."

"You did great, superstar."

"Thanks!" She does a tendu that leads into a step

touch sequence, then bends into a plié and ends with a bow.

I clap with extra enthusiasm while attempting to swipe at my unshed tears. "Beautiful."

"Why are you crying? Is your car broken?" Her blue eyes hold a glimmer of concern. "My daddy can fix it."

"No, my car is fine." It's my impulsive attitude that requires repair. I'm beginning to realize this stunt could end in disaster.

Jake chooses that moment to saunter over. Masculine swagger drenches his towering stature. His faded jeans hug his muscular thighs in a way that should be criminal. A plain white shirt tries and fails to conceal the carved definition along his abdomen. The short sleeves put his biceps on prominent display and highlight the colorful ink decorating his skin. Those tattoos are my ultimate downfall. If I stare too long, I'm likely to slip in a puddle of my own drool.

"What can I do to you?"

I blink myself back to reality. "Huh?"

"Oil change? Tire pressure? New windshield wiper blades?" His slip of the tongue doesn't go unnoticed, but I choose to let it slide.

"Sydney asked if I'd come to your house for dinner."

His eyebrows take a hike so high I'm surprised they don't disappear into his hairline. "Is that so?"

The little girl gasps. "I'll start cooking!" Then she dashes to a kitchen playset in the corner that appears designated for her toys. Glitzy lets a shrill ruff fly free before bounding after her.

With Syd out of earshot, Jake ditches the tolerant pretense and spits a curse. She's the only one who softens his jagged edges. The rest get piss, vinegar, and a heaping dose of disdain.

The glare he shoots at me confirms as much. "I wasn't aware we were expecting company."

"Funny," I quip. "I could say the same about dinner last night."

His glare is lethal. "This is you getting back at me."

"Why would I need to get back at you?"

"Cut the shit," he growls.

"Does that mean you're ready to admit that you sabotaged my date on purpose?"

His scoff is dipped in arrogance. "Should've thought of that before telling my daughter about it. Like I said, you're her second favorite person. Might as well have sent her a personalized invitation."

"I didn't spell out the details," I retort. The conversation with Syd at the studio filters through my mind. "Well, not exactly. She's very clever and sneaky. Just pulled the info right out of me."

"Or you secretly wanted us to crash your date." The satisfied gleam in his gaze isn't appreciated.

That serves to remind me of all the snarky crap he dished out last night. "You're quite capable of turning into a charismatic asshole when the mood strikes. I wasn't aware you had such experience in bullshitting."

Jake kept Daniel engaged in meaningless conversation the entire meal. I'd be impressed if I wasn't ambushed.

His chuckle is too cocky. "I'll take that as a compliment."

My eyes narrow until our glares clash. "You shouldn't. It was a distraction tactic, and you know it."

Jake wrenches his gaze off mine, choosing a random spot behind me as his next target. "What would I have to gain?"

"That's what I'm trying to find out."

And it's an itch I can't freaking scratch. Steam is about to whistle from my ears in a frustrated spew. There's always been an attraction between us. That level of chemistry doesn't just evaporate. But in the years since our fleeting relationship, Jake has given me nothing but hostility. There's more to the story, an angle he's playing at, and I'm determined to figure out what it is.

As if hearing my mental plotting, he grunts and crosses his arms. "Good luck with that."

Kade and Penn—both hidden from view under the hoods of their current ticket—must read the room. The pair straightens to assess our tense standoff. After a matching set of silent nods, they make a hasty escape into the office and shut the blinds.

Jake clenches his jaw. "Real nice, Pitch. Your temper tantrum is disrupting my employees."

"Should've thought of that before interrupting my plans." I pin his flimsy excuse back on him.

Once again, his eyes reveal the thrashing upset brewing inside of him. Light fades into darkness as he glowers at me. "You expect me to believe you actually like that guy?"

"So what if I do? It's no business of yours to interfere." I'm not upset about Daniel, but it's the principle.

He rips the hat off his head and flips it backward. Between that agitated motion and the thick veins snaking along his forearms, I'm likely to launch myself at him. Or walk out before I do something stupid.

Syd is suddenly beside me, stalling any attempt I had to flee. "Daddy wanted to meet your boyfriend. I did too, but I didn't say it all grouchy like Oscar."

Well, that's certainly an intriguing development. "What did you think of him?"

She wrinkles her nose. "My dad is way better."

I cough to cover my surprise. Her blunt honesty is a trait to admire. It's not like I'm offended by her remark. Daniel isn't my anything to defend. In fact, I'll be surprised if he bothers to call me again. Jake saw to that with a ferocity I don't appreciate. Which is precisely why I'm not eager to reveal the success of his efforts. The gloating smirk he's wearing isn't helping his case.

"Your dad is all yours." That explanation is reasonable enough.

"But I can share. I'm super good at it."

"That's very generous, but I… already have a boyfriend?" It's not a total lie. There's a battery-operated version in my nightstand drawer. Bob is very reliable.

"Isn't my dad your friend?" She's already put me on the spot with this question.

I falter with the answer just the same. "Um…"

"You said he was," Syd reminds me. "That's why you're having dinner with us."

A hot sting blooms on my cheeks. Regret is a sticky substance I can't escape from. I'm not going to get saved by a well-timed knock this round.

My gaze lifts to Jake, as if he's going to provide me with a rescue raft. The smolder I find directed at me is unexpected. A shiver races over my skin, but there's no drafty chill to blame. It prompts me to take a breath and inspect the shop.

With the roller doors sealed shut, the heat is trapped and creates a toasty environment. Organized shelves and cabinets frame the outer edge. Three spacious stalls occupy the middle. Syd has an entire corner dedicated to her. I smile at the pink frills making a loud statement in the otherwise standard industrial building. Motor oil and rubber cling to the open space, but the scents aren't oppressive. I fill my lungs with another long inhale. "It smells... clean."

Jake scrubs over his mouth with stained fingers in an attempt to hide a smirk. "Our filtration system is solid. It sucks breathing dirty air all day. Plus, I don't want Syd fussing at me."

"I don't like when it's stinky." She waves a hand in front of her nose.

"Wrapped around her pinky," I murmur.

He shrugs while hitching his thumbs into his belt loops. "Won't deny it."

I shift my focus off him to track Syd twirling around neatly stacked tires. There's an underlying sense of comfort emanating from the walls. Every item has a home and belongs right where it rests. The owner has taken great care to create an atmosphere people want to enter. I imagine Kade and Penn treat the garage as more than a job. It's the respect of the trade.

"This is different from what I envisioned," I choose to admit.

"What do you visualize while dreaming of my shop?"

My eyes roll at his salacious tone. I won't feed his ego more than necessary. "Grime and grease."

Jake clutches his chest like it's wounded. "My reputation is important to me."

I snort, but it lacks conviction. "Yeah, okay. I'm sure your customer service is award-winning."

"Have you heard any complaints?"

"No, but that's beside the point."

"And what's the point?" It might be my imagination, but I think he's moved closer.

I stare into his eyes that reveal too much. "You're—"

"Daddy, I'm hungry. We can't eat plastic food. It was a joke." Sydney has impeccable timing. I could've used this interruption during her earlier interrogation.

Acceptance squares Jake's shoulders. He slides a stoic glance my way. "You like pizza?"

chapter ten

Harper

"MY TUMMY IS SOOOO STUFFED. LOOK HOW BIG IT IS." Sydney leaps from her chair and puffs out her stomach for our inspection.

"Wow," I gush. "Three slices. You're a good eater."

"I wanna be tall and strong like you."

Those are two traits I hadn't previously assigned myself. "That's very sweet."

"Oh! And I wanna be a ballerina." She does a rapid routine of unchoreographed steps that are mostly a blur.

"Goals are important. Practice, exercise, healthy food, and sleep are the recipe for success, cutie pie." Pretty sure Jake snorts at my pep talk, but I ignore him.

Syd gasps and whirls toward her dad. "Can I have dessert?"

He glances at the clock. "It's almost time for bed. I thought you were full?"

"There's a little room right here." She points to a small spot on her stomach.

"Then you can have a little something."

Genuine delight resembles a squeal as she races to the cabinet. While she rummages in the contents, I let my gaze drift to the man still seated at the table with me. His posture is relaxed, one arm slung over the back of the neighboring chair. We sit in a peaceful lull that I haven't felt around him in… well, maybe ever. There's always been a thread of tension for one reason or another.

"How 'bout these?" Syd rushes back to us with Gushers in her grip.

"Sure, Boop." His eyes crinkle in the corners as he watches Syd rip open the package. Then he catches me staring. "Do I have something on my face?"

I laugh and shake my head. "You're a great dad. I hope you know that."

He squints. "Because I let her have fruit snacks at eight o'clock?"

"Because she's your whole world and it shows." I'm fortunate to have a backstage pass.

Jake drops his gaze to trace a vein in the wood. "Better quit or she'll invite you to dinner again."

Warmth spreads through my chest. That idea holds more appeal than it should. I've probably overstayed my welcome as it is. Just as I'm about to begin the process of excusing myself, Syd yawns with an exaggerated roar fit for a lion.

"I'm sleepy," she murmurs.

"A full belly will do that to you." That's why I insist on a power walk after lunch.

"You know what that means," Jake says and rises to his feet.

Sydney peeks at him from under heavy lids. "Can Miss Harper put me to bed?"

"Uhhh," I flounder on dry land. Pressure seems to hold the entire room hostage. When I look to Jake for guidance, he appears equally shocked. The fear of intruding on quality time jostles my foot. This is far beyond my dance instructor duties, which is evident as I stand on shaky legs. "Shouldn't your dad do the honors?"

"But I want you to tuck me in. You just gotta read me a story. I can put on my own jammies." Her voice holds a whiny fuse that has the potential to explode.

"It's fine," he assures me.

"Is it really?" Girl code would suggest otherwise.

Rather than respond, Jake lowers to the floor and opens his arms. Syd rushes forward to wrap herself around him. They fold together in a heartfelt exchange that hitches my breath. It's obvious that affection doesn't run dry under this roof. The bond between father and daughter is something truly special to witness.

I'm swept into the past, to faded memories of my dad. He died in a car accident when I was Sydney's age. It's a tragedy I often block out since I was so young when it happened. My mom rallied despite losing her husband. She raised me with a support system equal to two parents, much like what the man crouched on this kitchen floor is doing for his child.

Jake presses his face into Sydney's hair. "Love you, Boop."

"Love you too, Daddy." She burrows into his trusting hold.

"Sweet dreams," he murmurs before releasing her.

Syd beams broadly at her adoring dad. "Nighty night. Don't let the beddy-bugs bite."

In response, the grumpiest man I've ever met blows his little girl a kiss. I sway into the wall with a thump. My elbow aches as the force of a swoon threatens to pull me under. Good grief, this man needs to come with a warning label. I'm still trying to gather my bearings while Sydney dashes into the hallway.

"C'mon, Miss Harper. It's time for bed!" She prances up the stairs with Glitzy hot on her heels.

"I'm just… going to… go do that." My statement is choppy, similar to the uneven breaths filling my lungs. I don't dare look at Jake for fear that he'll see the desire shining in my eyes. He'd never let me live that down. Instead, I spin on my heels with my cheeks burning.

Syd pokes her head out of the bathroom when I reach the landing. Her finger jabs at a door a few down. "Pick out a story to read while I get dressed, m'kay?"

"Sure, sweetie." That's easy enough to accomplish, I think.

"Thanks! I'll be done super soon."

My socked feet drag on the plush carpet as I inch toward her room. There's a strange sensation creeping along my spine, as if I'm an intruder in their house. I set out to give Jake a shock with my unexpected arrival. Sydney requesting for me to be in charge of bedtime is another surprise entirely.

A pink princess paradise greets me when I step over the threshold. I almost stumble back from the abrupt change in scenery. Floor to ceiling is covered in fluff, frills, and fun. It's like walking into every little girl's dream sequence.

I shake off the stupor and focus on my assigned task. There's a small shelf under the window stacked with options for me to choose from. My experience with children's books is outdated at best. I run a finger along the spines, stopping at a hilarious title.

"Did you find one?" Syd reappears, clad in My Little Pony pajamas and fresh breath.

"Yep." I whip my choice off the shelf for presentation.

She giggles. "That's one of my favorites. It's soooo funny."

Sydney leaps onto the bed and dives under the covers. Glitzy isn't far behind. She spins in several fast circles before curling up on a pillow. I perch on the edge, holding the book open at an optimal angle for Syd's viewing.

"Don't Let the Pigeon Drive the Bus!" I read the title aloud, adding a goofy tone for extra enjoyment.

The opening dialogue already has me laughing. Syd's eyelids droop lower with each page flip. By the fifth or sixth, she's snoozing soundly. I smile at the energic whirlwind finally at rest. Soft snores provide further confirmation a minute later. That's my cue. I tiptoe to turn off the lights and ease the door shut.

Jake is sprawled on one end of the couch when I return downstairs. The room is dim with only a small lamp casting a glow. His feet are kicked up on the low table, ankles crossed, beer in hand. He looks at home, which is only fitting.

"She's all tucked in," I say from my awkward stance near the foyer. Just a few paces to the left and I'll show myself out.

"Wanna stay for a drink?"

The offer is surprising, but this entire evening has thrown me through enough loops to build a rollercoaster. "Um, I guess I can hang out for a bit longer."

His chuckle is rich and raspy in the dark, beckoning me into the shadows. He's probably been waiting all night to give me a piece of his mind. "Don't sound too excited about it."

"I just wasn't expecting the offer." Which fits the complex puzzle I'm still trying to solve.

I park my ass on the cushion, but my spine is stiff. Too many thoughts cloud my better judgment. Jake nudges an unopened beer toward me with his foot. Alcohol certainly won't deliver clarity. A distinct pop breaks the silence as I crack the tab, announcing my decision to stick around.

"Bottoms up." He lifts his own in the air.

Fizz and hops dance on my tongue before I swallow the bitter flavor. "Yummy."

"Gets the job done." He rolls the can between his palms, appearing deep in thought. "What were you gonna call me earlier?"

Several terms and choice words come to mind, most of them unflattering. "When?"

"In the garage before Syd cut you off about dinner. You started saying I was something. I'm curious as to what that might be."

I gnaw at my inner cheek as another fierce blush takes root. "Impressive."

His beer pauses halfway to his mouth. "Impressive?"

"You impress me," I admit in a breathy voice that doesn't sound like my own.

He rolls his head along the back of the couch until our gazes meet. "Will you let me eat your pussy?"

I sputter, wasting perfectly good oxygen. "W-what?"

"You heard me."

"Probably not correctly." If I had more than one sip of beer, I'd be willing to put a hefty wager on hearing things. "Who just asks something like that?"

"Someone impressive."

"You're taking my meaning out of context."

"Does it matter?"

No, not if the tingles spreading from my lower belly are any indication. The traitorous dry spell I'm stuck in insists on mocking me. "Will I let you…?"

"Eat your pussy," he finishes.

"Right," I exhale on a squirm. The hungry minx I haven't properly fed in years won't be silenced. She rises to the surface with snapping jaws. "Um, what girl wouldn't?"

"I'm only asking you."

For some stupid reason that makes me feel special, which means I should probably leave. "You actually want to… do that?"

Jake's hooded eyes follow the flush racing up my neck. "Do what? Say it for me."

I clench my eyes shut. "Eat my pussy."

His hat is pulled low, but I can see the restraint fraying in his gaze. "Fuck, you're sexy. And yes, I want to. Very much so."

"Really? I didn't think guys—"

A loud rumble in his throat stops me short. "You only need to worry about me."

"Do you expect me to reciprocate?" My gaze trails to

the bulge in his jeans, putting strain on the zipper. This isn't completely new territory for us. Our history didn't travel that far south, though.

He slices a hand through the space between us. "Absolutely not."

I scoff and cross my arms. "That's one way to make a girl feel warm and fuzzy."

"It's just honesty. I don't want anything in return."

It's baffling that I haven't denied his request. I should say no. That's the logical response. But I find myself wanting to be very illogical. Especially when this man is involved. "Why?"

"Too many complications."

"But you doing something extremely intimate to me isn't complicated?"

"Nope, it's simple. I'll take off your pants, eat you for dessert, and make you scream my name. But not too loud." He points upstairs before pressing a finger over his lips.

As if a reminder of where we are and who I'm with is necessary. "I'm not the vocal type."

"We'll see." His eyes flash, accepting a challenge I didn't intend to make.

That's when I notice I've been absently scooting backward on the sofa. My shoulders are flush with the pillows. "Are you sure this is a good idea?"

"No, but you get me hard just sitting there. I can't stop thinking about taking the edge off."

"By going down on me." I remove the question from my tone.

"That would do the trick." He traps his bottom lip

between his teeth. The flesh turns white under the force of his bite.

I want to feel that pressure on my skin, which is why I find myself nodding. "Okay."

"That's what I thought." He sinks to the floor, kneeling between my splayed thighs.

"Oh, you're just getting right after it."

Jake's palms settle my bouncing knees. "Why beat around the bush?"

"I'm freshly waxed, thanks for asking."

His chuckle is a gritty scrape against my rapidly building arousal. "I'd never dare to assume otherwise. But making pitstops just builds anticipation and gives the wrong impression. You already know where I'm headed."

"This is beginning to feel like a transaction." Yet I sink lower on the couch.

His hands roam along my bent legs. "I'm not going to kiss you or fill your head with romantic notions. This is just me giving you pleasure."

Am I actually considering this? A glance at the unfiltered lust in his gaze practically begs me to agree. "No strings?"

"Not a single one. Just sit back and let me do what I'm good at."

"Since you asked so nicely," I joke.

My snark spurs him into action. Jake strips my leggings from me in one deft motion. The carpet is cool beneath my suddenly bare feet, alerting me that my socks are gone too. My thong is treated with more regard. His fingers trace the lacy pattern before hooking into the elastic band. He peels the silky material down and off with a patience I wouldn't credit him for.

With my lower half naked, a prickling awareness prods at me. But Jake doesn't give me a moment for doubt to slither in. My left leg gets slung over his broad shoulder. He does the same with my right, lifting until I'm balanced at a slight diagonal.

As if I'm not already on display, Jake stretches me wider and wedges himself into the gap. He flips his hat backward while preparing to dive in. So much for not building anticipation. That practiced move is foreplay, a better aphrodisiac than an entire oyster buffet. His large palms grip my ass to haul me closer. This position puts me on a platter for his feasting.

His lips ghost along the sensitive skin of my inner thigh. "You wet for me?"

Why he insists on holding conversation while I'm spread eagle in his face is beyond me. "Touch me and find out."

"Tell me," he commands.

"Yes," I mutter in return. Drenched is more accurate. I can feel my hot arousal in contrast to the exposed chill.

A pleased noise spills from his mouth. He drags his nose to my center, inhaling loud and long. "Smells like frosting."

If I blush any harder, I'll combust. "I'm beginning to second guess this entire ordeal."

He shushes me, the reprimand blowing across my heated flesh. I'm rigid in his controlled grasp, draped over him like an erotic garment. My pulse thunders loud enough to serenade us both.

"Relax," he rasps against my exposed center.

"Kinda hard to do that when you're up close and personal with my hoo-ha. It's too weird."

"Let's see how you feel after I do this." Jake flattens his tongue and gives me a long lick that doesn't seem to end.

Sparks ignite under my skin and I surrender all restraint. My upper body sags into the couch. "Ohhhh."

He chuckles. "There we go. You're getting it now. I'm gonna make stars dance in your eyes."

His lips latch around my clit, that talented tongue lashing at the sensitive nerves. It's apparent after only a few swipes that I'm going to crest the peak very quickly. A tremble already tweaks my muscles. Heat is rapidly spreading through my legs. There's a telltale throb expanding from where his mouth works me into a frenzy.

"W-wow," I pant. "You're really good at this."

"You shouldn't doubt me," he rasps into my slit.

The ebb and flow have me delirious, desperation sinking its claws into my need. "K-keep going."

"I will," Jake taunts. "If you tell me what you want. Be specific."

"Make me come. I want to come," I blurt. Modesty fled after he put his mouth on me.

"That's what I want too."

I shiver as his lips return to my slippery center. He slides a finger into me, my inner walls clenching around that thick intrusion. Pressure doubles and coils faster with each pump from his swirling digit. My hunger spirals and expands until I'm filled with passion.

"S-shit, oh, oh. Holy, my goshhhhh." The babble spills like a waterfall from my gaping lips.

"That's right, Pitch. Let me hear you."

I tip my face skyward and let out a muffled wail. "Yesssssss."

"Taste too fucking sweet." The guttural words are spoken against my folds.

I tremble at the filth dripping off his tongue. "More."

As if satisfying my earlier curiosity, his teeth gently bite into a fleshy spot on my leg. "Ask nice."

"Please," I gasp.

His answer is a second finger gliding in with the first. The two curl to hit a sacred spot that makes me quiver. I press a cool palm against the blazing heat streaking across my face. There's a fever raging inside of me. Only Jake can extinguish the flames.

I peer at him from my sloped distortion and get light-headed. Jake's nose, mouth, and chin are buried in my lady business. He moans as if I'm a delicacy. From the way he's devouring me, I'm likely to believe it.

The visual shoots a fierce craving into my bloodstream. I feel consumed, and sexy. Powerful. It doesn't escape my notice that Jake of all people is the one inspiring these thoughts. Now isn't the moment to obsess over details.

Especially when his mouth clamps onto my clit with suction to make my vocal cords hoarse.

"Harder," I beg.

His chuckle is seductive. "Greedy girl."

But he complies. The coarse rub from his stubble is a friction I didn't know I was missing. My hips move with an agenda of their own, chasing the relief just beyond my grasp.

"There. Right there," I cry.

Jake sucks my clit between his lips, the storm brewing bigger with each pull, until I'm thrust into the abyss. The force chatters my teeth. I'm barely aware that I'm spasming in his hold as he continues his onslaught. His insistence doesn't relent even though I'm hurtling over the cliff into floating bliss. I'm suspended for several seconds—or maybe minutes. All I know is that the relief is unlike anything I've experienced. He claims the release from me until I'm drained.

And true to his words, I see stars dancing in my vision.

My body is the consistency of properly pleasured goop. This man has earned the impressive title I bestowed upon him. I'm lost to the aftershocks while Jake dips his wet fingers into his mouth.

"You taste better than I imagined. So. Fucking. Sweet." Each word is punctuated by a thorough lick across his joined digits.

I whimper at the sight. "You're dirty."

Jake swipes at his damp mouth and chin. "Only 'cause you made me so."

There's no denying my involvement. The evidence still glistens on his face. Maybe I should be ashamed, but he's wearing my release like a badge of honor. It sends a thrill through my slack limbs.

"Uh-huh," I mumble mutely. I've barely recovered from the best orgasm of my life when he returns to his spot on the couch.

He flicks heavy-lidded eyes at me. "Good eats, Pitch. Better than hot fudge."

"You're welcome," I quip with a lazy grin aimed at the ceiling.

"Although, I'd be willing to slurp some off you. That combo would be addictive. Might never get enough."

I jolt when he taps my outer thigh. "What's up?"

The arrogant ass smirks, well aware I'm basking in the afterglow. "Want another?"

"Um, that was plenty." My clit is freaking numb, likely to stage a revolt if I accept.

A chill bites at my exposed skin. It serves to remind me that I'm nude from the waist down. I cross my legs and draw them against me. That vulnerable sensation rattles my bones again. My shoulders curl inward as a cold and empty ache replaces the warmth.

What I could really go for is a hug. A sideways glance proves I'm alone in that yearning.

Jake is slumped against the armrest. A flinty guard is already slamming shut over his gaze. The space he's shoved between us is an icy expanse better left uncharted. Instead, I gather my discarded clothes to keep from overanalyzing.

An awkward lull creeps in as I get dressed. The silence allows confusion to enter the room, try as I might to remain unaffected. Turns out that an emotional connection—no matter how fleeting—is important to me. How he can be this detached agitates my pesky need for comfort.

"So," I mumble. "That was… interesting."

Jake snorts. "We don't have to do this."

"Do what?"

"Talk," he deadpans.

His flippant tone irks me. The casual dismissal tempts me to ask him if I can spend the night, just to watch his composure reel, but I won't appear clingy. I should've prepared for this. He's predictable in that sense. Even more so, he spelled out the terms before getting personally acquainted with my cooch. This misplaced hurt is on me.

"Welp," I yawn with an exaggerated stretch. It's a feat to stop my knees from wobbling as I stand. "I'm gonna sleep well tonight."

Steely eyes follow my measured backpedal toward the entryway. "Don't say I never gave you anything."

The urge to throttle him forms my hands into fists. My euphoria has fizzled out completely. What's left is the unfortunate realization that this was a shallow means to an unfulfilling end. I know the score, and he rightfully earned a win this round.

That doesn't mean I'm admitting defeat. "Give my best to Jill or Rosey Palmer or whoever keeps you company between the sheets. That fresh spank bank material should come in handy. Pun intended."

I turn and flounce to the door, my dignity giving Jacob Evans the middle finger behind my back.

chapter eleven

Jake

HARPER FUCKING WILSON.

Her name might as well be tattooed on my brain. It's a personalized plague, ruining me from the inside out with each passing day. The entire point of getting a taste was to snuff out this incessant need that never shuts up. In reality, all my down-under actions succeeded in accomplishing was ramping up my appetite for more.

That woman is finger-licking good, and I have a bad feeling my cravings for her are only going to get worse. I can still taste her pussy on my lips a week later. The unique honey blend has ruined me for any other flavor. She's too tempting. I surrendered in a weak moment, but there are bound to be more. On cue, another rush of longing hits and I almost crash to my knees.

It cements my resolve and the stalkerish behavior

that accompanies it. Although to be fair, it took zero effort to track Harper down. She's a creature of habit and I'm fucked on her enough to know her constant whereabouts.

Which is why I'm loitering on the sidewalk outside of Bean Me Up.

Knox Creek's beloved coffee house is mostly full when I enter. The rich scent of freshly caffeinated brews assaults my nostrils, but I barely notice as I scour the quaint space. Several curious gazes are quick to study my random appearance. Included in the onlookers are Susan and a few other recognizable faces. The mom squad is seated together with their eyes firmly pinned on me. Their interest is probably piqued higher seeing as I've never stepped foot inside this café until now. I'd stare at the man frozen in the doorway too.

Glossy hair the shade of a homing beacon attracts my attention in the correct direction. Just the sight of Harper swiping whipped foam off her upper lip gets me hard. It makes me want to drizzle hot fudge on her pussy and take my sweet ass time licking her clean. Feverish desire pumps hot in my veins until I nearly stagger where I stand. Fuck. Maybe this was a mistake.

Doubt hits me too damn late as the crowd stills with bated breath. A rapt audience isn't ideal, but providing fresh meat for the town's gossip rings is kind of our specialty. Harper will be made aware of my creeper status either way. To prove that undeniable point, the nosy onlookers track my direct route to her table. It's only a matter of seconds until conspiring whispers replace the idle chatter.

Harper's startled gaze leaps to mine while I erase the

remaining distance. Without waiting for her jaw to lift off the floor, I slide onto the chair opposite hers. A tense quiet settles as I make myself comfortable.

"Mornin', Pitchy." My tone is calm, collected, and utter bullshit.

She glances around, noticing the spectators. "Following me now?"

I shrug. "Keeps things interesting."

"As if you're boring."

"Careful with the compliments or I'll be under the table having you for breakfast. I'm all too eager to bury my face between your thighs again." Deflection is my finest defense mechanism, and she knows it.

That doesn't stop her cheeks from turning a hypnotic shade of red. "What're you doing here, Jake?"

"I thought we were routinely dropping in on one another unannounced. It's my turn based on that logic."

Her expression is wary, and rightfully so. "Where have you been since last Thursday? I didn't even see you bring Syd to the studio for her classes."

Which was dumb luck that I greatly appreciated.

"Did you miss me? That's cute." I tack on a cocky smirk to disguise what her remark does to me.

Harper frowns. "Cut the crap. Why are you here?"

"Thought I'd see what all the fuss is about." My eyes do a purposeful sweep of the trendy establishment.

"At my table," she grinds out.

"Making polite conversation."

"Since when? You're not polite about anything."

"Maybe I'm trying to make a change."

"I'm not sure how that involves me. We don't do… this. Whatever this is."

"Exchange pleasantries? Banter about the weather? Engage in civil chit-chat? Be social in general?" The options are laughable, but I manage to keep a straight face.

Meanwhile, her lips press into a flat line. "You made it quite clear that we don't need to talk."

"Still salty about that, huh?"

She huffs. "Nah, a cold shoulder brush-off was the cherry on top of that cliterizing performance."

"Cliterizing performance," I repeat. "Wow, that sounds like another compliment. Should I eat you now or later? I could be easily swayed to do both."

Her glare is a valid reprimand. "You discarded me like I'm a disposable toy. Excuse me if I'm not eager for another round."

"Pitch—"

"Don't." Harper averts her gaze to the coffee mug in front of her. "Does treating me like shit turn you on?"

My gut clenches at her somber tone. It serves to remind me of my actual purpose for this not-so-casual visit. Call me a hypocrite, but I'm suddenly in favor of beating around the bush. "I'm an asshole, We know this."

She cocks her head to the side while sipping from her drink. "Not sure I've heard you admit it."

"Funny you should mention that," I mutter. Wounded pride is a thick exhale that slumps my posture. "I actually came to… apologize."

Coffee sputters from her lips. It's impressive that her shirt remains dry. "Um, what was that?"

I scrub over my mouth to smother a grin. "You heard me."

Harper dabs at the splatter with a napkin. I want to make an entirely different mess with her, which is how

I got myself into this one. Her gaze lifts to mine as if hearing my filthy musings.

"It deserves to be repeated."

The least I can do is comply with her request. "I'm sorry."

"For what?"

I can't blame her need for specifics. The list is endless, if I'm willing to admit it. Most recent is at the top. "I crossed a line the other night, asking for something I shouldn't have."

"Silly me assumed you felt bad for shutting down after going down." She points at her lap like my dirty mind isn't already there.

"That too," I tack on with ease.

Her shrewd focus pins me in awkward silence for several agonizing seconds. "You're acting weird."

I rake a hand through my hair. "Thanks to you."

"Me?" She almost sounds offended.

"Your pussy is addictive. A delicacy I could eat for every meal." I smack my lips for emphasis.

Red splotches bloom on her cheeks. "Can you keep your voice down? We're in public."

"Let them listen," I scoff and blindly gesture at the eavesdroppers. "They're already talking about us."

As if choreographed, several heads whip away from us when I scan the room. Fucking vultures.

"We don't need to give them a sordid tale to twist," Harper reasons.

"Why else would I be here?"

Her breath hitches. "You better be joking."

I roll my eyes. "Get your head out of the gutter. I'm in enough trouble already."

"With yourself?"

"Yeah, for starters. I thought I could touch you and move on. Instead, I've thought of little else than you riding my face."

My hunger for her has left me unsatisfied for years. I could've survived those unfulfilled pangs. This insatiable appetite after sampling a single orgasm from her is another problem entirely. I shift on the chair as the memory pumps fire into my veins.

Her outraged squeak bursts into my lust bubble. "Good freaking grief, Jacob. Watch your mouth."

I hold my palms up in surrender. "To tell you the truth, Sydney is my main concern."

"What happened?" Worry clangs like a loud gong in Harper's voice.

It's endearing, and detrimental to my restraint. I have to reinforce my boundaries against this woman's magnetic pull more than ever. That's the real reason I crashed her morning routine.

When Syd blamed my recent brooding on missing Harper, I accepted the sign for what it was. This obsessive pattern has gone on long enough. The last thing I want is for my daughter to catch me distracted. That would defeat the entire purpose of fighting my attraction to this woman in the first place.

"Sydney is fine. That's how it has to stay," I say in response. "She comes first. Always."

Her sincere compassion shines bright as she nods. "Yeah, of course."

"It's no secret that she's very attached to you."

Harper's throat works with a thick swallow. "We've definitely formed a bond. Is that bad?"

"No, Syd thrives under your care and guidance. She really looks up to you."

She sniffs and fiddles with her coffee mug. "That might be the nicest thing you've ever said to me."

"I have my moments. You can thank Sydney."

"No surprise there. She's the sweetest. I try to tell her often."

"As you should. Same with saying you love her. Only if you mean it, though. She doesn't need fake sentiments." The thought is crushing.

Harper presses a palm flat to her chest. "I do mean it. How could I not?"

"Beats the hell outta me. The woman who's meant to love her the most isn't around, so I don't pretend to understand how others operate their emotions."

"That makes sense. It's something I've been thinking about a lot lately." She nibbles on her bottom lip. "I don't want to overstep."

A groan builds in my throat. Even her innocent consideration is sexy. Awareness thrums beneath my skin. Just sitting across the table from her is too much. Years of misplaced anger and residual guilt have piled up. I want to gather Harper in my arms, but I always push her away instead. The constant conflict fucks with my head.

"Syd is almost desperate to fill the void her mom left. I won't deny my daughter genuine relationships. It's bound to happen. Morgan makes her own decisions. If she wanted to be here, she would be. Simple as that."

She bobs her head at my explanation. "Okay, I guess that's reassuring. What're you concerned about then?"

This is where it gets more difficult. I scratch at my stubble while trying to find the right words. "There's a reason why I've been such a dick. You represent everything I won't let myself have, but that doesn't stop the want. I want and yearn and crave. *Desperately*. That's why I gave in last week when I shouldn't have."

Her lashes flutter with rapid blinks. "Huh?"

"It was meant to be once, to offer momentary relief. To prove I could have a taste and walk away. You got off. I got what I wanted. No complications. That's all it was supposed to be."

"But it isn't?"

"It's never that easy with you."

She wrinkles her nose. "Um, thanks?"

"What I mean is that you aren't meaningless fling material to me. We can't just fuck around without feelings getting involved. Your connection to Syd makes it impossible." Not to mention how crazy I already am about her.

Harper scoffs. "You wouldn't get me to agree to those terms anyway."

"Exactly, you shouldn't. But I can't have serious romantic relationships. Period. Syd is going through enough with Morgan's unreliable actions. If someone else she loves were to leave, that would destroy her. It's a risk I won't take. I also won't compromise what she gets from me, which is everything."

"Any woman you date will understand your daughter comes first."

Heat creeps along the back of my neck. "I don't want to date just any woman."

"Okay, Mr. High Standards. Then the lucky lady you deem worthy of a quick bang in the Roosters bathroom." She pretends to retch. "Please keep it in your pants while I'm on shift. I don't want to witness that."

"Jealous?" The spike in my pulse reveals just how much that idea appeals to me.

"In your dreams, Prince Charming. This conversation aside, you've made it your mission to be an asshole." Harper smiles despite the edge in her tone.

The crack in pressure allows me to sit more comfortably. "I thought it would be easier if you hated me."

She blanches. "Why?"

"Then you'll stay away. It will be easier to fight… this."

"What's this?"

"Endless longing. Otherwise I'm damning both of us to this misery." I stab a finger into my temple. "I refuse to lead you on, or let you believe more could happen for us."

"Maybe I'm a glutton for heartbreak," Harper quips. Her sunny disposition doesn't falter, even while discussing emotional turmoil.

"That's your choice, but it won't be from me taking liberties I have no intention of repeating." Jaded barbs attempt to replace the next conviction. Old habits are hard to break and all that. "I won't interfere anymore. Date whoever you want. Accept candy bars from desperate customers. Share your smiles and laughter freely. I won't steal more moments from you."

Harper pinches her brows into a deep furrow. "Why does it feel like you're breaking up with me again?"

"Maybe we never got the closure we needed."

"Is that what this is?"

I pause to admire her beauty that never fails to tie my tongue into knots. "Can't fault a guy for trying to make amends."

"By telling me we can only be connected through Syd." It looks like she's trying to fit the misshaped pieces together.

Good luck to her. I've been at it for years with no success. Responsibility weighs heavy on my shoulders.

"That's the only way it can be for us. I won't sacrifice Sydney's happiness." Just the small amount of my own that's not tied to her. It's not the most balanced method for my identity beyond fatherhood, but I find it necessary. Raw honesty burns in my chest. "I'm constantly afraid I'm fucking this parenting gig up. You know how it started."

"Don't remind me." Her face puckers, as if her coffee is suddenly sour. "You don't plan to date, like ever?"

"We wouldn't be just dating, so no. You'd consume me in a sense I can't afford."

Her mouth works soundlessly. "Um, okay. That's… intense."

My gaze dives into hers, drowning in the depths I'll never truly feel. Love is hilarious like that. "You have no idea."

"I really don't." She rests a palm on her forehead. "This is very off-brand for you. It's making my mind whirl. I would expect you to ignore my existence rather than admit I mean something to you."

I shrug, my focus trailing to the window casting a glow behind her. "Ending this rift is long overdue."

"If I didn't know better, I'd guess you're trying to establish a truce or something."

A noncommittal grunt is my immediate response. "It's obvious I can't avoid you. The alternative is to continue behaving like a surly bastard, which hasn't worked out too well."

"I could do without the hateful spite," she confirms.

"There's always going to be more between us, but we can't act on it."

Harper snorts. "There you go making assumptions again. Who's to say I feel anything but repressed animosity toward you?"

A raspy chuckle shakes my relaxed pose. "Trying to downplay you coming undone on my tongue? Your pussy doesn't lie."

That telling flush reappears, betraying her feigned indifference. "I thought we moved past the crude comments?"

"You forced me to prove the point."

She hangs her head with a groan. "Fine. Well done. I like you enough to let you eat me out. But it's over now."

"It was all that I wanted, now I'm living without." I recite the "Must Have Been Love" lyrics like a lovesick fool.

"Quit being cute," she giggles. Then her amusement sobers. "You're wrong, Jake."

"For you? I'm well aware."

"No, I don't need to hate you. I'm not sure that's even possible. It's just not inside of me to feel that way for you. That doesn't mean I always like you, though."

The smirk I shoot her lacks the usual cocksure slant. "That'll have to be enough then."

Harper cocks her head to the side, sending golden waves to spill over her shoulder. "If you say so."

chapter twelve

Harper

THE PINK BUNDLE SWADDLED IN MY ARMS COOS peacefully in slumber. Pursed lips pout at me while I stare in awe. Even the slight flicker from her closed eyelids mesmerizes me. Emotions clog my throat until my vision get misty. This precious blessing is already loved beyond words.

"I could just look at this darling face all day. Her poops are probably cute too."

Joy shifts beside me, a hiss escaping her with the subtle movement. "They kinda are, gross as that seems. Cole and I fight over who gets to change her."

"How will you get anything done?" The gah-gah babbled tone spills out naturally.

"Good question. I might just stay home with her until she goes to school."

That gets me to swing my gaze to her. "Not funny. I can't run the studio without you."

My bestie flicks lint off the blanket covering her lap. "Maybe she'll be our sidekick then."

"I'm good with that," I croon at the sleeping beauty.

"Can I have that in writing?"

Amusement bursts from me, startling the newborn wide awake. I begin a gentle sway while humming and her lashes flutter closed. Crisis averted. "Don't worry about proof. If it were up to me, I'd never leave this baby's side."

"Crazy how fast the bond forms, huh?"

"I'm literally wrapped around her little fingers." I hold up my thumb that she's clutching with all her might.

Belle Everly Baker was born last night on March ninth, just a few days after her due date. The late arrival is only fitting, seeing as Joy has the tendency to run several minutes behind schedule. This tiny treasure is already teaching her mother a valuable lesson in tardiness etiquette.

I watch in complete fascination as a huge yawn stretches Belle's squished features. A contented sigh breezes from her next. She wriggles a bit and I adjust my hold. Praise for my efforts comes in the form of quiet snores.

"Good work, Mama. She's perfect."

"She is, isn't she?" Well-deserved pride radiates from Joy's voice.

"Is Cole head over heels?"

"Totally smitten. I'm shocked he willingly left to get food."

"Mama has to make the milk, doesn't she?" This goo-goo voice might be permanent.

"The manufacturing equipment has switched on. My boobs suddenly get really hot and hard. It's a strange sensation." She tugs at her tied robe to inspect the ladies.

I lift my brows. "Wow, that's fast. Doesn't it usually take a few days?"

Joy shrugs. "She latched on almost instantly, which probably jump starts production."

Makes sense, not that I have any real knowledge. "How was labor and delivery?"

"A painful blur. But once they put Belle on my chest, nothing else mattered."

"No complications?"

"None. She took it easy on me."

"Just saving it up for when she's older," I tease.

She sputters in exaggerated outrage. "Why would you even joke about that?"

"Eh, it's an old wives' tale or whatever. You know you're getting the sass handed right back to you."

"I wasn't that bad," she mutters.

My snort calls her bullshit. "Your mom might disagree."

Her arms cross in defense. "That was *your* bad influence."

"Oh, sure. Blame the teenage trouble on me. Maybe that will stop the traits from manifesting."

"I blame you for suggesting it might in the first place. Baby Belle can do no wrong."

"Of course she can't," I agree. A quiet gasp escapes me when her lips curl into a serene grin. "She's smiling at me."

"That's just gas," her mother states automatically.

I send my bestie a pointed stare. "Let an auntie believe in small miracles. This angel baby is advanced."

"Oh, my apologies." Her palm flutters to her chest with theatrical flair. "You're right. My daughter is exceptionally smart fresh from the oven. I'm talking off the charts."

"That's better," I commend while stroking a bent knuckle along Belle's petal-soft cheek.

"Speaking of miracles, how did your brunch with Jake go?"

It takes me several seconds to process her statement, but I still can't compute the message. The flutters in my belly are extremely distracting too. "Huh?"

Her brows wiggle. "I heard you looked pretty cozy sharing a table at Bean Me Up a few days ago. Thanks for holding out on your best friend. I specifically told you I need to live vicariously."

I let my jaw go slack. "How did you hear about that? You've been holed up on bed rest."

"Puh-lease. Word travels." She swats at the air like it's a pest that needs to be cleared. "Besides, my mom is close with Claudia. You know that woman makes it her daily duty to run the Knox Creek rumor mill. Susan is next in line, who is the one that reported you were cuddled up with the grumpy mechanic."

"We were not cuddled up," I grumble.

"Then what were you?"

"Just… talking."

Her eyes nearly roll from their sockets. "Don't think you can evade the inquisition just because this day is all about my baby. Spill. No skimping on the details."

After I chase off the giddy hive in my stomach, I give her a brief recap of my somewhat civil conversation with the notorious ass. I gloss over Jake's pussy comments and my full-body blush that followed each one. Instead, I focus more on our so-called truce. His niceties have yet to make an appearance.

"We'll see," I say in conclusion. "He was actually decent and honest. Admitted to being a dick to me on purpose. It was a healthy discussion. I'm tempted to believe him."

Joy is quiet for several moments. "Jake Evans?"

"Yep. Trust me, it was a shock to my system too."

"I'd say." She shakes her head. "So, that's it?"

Other than my lingering confusion about his refusal to date, and the subtle suggestion that choice is tied to me somehow. But that's a can I'm not interested in opening. "I guess."

"Why do you sound disappointed?"

My gaze lowers to Belle cuddled against me. A pang rattles around in the unoccupied space behind my sternum. "I'm not sure. There's always been a small part of me that wished things worked out between us. Now it seems like that chance has officially been squashed."

"Forget Jake. He's had countless opportunities and squandered them. His loss. Plenty of eligible bachelors are just waiting to sweep you off your feet," Joy insists.

A heavy exhale deflates my posture. "I've already heard that from you recently."

"It's true. Have you been keeping an open heart?"

"I mean, kinda? The catastrophe with Daniel spooked me."

"That doesn't count." She scowls. "Jake sabotaged you."

"Dr. Pumper wasn't the one anyways. Maybe the date crasher did me a favor."

My friend scoffs. "Don't give him more credit. He's scaring guys off for no reason."

"It doesn't matter. I'm a long ways off from starting my own family." And that's putting it optimistically. Somehow, that stage appears even further away than it did when I felt the non-envious pinch weeks ago.

Joy leans over to squeeze my arm. "You can get your baby fix with my little one whenever you need."

I dip my chin to get a calming whiff of Belle's wispy hair. "She's got that powdery newborn scent. Really hits the spot."

Her nap comes to an abrupt end with a squeaky whimper. She drags her tiny fist toward her mouth and begins sucking. When that proves unsatisfying, she begins rooting for a nipple in the blanket.

"Uh-oh. Someone is hungry."

Joy shucks her robe, unclips the cup from her nursing bra, and lets her boob pop out. "All set. Come to Mama, Baby Belle."

I pass her over with a muffled laugh. How natural these motions kick in. My humor is drowned out by loud suckling noises.

My eyebrows fling upward. "You weren't kidding. She really goes after it."

Joy hums in agreement and slumps against her mountain of pillows. A soft smile appears as she watches her baby drink. My bestie looks tired but blissful. She's glowing with pure happiness shining from her pores.

"Motherhood looks really great on you, babe."

She blinks sleepy eyes at me. "Aww, thanks. And don't get down about being single. You could meet your future husband this afternoon." A twinkle enters her gaze. "Or maybe yet this morning. I spotted a cute doctor on this floor yesterday. He might be doing rounds right now. You should check. I think his name is—"

"None of your concern, fiancée." Cole saunters into the room wearing a cheeky smirk. His arms are loaded with sugary treats from Dunkin' Donuts.

"For Harper," she counters. "You handle all my needs."

He chuckles at her grabby hand reaching toward their breakfast. "You just use me for the dirty deeds."

"Um, yeah. Have you seen your penis?" She makes the announcement candidly like it's a weather update. "Oh, and your baby batter. Our daughter is a genetic marvel."

Cole sits on the bed and scoots over to wrap an arm around his girls. As if that isn't swoony enough, the jaw-dropper presses a kiss to his fiancé's forehead and begins massaging Belle's tiny foot. The scene melts my heart.

That's when I recognize that this moment is meant

to be private. They're sharing an intimate exchange as a new family. The trio blends seamlessly while I lurk off to the side like a shadow. My stomach sinks lower the longer I intrude.

I launch to my feet. "I'm gonna go."

Joy startles at my abrupt movement. "What? Why?"

"There's some stuff I should do." It's not a total lie.

Her eyes narrow. "Since when?"

I shoo off her probing. "You three need to bond. I'll visit again later, or tomorrow."

An argument parts her lips, but then she nods. "Yeah, okay. I just feel like you're rushing out."

"To find Dr. Hottie." I hitch a thumb at the hallway, tacking on a wink for diversion's sake.

The suspicion flees her expression, replaced by animated enthusiasm. "Yay! Good luck, and let me know how it goes. Like immediately. Do. Not. Delay. I'm out of commission for at least six weeks and need the juice."

Cole groans. "Don't remind me."

She elbows him. "As if you have it rough. I just pushed a tiny human out of my vagina."

He winces. "Have I told you lately that I love you?"

Joy nuzzles her nose against his. "Not for at least two hours."

The tension returns to my stance, forcing my legs to pedal backward. "Okay, okay, I'm going."

"You can stay." My best friend pouts, but her attention quickly strays to Belle and Cole where it belongs.

"I really can't. Another minute in this romantic bubble and I'll get knocked up on the fumes." My laugh is choppy as I wave a hand in front of my face. "Holy hearts and flowers, the potency is enough to make a girl weak in the knees."

And hold onto hope for the one who doesn't deserve it.

chapter thirteen

Jake

SYDNEY IS A TWIRLING MACHINE. I'M NOT AT ALL SURPRISED, considering her preference for moving nonstop. My eyes can barely track her fast spins on the live feed. It helps that the other students appear to be soaked in molasses.

The folding chair creaks beneath my weight. I glare at the thin metal legs ready to collapse. If Harper wants family and friends to watch their kiddos perform, the least she could do is provide seating meant for actual adults. It's almost tempting to walk out on principle alone. But that would unravel a few threads from our newfound agreement to be… friends.

My upper lip curls at the bland term. That bubbly blonde couldn't be my platonic pal by any stretch of her skintight leggings. I snarl a silent curse when she bends forward in direct view to test my theory. Nope, not even if I got a brain transplant and lost every drop of testosterone.

Frustration burns from the inside out. My nonexistent restraint doesn't matter. We haven't exchanged more than a handful of clipped words since establishing the so-called truce.

"Well, hello. Fancy seeing you here."

I turn on the rickety chair to find Susan entering the studio viewing area. My thumb jabs toward the bank of televisions. "Decided to see what all the fuss is about."

"Aren't they adorable?" She clutches her clasped palms to her chest. "Syd certainly steals the show. She's very advanced."

"Really?" My gaze returns to the live stream. I couldn't decipher good from bad if I sat here all night.

Susan titters, finding amusement in my dumbstruck expression. "Yes, your daughter has a natural ability. They're all lucky to have such a patient instructor. Harper provides a nurturing environment that encourages their unique talents to thrive."

I roll my eyes at the syrupy sweet compliments. "How special."

"Extremely. She's very great with children."

"Uh-huh, Syd is a huge fan."

Susan's keen gaze narrows on my lacking enthusiasm for this topic. "I saw you together at Bean Me Up."

I'd like to say she's the first to railroad me about my casual chat with Harper. In truth, she's more like fifth or sixth. Damn vultures don't know when to quit swarming. "That was nothing."

She arches a catty brow. "Sure didn't look like nothing."

"We're just friends," I grind out. I remind myself that

this woman is kind and generous under most circumstances. This just doesn't happen to be one of them.

"My daddy is Miss Harper's boyfriend," Sydney blurts from beside me.

I damn near launch five feet in the air. My startled focus swivels between my daughter and the screen she's supposed to be on. "Where did you come from?"

Her giggle is a loud peal. "The studio. You're silly, Daddy."

Meanwhile, Susan's eyes hold a concerning twinkle. "Oh, isn't that precious? Harper is your dad's girlfriend?"

"Uh-huh. She came over to our house for dinner and everything. Is she gonna come over again soon, Daddy?"

"I'm not sure. You'll have to ask her." I scrub a palm down my face in an attempt to calm my frazzled nerves. "Are you already done, Boop?"

"No, Daddy! It's your turn to dance."

"Wha—?" I feel my eyes bulge.

That's when Harper appears from the hallway. Her polite smile serves to further agitate the itch spreading from the back of my neck. "Hello, brave partners. I'm happy you could make it for our first practice."

"A little warning would be nice," I mutter.

"Check your email," she chirps.

Fuck email, I silently spew. My personal inbox is flooded with over two thousand unread messages. "Can't you text me?"

"Can't you read your emails? Everyone else got the memo." She lifts her chin to a spot behind me.

I let my gaze follow hers. Ten other adults are crowded in the lobby, ready and waiting to learn. The prepared crew is dressed appropriately in athletic gear. My flannel and jeans are no match for the task. Their expectant expressions are too eager, especially the three men ogling Harper's curves.

My gut clenches. "We're doing this now?"

She crosses her arms, shoving her luscious tits up for my viewing pleasure. "If you're willing. No pressure. It's meant to be fun."

"C'mon, Daddy." Syd yanks at my arm with the strength of a Clydesdale. "I wanna be in the front row."

"Of course you do," I mutter.

But my feet obediently follow her into a long, narrow room. She guides me to a pink dot on the glossy floor. Mirrors cover three walls from floor to ceiling. My own fierce grimace glares back at me until Sydney's infectious glee smooths the upset.

Her skinny form snuggles into my side. "Thanks for being my partner, Daddy. I can't wait to dance with you."

And just like that, I become putty in her small palm. "Anything for you, Boop."

Harper glides into the studio with a practiced stride of authority. "Welcome to our class, family and friends. We're happy to have you."

A chorus of mixed greetings fills the space in response.

She nods and claps twice. "Thanks for squeezing these short practices into your busy schedules. I'm aware that your time is valuable, and I won't ask for too much. We're going to keep this basic but adorable. Since we're taking it easy, there's no need to stretch or do a formal warm-up. Bonus, right?"

Someone in the back clears their throat. "How many times are we meeting again?"

"Just three. But we can add more if needed. Everyone learns at their own pace."

Mumbled agreements come from the group.

Harper smiles. "I created a simple choreography that should be easy to memorize. This short routine involves a combination of step touches, timed toe taps, ball changes, tendus, and pivot turns. Maybe a few hip dips and top rocks if we're feeling fancy. We'll incorporate a traveling basket and several turnaround lifts for the pair sections."

I sure as shit assume I'm not the only one gawking like she's speaking a foreign language.

"Don't worry," she laughs. "I'll demonstrate each, and we'll go slow. There's a packet with step-by-step directions as well. This lesson will focus on the individual basics. Then next time we'll add the partner pieces. Ready to begin?"

"Yes," is our unified reply.

"Excellent," she cheers and grabs a remote.

A heavy beat floods the silence. The music almost makes me want to dance. Many of the other adults surrender to the temptation. Several shoulders are already wiggling to the fast tempo. The kids join us, laughter blending in with the song.

"Yes!" Harper hoots. "You're already in the mood. I love it."

A foul curse tickles my tongue when I find my heel stomping along to the rhythm. Syd giggles and begins mimicking the involuntary action. I pinch the bridge of my nose while unease bunches my muscles.

"We're going to start with the step touch. This is the foundation for most dance moves. It's a total breeze, and also fairly self-explanatory."

Sydney and her fellow dancers begin moving in what I guess is the step touch. Their arms roll between each transition, ending on a clap when their feet meet.

"Hey, hey." Harper wags her finger in a teasing manner. "We need to explain the steps."

"Oh, oh!" My daughter thrusts her hand in the air. "We start at first position."

"Yep, very good. Let's find our center," she instructs.

Harper turns to face the mirror while rolling her shoulders. Her stance is straight, legs and feet pressed together, but her toes are pointed out. The group is quick to follow her directions until we're all in the same pose.

"We'll keep our hands on our hips to maintain balance." She holds herself still for emphasis. "It also helps us stay focused on our feet."

Not in my case while I stare at her fingers digging into the clingy fabric. This friendship shit was doomed before I even suggested it. Or maybe she did. That would make more sense as my eyes linger on her ass.

"Just watch me." She doesn't have to tell me twice. "Step out with your right, then bring them back together with your left. The weight stays on your right. Just a toe tap from the left that sets you up to move back. Step out with your left, then close with your right. Open and shut. Back and forth. See how the steps match the beat?" She does several passes in steady succession. "That's eight counts."

"Why do we only count to eight?" The question comes from Susan, whose eye contact I've made a point to avoid.

"It's easy to break the music up into sections, and using a lower number makes it faster to follow. That's what I was taught way back when." Harper winks at our reflections, upbeat as ever. She breaks from the sequence when the song changes. "Your turn to try."

We wait in the centered position. For what, I'm not sure. Maybe for foolishness to creep in. The amount of dance lingo now in my vocabulary is appalling. Not to mention how far removed I currently am from my usual self. I rock on my thick soles under the weight.

That catches Harper's attention. "Oh, shoot. Your shoes need to go."

I narrow my eyes at her insistence in the mirror. "Why?"

"You'll scuff my floor more than you already have." She points to a black mark near my boot.

"These are all I have with me."

"Should've read the email," she whispers. "For now, you can wear socks or go bare."

Flames lick my skin despite our audience. Rather than feed the fire by picturing her naked, I remove my boots and carry them to the nearest wall. Then I reclaim my spot front and center.

My brows lift in expectation as I lift a socked foot. "Better?"

"Much," she says. "Okay, back to business. I'll count us in. Five, six, seven, eight…"

As a whole, we step out to the right. I slide my left foot over and nearly slip on the zero traction. Sydney gasps at my clumsy footwork.

"Daddy, you gotta be careful." Her concerned gaze peers down to assess the problem.

"Just gonna ditch these before I break a leg." I wrench off my socks and toss them away in a discarded ball.

"Okay, I'll help you catch up. I'm super good." Syd bops in a seamless step touch like the pro she apparently is.

I copy her movements, hiding my shame behind a smirk. "This isn't so hard."

Harper had been walking around to inspect everyone's progress, but her assessment falters when she reaches me. I notice her giving me a thorough once-over, stalling on my bare feet.

"Problem?" If she picks on me again, I'm likely to storm out. But I get the impression this is more of a personal… interest.

Her throat works with a thick gulp. "Uh, no. All good."

In the next second, she scurries back to her place at the head of the room. Her reaction loosens my muscles, allowing me to move more freely despite the strange maneuvers. I even shake out my hands when the beat pounds.

"You're doing awesome," Harper shouts over the din. "We're going to do six more repetitions at this speed. After that, we'll go faster. We can add a twist to give the simple sequence more impact. Then I'll introduce you to the ball change and some arm actions."

Then she flies into motion. Her movements are graceful and sleek. I'm lost in the sway of her hips until she spins to face us, never breaking form. Her gaze scans us while she maintains the fluid motions. My steps are robotic as I follow along, but I manage to pull through with my pride intact.

Harper leaves her post in between to stroll the room. Her encouragement radiates from each person, boosting their spirits. Even I feel lighter on my feet after learning what the fuck a ball change actually is. The children take on an assistant role while flitting about. Each tiny dancer guides their parent or trusted adult in the choreography.

Syd twirls her signature circles around me while keeping count.

"Phew," Harper breathes. She wipes fake sweat off her forehead. "I wasn't sure if twenty minutes would be enough, but you're fast learners."

"Only 'cause they have the bestest teacher," Sydney coos.

Harper clutches a spot near her heart. "Aww, my students are the bestest. You make my job very rewarding."

The children release a synchronized sigh under their instructor's praise.

She holds her arms out. "Well, that's all I'm going to teach you tonight. Before we go, does anyone want to show off what they've learned?"

"My daddy will!" Syd shoves me from behind.

I hang my head at my daughter's exuberance to immediately volunteer at my expense. "Is that really necessary, Boop?"

"Uh-huh. Do you wanna borrow my tutu?" She tugs at the rainbow tulle around her waist.

"No, you keep that on. There will be enough eyes on me already." My stride is painfully slow as I shuffle to where Harper stands.

She steps to the side, giving me the floor. "You don't have to do this."

One look at my daughter strongly suggests otherwise. Both of her little thumbs are pointed straight up in giddy support. Besides, denying her simple wishes isn't my style.

"I'll survive." This stunt might improve my reputation around town.

But it's the approval gleaming in Harper's gaze that makes me want to put my best barefoot forward. "Then let's see what you've got, stud."

chapter fourteen

Harper

CLASP MY PALMS FLAT TOGETHER AGAINST MY CHEST AND prepare to try again. "Please, Garrett? You haven't let us since I started working here. This is my first Friday off the clock. I think you owe me."

"Sure," my boss mumbles.

My lips part on a disbelieving breath. "Sure?"

"Do whatever you want, Wilson." The free rein is extremely out of character for him, along with his averted gaze.

That doesn't stop my excitement from bubbling to the surface, though. "Really?"

"Uh-huh, it's fine." His distracted focus is zeroed in on something over my shoulder.

I swivel on my stool to search for what's captured his attention. It takes less than two seconds to spot the culprit.

A curvaceous beauty is seated alone at a table across the bar. Her presence is magnetic, as if we're being pulled into her orbit. The unsuspecting saps in her direct vicinity are about to be locked in a trance. By the look on Garrett's face, it's already too late for him. I'd be willing to wager that he'd agree to do just about anything with her in his sights.

Confidence oozes from her relaxed pose. She scans the evening crowd with a lazy perusal that reminds me of a fierce lioness about to play with her food. As if to confirm my comparison, black polished nails pluck a cherry from her glass. Then she sucks the dangling fruit into her mouth while a coy smile grows at the taste of victory. Yep, this is a woman in her element.

And I'm totally taking advantage. Consider it an employee bonus.

"Thanks, boss. You're the best!" My voice fights the music pumping from the speakers. "I'd kiss you, but you're like a brother to me."

Garrett recoils, suddenly very alert. "Gross, Harper. I don't wanna make out with you."

"Umm," I pop my lips. "That's not what I said, but good to know we're on the same page."

"Huh?"

A chastising groan announces my disappointment. "Head in the game, Foster."

His shoulders straighten into an imposing image of authority. "Not sure what you mean."

"You're not listening to me, which has really worked out in my favor."

He grumbles something under his breath

about having an off day or something along those lines. "Might need some fresh air."

"Go right ahead. It doesn't matter if the fog clears, though. You already agreed to let us have a dance party."

"I did?" His shock is genuine considering he's been shooting down my requests for nearly a month.

My palm smacks my forehead. "Good grief. Go over there and hump her leg already. You know you want to."

Garrett scoffs. "Do not."

"Then it won't bother you that her date showed up." I blindly gesture at the man I spied snagging the seat across from her.

"The fuck?" His hands slam onto the counter, ready to propel himself over the wood and haul ass in the vixen's direction.

"Oh, my. Are you seeing this, ladies?" I swing my gaze from right to left. My two friends flank me, one on each side. "Knox Creek's most eligible bachelor has finally found the one who makes his charm falter."

Ginger hums in agreement. She props an elbow on the bar and rests her chin on a closed fist. "Never thought I'd see the day, or have a front-row seat for the show."

Garrett scowls at our antics. "Her drink is almost empty. She's a paying customer, and it's my business to fill her up."

"Let's be honest. You wanna fill her up with more than vodka and soda," Ginger jests.

I snort into my margarita. "Yeah, boss. The

expectations are real classy in this joint. Maybe that should go on a coaster."

"That the cock den attracts gorgeous women? Helluva slogan," he boasts.

"She's very attractive," I agree with a play on his words that supports my earlier assessment.

"More like smoking fucking hot." The fact that his filter is on the fritz cracks me up.

My entire upper body shakes until wasted booze sloshes from my glass. "Wow, tell me how you really feel."

"Already did and you're cracking jokes." His fingers tunnel into his already mused hair.

"Can you blame me? Your feathers are ruffled."

"I'm fine." Garrett smooths a palm down his shirt and turns away. There's a cluster of loyal regulars who won't bat an eyelash at his unusual behavior.

"Uh-huh. Put her next round on our tab. She lowered your guard," I call to his retreating form.

"Cheers to that." Ginger clinks her glass against mine.

"Now we get to shake our booties until the lights go off," I whoop.

Callie's wide eyes appear positively horrified by the thought alone. "Count me out."

That's the first time I've heard her speak since we sat down. Her meek demeanor stems from being trapped under strict archaic values for twenty-one years. It's going to take more than a rebellious raspberry lemonade to shed her oppressive upbringing. Small steps in the right direction, though. She was the one—shockingly enough—to initiate this outing.

Her downcast gaze slides to the right, peeking upward ever so slightly. Ridge is towering over that general area in his typical stoic stance. The guy exudes intimidation, but he's a total gentle giant to those who matter. A smile tugs at my lips while I glance at the timid girl beside me. Maybe Callie just needs stronger motivation.

"Oh, Garrett." I beckon him over with a deceptively polite wave. "Do you mind if we clear some space for our bumping and grinding? Also, is the smoke machine still hooked up?"

A defeated sigh escapes him. "Ridge and Drake can move shit for you."

"Where's Drake? I haven't seen him." Leather creaks as I lift off the stool to do a visual sweep.

"In the office, probably licking his wounds."

Ginger leans forward with a gasp. "Did he finally end things with Marissa?"

"Either that or it's his time of the month to be a grumpy asshole."

"Sounds familiar," I mumble at the latter part of his statement.

The only difference is that *my* grumpy asshole follows a continuous flow cycle. That instinctual claim gives me pause. *Shit.* Jake isn't my anything.

Garrett lifts his chin at Ridge, unaware of my mental bumbling. "Hey, be sure to make extra room. It's gonna get fucking rowdy with Harper spinning circles around everyone."

My other boss offers a silent salute before leaving his perch to fulfill our request.

"Maybe I could help Ridge stack the chairs," Callie

murmurs while tracking his hulking form across the room.

"You should," I urge. I'd encourage almost any excuse to get her cute butt off the stool to spread those clipped wings.

Her posture slumps more than it already was. "I'd probably just be in his way."

"Girl, even if you just lift a napkin, he'd be grateful for your assistance."

She visibly brightens. "Really?"

"You'll never know if you don't try, but only if you want to. Don't make yourself uncomfortable." I wrap my arm around her for a quick squeeze.

She nods and nibbles on her bottom lip.

Garrett drums his fingers on the bar. "You should listen to the woman who always gets what she wants."

"Oh, puh-lease. Not always," I insist.

"Sure about that?" He points to the area near the far wall where there's already a decent amount of space cleared out.

"Thank you, thank you, thank you," I gush.

He flicks his wrist, shooing off my gratitude. "Not a problem, Harps. Long overdue, like you said."

"You won't regret it."

"Better not. At least Evans isn't here to burn the place down if another guy so much as looks sideways at you."

I huff good-naturedly, but my pulse skips a beat at the idea. "Don't worry, I haven't seen him darkening the corner section for almost two weeks."

"Miss him?"

"Hardly." But the flip in my belly betrays me. Not

to mention that our paths cross at Barre Twirl. "My tips have tripled without him constantly breathing down my neck."

Garrett smirks while staring at the entrance. "Well, I guess it's a good thing you're not working tonight."

"Right? I'd hate to miss out on dancing." My head bobs to the peppy country song that just started.

"Nah, otherwise you'd get shitty tips."

The shiver ghosting down my spine has me turning toward the door. Jake is there, just barely over the threshold. It almost looks like he's still deciding whether to stay or go. His gaze searches the bar with an intensity that almost has me flailing my arms.

Then our eyes collide in a heated exchange that I feel in the depths of my core. There's a pounding in my ears that drowns out all other noise until all I can hear is the echo from his pulse matching mine. I suck in a sharp breath as several emotions battle against his stony expression. Jake allows relief and frustration and longing and raw hunger to be put on full display.

It gives me the courage to wiggle my fingers at him in welcome. My smile combats his frown. Thunder crashes over his already stormy features. Then he rips his eyes off me and stalks toward an available stool basked in shadows.

"Oh, shit. This night just got a lot more interesting," Ginger laughs.

I brush off her comment with an easy grin. "Nothing crazy is going to happen. We put the past to rest and decided to move forward as friends."

Garrett chuckles, which turns into a booming

laugh. "That's a load of bullshit I could smell from across town."

"Ha ha, very funny. Your support is greatly appreciated."

"Which I'd freely offer if I believed you," he counters.

I tuck my arms tight across my chest, prepared to defend my truce with Jake. The doubt and disappointment can take a hike. "Then I suppose we'll just have to wait and see where the night takes us."

Ridge—who I didn't even realize returned to his post behind the bar—slides an overflowing shot glass in front of me. "For you."

I give the suspicious peachy-colored liquid a cursory glance. "What is it?"

A deep dimple dents his cheek when he smirks. Almost positive Callie sways in her seat. "Pink Panty Dropper."

Laughter spews from between my pressed lips. "For real?"

"Yep, mixed it myself."

"From who?" Better not be him. My eyes narrow on Callie's behalf.

Ridge jabs his thumb at a very specific target. "Evans."

A fierce blush stings my cheeks. "He wouldn't."

"He did," Ridge confirms with a straight face.

"Just friends," Garrett grunts. "Just like I didn't get hard when that hot chick tongued her cherry."

My laugh holds more snort than humorous notes. "Real classy."

He winks. "I'm beginning to think that should be our slogan."

"Ask Jake. He's clever as fuck." Ginger hasn't stopped giggling and nudges the shot toward me. "Bottoms up, babe. We'll see how long it takes for those pink panties to drop."

chapter fifteen

Jake

It was a mistake coming to Roosters. That couldn't be more glaringly obvious as I simmer in a furious stew of my own making. I almost canceled Syd's sleepover with Polly as a last-ditch effort to force myself to stay home. But that would be selfish, and proof that my restraint has crumbled.

The evidence accompanies me where I currently sit, though. My weakness is on display right in front of me, mocking my most recent failed attempt. I can't control the demand to watch Harper. All else disappears as usual. Even the cold bottle in my grip is forgotten.

Lush hips swing at a hypnotic pace that has my mouth watering. A feverish beat pounds from the speakers to sync with her allure. Colorful beams of light swoop down to bathe her features in a pulsing glow. She's seductive, her sensual rhythm too intimate for a public place. The shot I bought her no doubt lubricated these already fluid motions. Another careless error on my part.

I absently take a swig from my beer but taste nothing. Harper's captivating spectacle has gained the attention of everyone within viewing distance. Bodies revolve around her like she's the sun. Nobody gets too close, probably in fear of burning. Or maybe they can feel my wrath ready to strike.

She grinds against the steam that billows from her intoxicating efforts. The temptress knows she's irresistible. Her arms lift and curl to embrace empty space. I could fill that void. Fuck, the temptation almost shifts me into drive. If she so much as crooks a finger, I'll come running with my tongue lolling.

"Why do you insist on torturing yourself?" Garrett blocks my direct line of sight. His smirk reveals that the position is intentional.

Tension radiates across my strained posture. "Why do you care?"

"You're spoiling the mood for my customers." His explanation is similar to the shitty excuse that Ridge spewed not too long ago.

My tolerance for their complaints has decreased significantly since then. "Too fucking bad."

Garrett's glare threatens to kick my ass to the curb. "Wanna try that again?"

"No."

"Then allow me to give you some much-needed guidance."

If the bottle in my hand was a can, it'd be crushed. "I'd rather you didn't."

"Too fucking bad," he repeats my foul attitude. Then he leans in as if this is a private conversation. "I want you to get off your cranky ass, stalk over to the spot you haven't quit glaring at, and officially claim the girl you're crazy about."

"Bother someone else with your meddling." My gaze attempts to return to Harper like an addiction that craves its next fix.

"No one else caught the love bug nearly as bad," he drawls.

"The love bug?" I scrub a palm down my face, seconds away from showing myself out after that comment. "Are you serious with that shit?"

"Nah, you're just fun to fuck with."

I rip at the soggy coaster under my beer, crushing the cardboard in my fist. "Can I tell you how happy it makes me to be your entertainment?"

"No need. It's written in your signature grimace. Why don't you do us all a favor? Get it over with. It's for the good of the group at this point." He gestures behind him as if I need directions.

"If it were that easy, I would." The honesty pours from me. "We can't be together."

"But you can glower and grump and be an unreasonable jackass whenever she's around?"

"You're one to talk about being an unreasonable jackass," I counter.

"Least I know what I am," he says. "There's a simple solution."

"That's not gonna happen," I say to round off the statement.

"Why not? Harper is fantastic with kids, which is a huge bonus. Your daughter already loves her. I'm certain the feeling is mutual. She's the only one other than Syd who gets you to smile." He holds up a finger, saving the best for last. "Don't bother denying that she's special to you."

"It's not that cut and dry."

"Enlighten me." His spinning wrist motions my refusal onward.

"I have to think about what's best for my daughter."

"And providing her with a supportive, reliable female role model wouldn't fit that priority?"

My muscles flex under the strain of his pestering. "What if she leaves us, huh?"

"Don't give her a reason to."

"Fuck, Foster. Why didn't I think of that?" I roll my eyes to pair with the sarcasm.

"Harper isn't Morgan. Hasn't she already proved that? That woman is loyal to you for no reason. Take the fucking risk, and put us out of our misery." He's making too much sense.

I peel at the label on my bottle, using any distraction to avoid the obvious. "Are you my therapist now?"

Garrett snorts. "You couldn't pay me enough to fill that role. This is more of a… civil service."

"So you've said."

"Yet you still haven't budged. It's almost like you enjoy being angry and spiteful."

"Especially when pushy bartenders insist on getting in my business."

"Fine, I relent." He holds his arms up in surrender and begins backing away.

"How 'bout another beer while you're at it." I finish what's left of the warm one in front of me.

He snags the empty Coors. "Sure, Evans. Let me grab that while you sit back and watch your soulmate get groped by another man."

I'm across the room at the edge of the dance floor before he even finishes the sentence. A red mist covers my vision while I approach the guy grinding into Harper. He doesn't even seem to notice the rage painted all over my features, choosing that moment to fondle her ass with both palms.

The instinct to dismember this dumbass is barely restrained by a single thread. Garrett's pep talk mixes with irrational jealousy to blend a potent concoction that inebriates my common sense. I clench my fists until the knuckles turn white. Absent of sound logic or not, even I can recognize that wouldn't slide me into Harper's good graces.

"If you want to keep your hands, I suggest you refrain from touching her." It's a miracle my voice remains level.

Bleary eyes try to focus on me. "This your girl?"

"She's my everything as far as you're concerned," I snarl.

The asshole takes a breath and squares up like he wants to challenge me, but one look at my face and the tipsy groper wisely retreats. My glare follows his stumbled stride to the bathroom. Good fucking riddance.

Harper whirls to confront me. The lit fuse in her gaze sparks my arousal. When we finally get to fucking, our combined passion will be explosive. My body thrums in anticipation of joining hers.

"What do you think you're doing?" Her sharp tone rises above the thumping music to smack my wayward thoughts.

"Saving you." My possessive tendencies belong to her. It's no surprise that my protective side manifests for her too.

"From what?" She pauses to scan the crowd, fake concern replacing the fire in her expression. "Dancing?"

"Did you want him pawing at you like a feral cat in mating season?"

Her hip cocks to the side. "I was about to handle it."

"How?"

"A sharp elbow to the ribs usually does the trick." She demonstrates and narrowly misses the person behind her.

The storm wreaking havoc on my composure regains momentum. I go rigid as more failures against her pour down on me. "Are you often in situations where you need to defend yourself?"

"Why does it matter to you? I'm single and free to dance with anybody I like."

"Well, I don't like to see my friends treated that way." That casual title is wrong for her on too many levels to count.

Harper catches the distaste curling my upper lip. "Oh, please. That bullshit is stinking up the bar. Ginger and Callie aren't far if I require reinforcements. Stand down, buddy."

"Too late. I'm already off my stool."

She clutches her forehead with a groan. "We just had this conversation. You weren't going to intervene, remember? It was your grand plan."

"There's an adjustment period," I grumble. And I'm a total fraud.

Her smile is pure satisfaction, as if she predicted this exact event. "Having regrets the second another man's hands land on my ass?"

I clench my jaw against the impulse to immediately agree. "What'd you think about my peace offering?"

Or—more accurately—fuel for her blaze.

"Weak at best. These panties aren't dropping." Harper tugs at her fastened jeans. The truth is in her alert awareness. She's sober, which is how I prefer her for this altercation.

I prowl further into her space. "Are your panties pink? The thong I peeled off you—"

She claps a palm over my mouth. "Knock it off, Jake. That's behind us, remember?"

My fingers circle her wrist to remove the gag before I lick her soft skin. "I'm not so sure about that anymore."

"You better be joking," she snaps.

"And if I wasn't?"

"I'm not interested." Daggers glint at me from

her glare. "I won't be your fuck buddy. We're barely friends as it is, and even that's a stretch."

That final word reminds me of Harper's graceful movements. Static stirs in the air, drawing my attention to the space separating us. I push my luck and cinch an arm around her waist. A solid pull delivers her snug against me.

Our nearness soothes the demand that's been pacing under the surface. The irritation flees entirely as my lungs expand with a greedy inhale. She smells like flowers and rain after a drought and long-awaited comfort. The combined fragrance labels her as mine. I tighten my hold, daring to duck my head until our foreheads touch.

Harper's breath catches at our flush position. "What're you doing now?"

"Will you dance with me, Miss Harper?" I nudge my hips into hers.

She sputters and wiggles in my grasp. "Don't try to sexualize that. It's for students only."

I give her an inch of slack. "You're teaching me."

"As Syd's partner in the safety of my studio," she deflects.

"Afraid you'll fall into my arms and want to stay?"

"Not even a little bit." But she makes no further attempt to leave my clutches.

"Then how about another lesson?" I slide my feet to do a step touch, adding a ball change for a bigger reaction.

Harper gives it to me, her jaw hanging slack. "Did you just…? What's gotten into you?"

"Sound judgment from several sources," I admit.

"Just like that?" She snaps her fingers.

"It's long overdue. I've been blind, and stubborn."

"You've been different lately," she notes. "Why this sudden change of heart?"

Clarity washes over me in a rush. "I'm tired of fighting."

"That's why we agreed to stop."

"No, I mean fighting us."

Shadows dance across her conflicted features. I've been slowly steering us toward the corner that's shrouded in darkness. It's a false sense of privacy away from prying eyes and grinding bodies. Harper only notices my relocation methods when her ass meets the rough wall. Her gasp pulses through my chest.

"I can't stay away from you." My voice is gruff from the confession.

Her gaze studies mine. "You haven't tried very hard."

"What do you call the last six years?"

"Denial," she exhales.

"Yeah," I chuckle. "And I'm finally ready to admit the truth."

Harper consumes my senses. I watch her breasts rise and fall as she assesses me. Her heartbeat drums above the buzz in the background. The curve at her hip fills my palm, her thighs tucked between mine. Her intoxicating scent swirls in the air until she's breath in my lungs. A phantom drop of tangy honey hits my tongue, the memory still rich enough to taste. She's my anchor to this moment and battles the chaotic tide of our past.

The guard I once slammed down against her

falls into a useless heap. I feel desperate for her in a way I can't comprehend. This conviction thrumming through me is absolute, an insistence that won't be deterred.

I dip my face until our noses bump. Reckless decisions barrel through my mind. "Tell me I'm not alone in this madness."

Her throat works with a gulp. "I don't want to be a complication."

"You're not, Pitch. If anything, you're the missing piece."

"Since when?" Our conversation at the coffee shop seems to replay in her mind.

"It's all been a lie. Let me show you." My hand roams upward to cup her cheek.

"I can't do this with you." But the protest is weak.

"You're all I think about," I rasp inches from her lips. "This is how it's meant to be between us, how it always should've been."

"No, we're wrong for each other."

"Maybe that's what makes us right."

I lower my mouth to greet hers in a swift reunion. Our first second chance kiss is chaste, a test to seek permission. Harper whimpers, but doesn't pull away. Her body trembles against mine. That slight reaction has my lips parting over hers to expose what we've allowed to hang in the balance. She opens for me with a muffled sigh.

Our tongues move in unison. Memories assault me from days long past as we dive into familiar territory. It's been years since I've kissed Harper, but right now it doesn't feel like time has passed at all. My knuckles scrape against abrasive brick while I tangle my fingers in her hair. I gently cradle the back of her head to act as a cushion. She sucks my bottom lip while I stake a claim on her mouth. My arm that's still looped around her waist locks us together. These motions are natural between us, an exchange lost but not forgotten.

Heat floods my veins in a wave that makes me dizzy. *Fucking combustible.* Each second is a reminder of the chemistry we share. The flames spreading warmth through me only burn for her. As if sensing my urgency to reconnect, her fingers curl into my shirt just above my thumping heart. She uses the grip to pull me closer. I go willingly, seeking more contact from her. Then, just as suddenly, Harper flattens her palm and shoves to break us apart.

"We need to stop." Her lashes are wet.

"Fuck, Pitch. What's wrong?" My thumb traces her upturned jaw.

She takes a moment to gather her thoughts, blinking at the unshed tears. "Everything."

"Can you be more specific?" Pressure lodges in my chest. "Did I push you too fast?"

The edges of her mouth wobble. "No, not really."

"I didn't mean to maul you. It just felt nice to hold you close again."

Harper's eyes drift from mine. "I can't let you kiss me and pretend everything is okay. We're not okay, Jake."

My stomach knots against her upset. "I didn't assume we were."

"No?" Her laugh is hollow. "I might've spread my

legs for you the other night, but that doesn't mean I'm easy. It's just a shitty position I put myself in."

I flinch, her words striking like a physical blow. "Shit, you think I'm taking advantage of you. Am I that bad?"

"You certainly haven't been good." Harper scoffs hard enough to send stray hairs flying off her forehead. "I've done my best to move on and forgive, but you've hurt me. A lot. Not just when we broke up. You've directed hostility at me ever since. It's one thing to let the painful comments slide for the sake of remaining civil, but this"—she motions between us—"is a different story."

"It isn't a secret that I'm an asshole, especially to you."

"Yes, that's the common excuse you tend to spew whenever we argue." And she doesn't sound the least bit impressed.

Gnarled, finely-tuned defenses rise to take control. "What do you want me to say? That I'm sorry?"

"It would be a decent start."

My chuckle is dry, the brittle edges flaking off with each humorless note. "You don't think I know who takes the blame? I fucked us over then, just like I'm doing now."

"Then own it," Harper presses.

"I'm trying." The conviction lashes out from my clamped jaw.

Her chin lifts at a proud angle. She isn't shying away. A serene whisper parts her lips. "Try harder."

My destructive temper lurks at the ready. I choke down the bellow trying to rip from my throat. Instead,

I surrender to the pull Harper has on me. Lord only knows when I'll have another opportunity to fuck this up. My arms wrap around her, tugging until she's tight against me again. She doesn't struggle, but her body is stiff.

I bury my nose into the crook of her neck, inhaling the calm only she provides. "Every damn day when you're not beside me, I'm paying for my mistake. You belong with me but you're not and it's my fault."

Her fingers clutch at my shirt, keeping me grounded. "We don't just... do this."

"Am I making you uncomfortable?"

"If I said yes?"

"It'd break my bitter heart, but I'd let you go."

"Once and for all?"

My gut plunges to the floor. "If that's what you want. I've already been mourning the loss of what could've been. Seems only fair to suffer alone after you ruined me."

Harper pulls back to search my gaze. "How did I ruin you?"

"There's no replacing you, Pitchy. Nobody else comes close."

"But we only dated for a few months," she reasons.

"Didn't have to be mine for long to leave a permanent mark." The tattoo on my inner forearm burns in acknowledgment.

"It's not that simple for me to forgive and forget." Pain flashes over her features. "You already destroyed me once. Excuse me if I'm not waiting in line for an encore."

"I don't expect you to," I rasp.

"Then what's your plan?"

My brain sputters with the effort to compute a sensible answer. It couldn't be more obvious that I didn't consider the long haul. There are too many obstacles that I have yet to obliterate. But Harper Wilson is the only one for me. That has to count as a chance to prove myself.

"We can go slow." My tone is steady despite the feverish instincts demanding escalation.

"As friends?"

I grunt as my palms remain firmly planted on her ass. "You know we're more than friends."

"And that's supposed to sway me?"

"Yes?"

Harper gawks at my stalling tactics. "Wow, you're something else."

"That's not a compliment, huh?"

"Definitely not." She pushes me until there's a sizeable gap separating us.

"Let's talk about this," I plead, grasping for straws or anything else at this point.

"What's left to say?"

"Everything." Yet the most important declarations stick to my vocal cords.

Her shoulders slump in defeat. "This isn't what I want."

I reach for her limp fingers, threading them with mine. "We can start over. A fresh slate."

She's shaking her head before I'm done talking. "I won't agree to that. Not like this."

"Then how?"

"That's for you to figure out." Her expression is blank as she withdraws behind a shield.

The urge to silence her retreat has me leaning in, but a kiss won't diffuse this situation. "Give me a chance to right my wrongs. I'll be the man who deserves you, Pitch."

Harper's smile is sad as she ducks beneath my arm and begins backing away. "I would love to see you actually try, Jerky Jacob."

chapter sixteen

Harper

ANOTHER IMPATIENT KNOCK DEMANDS ENTRANCE AS I finish my bathroom business. A lady can't halt mid-stream to welcome uninvited company. I button my jeans and hop to the sink while the determined visitor begins pounding louder.

"One second," I call over my shoulder.

After rushing through the hand-washing process, I hustle across my apartment to the front door. I fully expect Joy to be waiting on the other side with a poop emergency from Baby Belle. For such a tiny thing, that newborn can explode like a geyser. The breath sputters from my lungs at who I find instead.

"Sydney?"

The little girl smiles at me like I've made her morning even brighter. "Hi, Miss Harper!"

"Hey, you," I greet and slump against the jamb.

With my guest's identity revealed, I take a moment to process her appearance. It takes less than a second to determine that she's hiding something behind her back. The crinkle of cellophane gives me a hint but doesn't solve the main mystery.

"Can I help you with something?"

Syd blinks at me. "No."

"Um, okay. Is there a reason you dropped by?"

"I brought you a surprise." She giggles and rocks on her heels, keeping the object out of sight.

My heart warms, regardless of whatever she's offering. "That's so sweet. What is it?"

She thrusts the gift forward without fanfare. "A whole bunch of KitKats."

And it truly is just that. At least a dozen are arranged to resemble a bouquet. It's an impressive—and mouth-watering—display if I'm being honest.

I accept the wrapped bundle with a grin that attempts to match her magnitude. "Thank you, superstar. These look yummy."

"You love KitKats the mostest of any candy, right?" Her earnest stare would get me to agree even if it wasn't entirely true.

"Yep, they're my favorite indulgence." I rub my empty stomach for emphasis.

"Phew." She wipes fake sweat off her forehead. "He didn't goof."

There's only one *he* who could be involved in this scheme. And now that I'm thinking about Jake, his absence is cause for concern.

I poke my head out in the wide hallway and look both ways. "Where's your dad?"

"In his truck."

"Does he know you're in here?" I would assume so, but it's important to get confirmation.

Sydney bobs her head, sending dark hair flying in all directions. "Uh-huh. He didn't let me out of his sight until you opened the door."

"Who let you into the building?" Which is another matter entirely.

She thrusts an arm toward the only other apartment on this floor. "The lady who lives next to you. She's very nice."

"And trusting," I mumble.

Although to be fair, Knox Creek is pretty lax on security in general. It's almost a shock to have a main entrance that's locked. More so, Sydney Evans isn't a threat. Her father, on the other hand, is capable of catastrophic damage.

I steel myself at the reminder. "Is your dad coming back in?"

"Nope," she chirps.

"Why not?"

Syd bounces her shoulders. "I dunno."

That gives me pause. It isn't as if Jake needs me to watch his daughter while he runs errands. Half the town volunteers on a daily basis for that honor. Exaggeration or not, she isn't on my doorstep to be looked after.

I study Sydney while trying to tease apart his motives. "Is there another reason you stopped over?"

Her eyes roll skyward. "Well, duh. I wanted to see you."

The noise that wheezes from me is what it sounds

like to melt in a child's hand. My eyes sting as I try to re-gain my composure. "Good grief. You're the cutest ever."

She preens under my praise, ending on a curtsy. "I know."

"And so modest. Do you get whatever you want, whenever you want it?"

Syd nods with another extra dose of enthusiasm. "My daddy says I'll be lotsa trouble when I'm older."

I'm tempted to believe it. "You'll always be adorable. Use that in your favor."

"Like to get a boyfriend? Daddy is gonna get a big stick to chase them away." She claps a palm over her mouth at the funny thought.

"That's good. You're too young to date." Even if it's totally innocent and only used as a meaningless title.

She sticks out her tongue. "That's what my dad said."

"He's right. No boyfriends until you're twenty-five or whatever age he thinks is best." It won't end well for me if I go against his parenting advice.

"But that's super old. I can't wait that long to meet Prince Charming." Her pout almost weakens my resolve.

"I turned twenty-five in December."

Sydney gasps. "Really?"

"Yep. Does that make me super old?"

"Nuh-huh." Her eyes twinkle. "But you're gonna find true love soon."

A strangled laugh steals my breath. "Oh, I don't think so."

She squeaks and begins clapping. "Are you already in love?"

I feel my eyes widen to twice their size. Words stick to my throat as I fumble for a response. The longer my delay, the hotter my face flames. All I manage is a muffled croak.

Her brows crinkle inward. "Huh?"

"No," I blurt through a clogged windpipe.

Her sneaking suspicion narrows on me. "I think you're in love, Miss Harper. Who is he?"

If this guessing game continues, Sydney is bound to assume I'm infatuated with her father. Which, well, I don't know if I can deny. But that's a sticky subject I don't want to stumble into. I'd rather address any other topic her wild imagination can conjure.

My gaze swings in a blurred arc for a worthy distraction. That's when I belatedly notice she's still lingering in the hallway.

"Do you want to come in?" Maybe I'm crossing a line, but Jake should've considered that when he tucked tail to his truck. "Should we ask your dad?"

"He says it's okay." Syd rocket blasts into my apartment before I can step aside to grant her entry.

The KitKat bouquet nearly tumbles from my grip before I can set it aside out of harm's way. I chew on my thumbnail while watching her dart around the confined space like a pinball. "It's probably best to check with him. Just in case."

"Whatever." She shrugs before flinging herself onto my couch.

After a few trial wiggles to test the softness, Syd begins bouncing on her butt. The cushions puff and whine from the unexpected exertion. She doesn't acknowledge the furniture's distress, too preoccupied with the search for the next spot to explore. On cue, she launches from her seat in a graceful dismount. Then the mighty whirl-wind dashes toward the kitchen.

My feet shuffle on the floor as I follow at a careful distance. It'd be a shame to disrupt her controlled chaos for no reason. "I'm just going to text your dad, okay?"

"Uh-huh," she mumbles while inspecting the contents in my cabinets. The hinges squeak in protest from the abrupt open and shut motions. She doesn't reach for anything sharp, which gives me the confidence to take my eyes off her long enough to send a message to Jake.

> **Me:** *Hey. I invited Syd to hang out for a bit. Cool?*
> **Jerky Jacob:** 👍

I let my jaw hang loose at his flippant—albeit expected—response.

> **Me:** *Did you srsly thumbs up me?*
> **Jerky Jacob:** *Sure did*

"Miss Harper, look! I'm sooooo beautiful, just like you." Sydney appears in front of me without warning.

The startle tactic almost squeezes a little pee out of me. Then I see her face, or mostly her mouth. It's apparent I made the fatal error of leaving her unattended for thirty seconds.

My heart threatens to pound right out of my chest. "*Holy shhhhi…* ish kebab. Did you find my lipstick stash?"

She puckers her paint job for approval. "Whadayuh you think?"

"Ummm, you'll certainly turn heads on the street. Probably stop traffic too."

Her gasp is pure delight. "Whoa. I did that good?"

"Yeah, you even colored outside the lines to be sure."
I roll my lips together to stifle a giggle.

"Yay!" Her fist flies straight into the air while she blows rapid-fire kisses.

Based on the shade, she chose a long-lasting stain. That stuff won't come off until tomorrow unless we scrub it with a makeup removal wipe. It's a blessing that Jake isn't here to witness her creativity. But that's an issue I'll concern myself with once her motor shifts into park. If she even hits that gear during waking hours. I'm convinced her energy runs from a nonstop tap.

On cue, Syd's gaze swings to a spot behind me. "Ooooooh, I love to read."

I brace myself when her attention sticks to the bookshelf. "There aren't any for kiddos."

And that's putting it mildly. My collection consists of smutty romance and dramatic thrillers.

"Are you positive?" She's already en route to fact-check.

"Pretty sure," I insist while jogging to catch her stride.

Sydney screeches to a sudden halt in front of the fireplace. She whirls to study the picture hanging above the mantle. "Wowwwww. Is that you, Miss Harper?"

My eyes take several seconds to stop spinning after so much action. I glance at the framed photograph that's stalled her progress. The picture behind the glass captures me in an elegant grand jeté. My left ankle throbs at the memory of a failed landing not too long after this shot was taken.

I sniff at the emotions threatening to rise. "Yep, that's me in college."

Her stained lips part in awe. "I've never seen you dance like that."

"It's been a while since I've danced like that. I got hurt and had to take a break from the really tricky moves." Not that those advanced steps were sending me farther than the campus theater. "That's why teaching is better for me."

Concern splashes across her pinched features. "Are you okay?"

"Yeah, of course." I lift into en pointe, or as close to it as I can get with bare toes.

Syd offers a round of applause, appearing satisfied with my demonstration. She stares at the photo for another moment. Then her body curls forward in an exaggerated hunch.

"I'm hungry." It seems the bookshelf adventure is officially forgotten as she pats her tummy.

"Oh, uh… I can probably find you something to eat." Grocery shopping just so happens to be on my list for this weekend. My hunt for sustenance lands on the discarded candy she delivered. "How about a KitKat?"

She jumps in place to approve of my suggestion. "Yes, please. Those are my favorite."

"Really?" I set myself in motion to separate one package from the bunch.

"Uh-huh. Just like you, and thanks so super much." Sydney eagerly snatches the chocolate from my outstretched hand.

"We have good taste in common, huh?" I lift mine to tap against hers.

She flops onto the rug that extends beyond my dining table and begins happily munching on her snack. "No, I mean you're my favorite."

I sit down on the floor beside her. A previous conversation

with Jake floats to the surface. "You're my favorite too. Just don't tell the others."

Syd giggles. A skinny finger presses to her mouth that's now smeared with chocolate on top of the red lipstick. "I'm super good at secrets."

"Then this will be ours." I nudge her shoulder with mine.

She goes quiet for a moment, which immediately rouses my guard. "Do you wanna have babies like Miss Joy?"

I choke on my bite of KitKat. "Mhmm?"

Syd cuddles against me. "You'd be a super good mom."

And that comment creates a hot lump in my throat. After I manage to swallow the crispy wafer crumbs, I fix a strained smile at her. "That's a really great compliment, superstar. I'd like to have kids someday. We'll have to wait and see. But if I do, I hope they turn out to be as sweet as you."

She gives me her signature megawatt grin, but only for a moment. The gleeful expression slips into a crooked slant. "I don't think my mom is gonna visit me ever again."

Even a cannonball blast couldn't warn me that this bomb was following the first. My next inhale is noisy and sharp, betraying the drop in my belly. As I contemplate how to respond, I'm almost tempted to remind her about the nonexistent love of my life that held so much interest earlier. I was wrong about that sticky situation. As it turns out, this is the last topic I want to address.

My palm rubs soothing circles along her back. "I'm sure your mom will come see you soon, Syd. She must miss you a lot."

She sprawls flat on the floor. "If she missed me, she

would wanna be with me every single day. She doesn't even call anymore."

"Have you tried to call her?"

"Uh-huh." Her head bobs to a defeated beat. "She doesn't answer, though."

The ache that spreads through me is crippling. Heat fills my eyes as I try to find words that will comfort her. "Your dad is really great. He loves you more than anything. His heart might burst with how much he cares for you."

"That's a lotta love." She spreads her arms as wide as they'll reach.

"It is. He'll always be there for you." Which serves to deliver another wave of moisture across my vision. My father isn't with me in the physical sense, but I can still feel him watching over me all these years later.

Sydney nods against the rug. "My daddy is the bestest."

"Which is pretty awesome to brag about, right?"

"Yep!" She bolts upright, nearly cracking our foreheads together. "Can you pretend to be my mom?"

I almost tip over sideways. My palm smacks the hardwood to regain some semblance of balance. "What?"

"You can be my fake mom." The determination in her voice sends dread skittering down my spine.

"I don't think that's a thing." Not to mention, extremely likely to create upset.

"Why not? It's just like when I play dress up with my imaginary friends. But you're real, which is soooo much better. Then I'd kinda sorta have a mom all the time."

"But you have a mom." My reminder is issued in a level tone that hides the tremble I'm experiencing everywhere else.

"Not really."

"Your mom would disagree," I insist. I can only imagine the hell I'd pay if Morgan caught wind of this.

"But she isn't here."

It's hard to argue with facts. My lungs strain under the pressure of holding my breath. I haven't been adequately trained to field these delicate—and potentially traumatizing—discussions. "How about I pretend to be your super cool aunt instead?"

"That's not as fun," she complains.

"Syd," I say and reach for her hands. "This feels like a big deal. I understand why you're asking me to be your fake mom. We have a close relationship and I love spending time with you." The lump in my throat returns tenfold. "But I'm worried about pretending to fill such an important role for you. It might bother your mom or dad."

"Should we ask my dad?"

"No, that's not really what I meant."

"We can keep it a secret." She whispers the compromise in a giddy rush that leads me to believe everyone in Knox Creek will hear about this by nightfall.

"It's an idea we can—"

A knock on the door interrupts me, and I cross my fingers that Joy has arrived with a poop emergency. I will gladly handle an explosive blowout to gain a few moments to unwind this clusterfuck I've gotten myself in.

Sydney leaps to her feet and races to the entryway. "I'll get it!"

"Let me check the peephole first," I blurt while scrambling to stand.

But it's too late, and another unexpected guest is about to be welcomed into our fake family drama.

chapter seventeen

Jake

SYDNEY IS THE ONE TO FLING OPEN THE DOOR. "DADDY! Come in. We've been waiting for you."

I almost fall flat on my ass at her appearance, but manage to stumble over the threshold instead. The loud slam that follows knocks me from the stupor. "Hey, Boop. What happened to your mouth?"

It's impossible to miss the grotesque smear across her lips that resembles blood. I glance behind my daughter to find Harper trying to blend in with the background. She wiggles her fingers in a wave but doesn't greet me otherwise. The flush coloring her slender throat makes me want to trace the splotches with my tongue.

"I found Miss Harper's lipstick." Syd's announcement swats my dirty thoughts into the gutter where they belong until after dark.

"Yes, I can see that." My gaze appraises her handy work. "You did… something special there."

She could probably get hired as a clown with a bit more practice. As if hearing my insight, she stretches her grin broad enough to scare her own reflection. "We're playing dress up."

I flick my eyes to Harper, noting her usual appeal. "Is that so?"

"Uh-huh. Harper is my fake mom."

The wind gets sucked from my sails and I double-over with a cough. "What was that?"

My daughter huffs. "She's gonna pretend to be my mom."

I stare at the woman involved in this farce. "Did you agree to this?"

She wrings her fingers until the knuckles turn white. "No, not really?"

"That's convincing." Sarcasm drips from my tone.

Her eyes are round, searching mine for guidance. "I didn't influence or encourage the idea."

"But you didn't discourage it either," I guess.

This game of make-believe could swing heavily in my favor. It would take minimal effort to plant the idea in Sydney's head that the three of us could be a family. A pleased rumble rolls through my chest. Fuck, that sounds like a dream I don't deserve to have. But using my daughter's attachment to Harper for my benefit is a dick move, even for me.

"It all happened so fast." Harper palms her forehead. "Sydney is a smooth talker. Her negotiation skills are better than mine."

"You're telling me," I chuckle. "Her quick wit gets me in trouble more often than I want to admit."

My daughter glows under our verbal applause. "You gotta be careful with talkin' too loud 'cause I'm always listening."

"And ready to turn the smallest crumb into a buffet to feed the town." Which is how I've found myself as a juicy snack for the gossip food chain.

Syd nods, then skips to Harper's side. She snuggles against her without an ounce of hesitation. Her eyelashes flutter shut in bliss when her second favorite person lifts an arm to wrap them in a tighter embrace.

The sight almost sends me crashing to my knees. Genuine relief like I've never felt floods me. This is a monumental moment that I've been desperate to witness.

"You're gonna be my new mom," Sydney murmurs.

"Umm, well…" Harper seems to struggle for a response. Her throat works overtime to gulp in oxygen.

"Does it bother you?" I tilt my chin while taking a long look at the satisfying picture they create.

"No." A serene smile curves her lips as she toys with Syd's hair. "I just don't want to cause complications, for either of you."

My gut seizes at the hurt in her voice. That careless comment will haunt me until I convince her it's a lie. "You're not a complication. Far from it."

Even if she were creating problems, the damage has been done for years. It's not a secret that my daughter is borderline obsessed with her dance teacher. Maybe it runs in the family.

Harper implores me with her soulful gaze. "How can you be so sure?"

"Have you seen the way my little girl looks at you? There's nothing wrong with that." Another layer of comfort blankets me.

She lowers her eyes to catch Syd's blatant adoration. "We have a bond, huh?"

"Yep. That's why you're gonna be my mom. Right, Harper?" The sugary plea in her tone has me on board, as if I wasn't invested already.

With the shock of her declaration fading, I notice she's dropped the formality. "Where did *Miss* Harper go?"

"Don't be silly. She's right here, Daddy." My daughter rolls her eyes. "But I'm not gonna call her Miss Harper anymore 'cause she's waaaaay more than my teacher. I only asked if she'd pretend to be my fake mom. But maybe if I wish hard enough, it'll come true."

My mind spins with the swift progression of her plan. "This is getting serious. How long did I leave you two alone?"

Something like suspicion narrows Harper's eyes as she studies me. "Are you behind this?"

"I wish I could take credit. That honor belongs solely to the mastermind attached to your hip."

Syd's sly grin reveals the truth. It's even easier to pin her as the guilty party when her mouth is stained red. "You'll always be with me, Daddy. That's what Harper said. I need a mama who wants to be with me too."

My head hangs under the weight of her hopes and

what's missing. Unfortunately, her mother doesn't share the belief that her involvement is necessary. It's suddenly hard to draw my next breath. Morgan doesn't have a clue about the pain her actions are causing. Our little girl just wants to feel loved by her parents. That's not much to ask as a child. It's what I've wanted for her since she was born.

Instead of letting regret consume me, I replay her full statement. The praise that I'm a reliable presence allows me to forget my shortcomings. It's especially beneficial where the blonde bombshell cuddling my daughter is concerned.

"You've got me no matter what, Boop." I lower into a crouch, spreading my arms wide.

Sydney flies at me in a blur of motion. We crash together in a well-practiced embrace. "Love you, Daddy. You're the bestest."

Warmth soaks my hardened exterior as I absorb her kindness. "Love you more, my sweet miracle."

Harper sighs from her spot several paces away. The reaction holds a slight edge that requests attention. Then she mutters, "I'm totally a complication."

Syd breaks apart from our hug to question me. "What's a complication?"

I stand, scrubbing a hand over my mouth to muffle the curse of that damn word. "It's like when something makes a situation difficult or more challenging. A bump in the road."

She gasps. "That's bad. Harper isn't a complication."

"You don't gotta tell me." I send a pointed stare

at the one who keeps reminding me of my terrible choices. "What can I do to prove it?"

"Probably shouldn't have said it to begin with," Harper mutters.

"If only I could reverse the clock."

Shit, the changes I'd make pile into a staggering heap. How different reality might be if I wiped out the huge mistake that lays a foundation for countless others. Or if I get a chance to correct it the old-fashioned way.

Sydney is busy watching Harper, but her gaze suddenly swerves onto me. The calculation swirling in those inherited baby blues has my heartbeat faltering. "Do you wanna have more kids, Daddy?"

"Uh, sure?" But only if a certain woman is interested in becoming a mommy.

"Harper wants to have babies. Like a whole bunch." She pretends to cradle an entire brood in her skinny arms.

"That's not exactly how the conversation went," Harper croaks.

But my daughter isn't listening. "Maybe I'll help change the pee-pee diapers. No poops."

It turns out planting a seed in her head won't be necessary. "You practice with your dolls."

"Uh-huh, and their butts are stinky." She plugs her nose.

"Better get used to it if you plan on being a big sister."

Her lips squish into a contemplative twist. "I need to ask Miss Joy where babies come from."

"It's magic." The safe explanation rolls off my tongue with ease.

Syd rolls her eyes. "How old are you, Daddy?"

"Twenty-eight. We celebrated my birthday last month, remember?" The ache in my joints makes that number feel double.

Her eyes expand. "Have you found true love?"

Instinct and routine habit sends my focus to Harper. Her stare is already locked on me. Tension bloats the standard gap between us until the dense force urges me forward. I curl my fingers against the demand to pull her in.

The connection is severed when I peek down at Syd. "I have."

My daughter squeaks. "Then why aren't you married?"

"Our fairy tale is"—I almost say complicated, but bite my tongue—"a long story. I'm hoping we find our happy ending soon, but first I have to prove myself worthy of her."

An unintelligible noise wheezes from Harper. My feet carry me three steps closer. If I stretch, our hands could touch.

Sydney coos. "That's sooo romantic. You're like Prince Charming."

More like the dragon who deserves to be slayed, but I'm not going to burst her bubble. "I'm glad you're rooting for me, Boop."

That's when my daughter glances between me and Harper, then at the minimal separation keeping us apart. She narrows her eyes. The lull that follows crackles with wishful thinking as she tries to eliminate the empty space entirely. I'm certain she can read the room better than most adults.

"I gotta go potty." Syd starts prancing in a circle, legs tightly crossed.

"Right down the hall where you found the lipstick." Harper points and moves to show her the way, but my little girl is already gone. "Well, someone is in a hurry."

"She's bad about waiting until the last minute." And extremely good about giving us a few private moments alone.

"Afraid to miss any fun in her absence."

"That's about right." But she volunteered in this case. I won't let her efforts go to waste.

Harper's concentration is still diverted, so she doesn't notice me creeping over. I slide a palm into the back pocket of her jeans, using the grip to tug her flush against me. Her body collides with mine as she sputters an exhale. Startled eyes leap upward to find my smirk waiting.

"Hey, Pitch." Heat is quick to spread through me while her curves are in my possession.

She recovers from the momentary shock and straightens in my hold. "What're you doing?"

I test the limits, letting my fingers dig into her denim-clad ass. "Getting comfortable. This is the first time I've been to your place."

Harper squints and quirks a knowing brow. "Which is funny since I don't recall inviting you."

"Want me to leave?"

Her glare shifts off mine, lowering to my throat. "I'm not rude."

"Then offer me a drink and see what happens."

"That's an unnecessary risk," she murmurs.

"What's the alternative? Sydney won't leave unless you kick us out."

She studies me, countless questions swirling in her gaze. "Were the KitKats your idea?"

I shrug. "Syd wanted to see you. She's been asking nonstop when you're coming over again for dinner. I'd prefer dessert, but that's a different discussion."

Harper blushes. "You're incorrigible."

"For you? Yes." My bent knuckle traces the heat blooming on her cheeks. "I might've let it slip that you're a sucker for certain treats."

"Where'd you find a whole bouquet of them?"

"Made it myself."

"You?" She scoffs a dry laugh, but her amusement sobers at my serious expression. "Oh, wow. That's... uncharacteristic."

I tug my bottom lip between my teeth. It's becoming increasingly difficult to resist kissing her. "Might surprise you yet, Pitchy."

Her gulp is audible. "I'm scared about interfering. Syd is getting really attached to me, which is fine. But pretending to be her mom? That's a lot."

"Too much?"

She gapes at me. "Why aren't you more concerned about this?"

"Should I be?" Little does she know it's an outcome I fantasize about constantly. "What I'm worried about is where this leads, the ideas it sprouts, and the impact on Syd if you're not committed."

"Right, of course. Again, it's never been my intention to overstep."

"That's not what you're doing. Sydney wants a reliable female figure in her life. You don't have to be her fake mom to give her that."

"Okay, I don't want her actual mother to be offended."

The possibility is comical. "You're no threat to Morgan."

"No?"

"Have you seen her lately? She hasn't visited since before Christmas."

Harper winces. "Maybe she's busy?"

"Don't give her excuses."

"I can't pretend to understand her circumstances." Her slumped shoulders reflect familiar defeat.

It's Morgan's priorities that confuse me. "I'll tell you one thing that's certain. If she wanted to be involved with her daughter, she would be. It's a choice."

"That makes sense," Harper sighs. "It's just tough to imagine."

"Not everyone wants to be a parent, or is fit to raise their child." Which is a crucial factor for Harper when it comes to my daughter. I tug my hand from her pocket to slide my arm around her waist. "I don't want you to feel pressured. You're not obligated to fill any role for Sydney other than teaching her how to dance."

She sags into me. "That's comforting to hear, but I don't mind if she wants to see me more often. I'm getting pretty attached to her, if I'm being honest. She's an amazing kid."

"Then just be there for her. That's all Sydney wants."

"I can do that," she confirms with an easy smile.

"Good," I chuckle. "That saves me some heartache and effort."

Harper stares at me—genuine, open, and unguarded. "Why's that?"

I bend until my forehead rests on hers. My restraint can only stretch so far. "I'm pretty sure you're stuck with both of us either way."

chapter eighteen

Harper

M Y SEEMINGLY UNEVENTFUL DRIVE IS INTERRUPTED
when dark vapor spills out from under the
car's hood. Internal alarm bells replace aimless
musings. Almost immediately after the sudden
appearance, several system alerts flash on the display
panel. Those red and yellow symbols are a taunt, as if I
couldn't already tell there's a major malfunction.

I gawk through the windshield as the smoke grows
thicker. An unmistakable jolt lurches me forward, narrowly bumping me into the steering wheel. Then my
faithful Camry sputters in what resembles a coughing
fit during a winter cold. Just as I'm pulling over onto
the shoulder, the darn thing stalls altogether. The silence that follows almost sounds like the vehicle's sigh
of relief.

"Just great," I mutter.

After shifting into park and stabbing the useless ignition button, I take a moment to contemplate my options. I hate to admit my sorely lacking skills in this area. My mom has many strengths, but handling repairs on her own isn't high on the list. She hired out even the most basic tasks. That damsel in distress trait unfortunately got passed down to me. I'm well aware I only have myself to blame.

Not that it matters if I had the knowledge to run general diagnostics. Between the stench of burning oil and inky clouds rising from the sealed hood, I can conclude that this mechanical failure will require a professional. I clutch my phone while mentally scrolling through people to call. This is my punishment for canceling roadside assistance.

It dawns on me that I might be in danger while waiting for divine intervention. I shove the door open and curse my delay in self-preservation. Fresh air envelops me, but there's still a putrid fog that hangs heavy. Maybe someone will smell my car imploding and come running. A judgmental scoff berates me.

At least it isn't below freezing or snowing. There are far worse conditions to be stranded in. I could use this as an opportunity to enjoy nature in spring.

Instead, I pace in a small circle while considering the next course of action. My mom probably has several capable folks on speed dial. Or I could put on my big girl panties and message—

A truck comes into view from around the bend on the opposite side. The beastly Ford demands recognition. Apparently, almost thinking his name conjures him.

Jake slows to a stop in the middle of the road. The right lane separates us, but I can feel his disapproval as if he's looming over me. I wince while his silence descends like a bone-deep chill. Then he flips his hat backward so I can appreciate the full view of his frustration.

"Fancy seeing you here," I greet him. My fingers wiggle in an attempt to smooth the deep creases between his brows.

His scowl isn't impressed with my nonchalant efforts. "Problem with your chariot, princess?"

I flutter a hand to my chest. "Are you calling me royalty? That's very sweet."

"Harper." Jake's voice rumbles like furious thunder. "What's wrong?"

"If I knew, I wouldn't be standing here."

"Why'd you get out?"

"I was worried it might explode." Which sounds silly, even to my own ears.

His tortured groan mirrors the sentiment. "What am I gonna do with you?"

Before I can answer, the back window rolls down. Sydney's adorable face pops out. A chipper bark tells me Glitzy is buckled in beside her. My heart warms into sappy goo over the fact that this grumpy man is out for a Sunday drive with his two girls.

Syd's exuberant wave matches her smile. "Hey, Harper."

I cough to dislodge the awe in Jake's honor. "Hi, superstar. What's new?"

Other than the fake mom topic we left hanging in the balance after our conversation yesterday. I'm not ready to rehash the details quite yet. Although, it's comforting to hear that she hasn't reinstated the formalities where my name is concerned.

Syd scrunches her expression in thought. An excited gasp reveals she's landed on an answer. "Oh, oh! Daddy had a tea party for me and Glitzy. He's the host with the most."

Rather than appear embarrassed by his daughter's gloating, the father of the year wears a proud grin. "My cookies were good too."

"Sooooo yummy," Sydney praises.

I lock my knees in a weak restraint to stop myself from running into Jake's arms and begging him to love me like that. There might be some repressed daddy issues at play. The notion turns my stomach and I almost gag. What's more likely is an underlying attachment to this jerky heartthrob that refuses to let go. I pity my resolve if he's serious about trying.

"Been stuck long?"

Six going on seven years.

I snap out of the false sense of calm Jake's raspy tone lulls me under. "Uh, five minutes at the most."

"Why didn't you call me?"

"Wasn't sure it was that serious." My pants might as well light on fire along with my smoldering motor.

His flat stare sweeps over my lie like a detector. "Serious enough to be worried it might explode."

"It's a valid concern," I mumble while my cheeks go up in flames.

"Did you even bother to look?"

I sigh rather than spill the truth. "What good would that do?"

His frown twitches at the edges. "For the record, it's pretty rare for a car to spontaneously combust."

"Listen, I don't claim to be a mechanic."

He grunts. "Nobody would make the mistake of assuming otherwise."

"Way to rub salt in the wound," I grumble.

"Are you okay, Harper? You look sad." Concern swims in Syd's eyes.

I paste on a smile that feels brittle. "Yep, I'm totally fine. My car isn't, though."

"Don't worry. My daddy is the bestest. He'll fix Ruby Red in a jiff-piff." Her measure of time is pure amusement.

My grin lifts effortlessly. "Ruby Red?"

She nods. "That's her name."

I stare at the plain sedan through a fresh lens. Newfound appreciation brightens the paint. "How cute. I love it."

"Just like you love her, right?"

"Of course." I give the trunk a gentle pat.

"And she's sick?"

"In a sense," I hedge.

"Daddy, did you hear that? You gotta make Ruby Red feel better." She glances back at me after addressing her father. "He's like a doctor for cars."

Accepting a favor from him, no matter how small, is a slippery slope. "Maybe you can just take a quick peek. I mean, if it's not too much trouble…"

"Glad that's settled." Jake mutters something else under his breath.

I'm about to ask when he whips around—not bothering to check for nonexistent traffic—and pulls over behind my car. The crunch of gravel beneath his boots drums in my ears as a warning. Bad news dressed as doom is approaching—for me or Ruby Red. Maybe both.

He strides past me and gets straight down to business. "Can you pop the latch?"

"Yeah, sure." But I'm too quick to agree. My pathetic inadequacies have me fumbling under the steering wheel. Lucky for me, the button is clearly labeled.

He's already got the hood up when I straighten and meet him at the front bumper. While stretching forward to fiddle with a knob, his shirt lifts to expose the ultimate distraction. I might whimper at the toned abs that slight motion puts on display. My mouth definitely waters.

Damn this attraction. I rip my gaze off Jake's chiseled stomach, only to fall victim to his bared forearms. The tattoos ripple with each precise shift. Watching this man in his element is a detrimental aphrodisiac. Despite our unfortunate circumstances, I feel the stirring of arousal tingle in my lower belly.

My mind reels as I try to fight temptation. Jake probably ditched his jacket on purpose. It might be warm by Minnesota standards, but short sleeves are a bold move.

I wave a hand to chase off the fumes. "What's the verdict?"

He abandons his inspection to stand upright to face me. "Tough to say."

My spirits sink. "Is it bad?"

He barely spares the engine a second glance. "Most likely."

"How can you tell?"

He crosses his arms, challenge thrumming from his wide stance. "Do I come into the studio or bar and tell you how to do your job?"

"Um, kinda?"

"That was before. This is a new version of me. I won't serve you any bullshit." It would be easier to believe if he kept a straight face. "Besides, this is what I do."

"This is just unreal. My Camry is very dependable. I don't understand what happened."

Jake shrugs his broad shoulders. "Things break. That's what keeps me in business."

I gnaw on my bottom lip while untangling the limited options. As recently revealed, tow trucks are a scarce commodity in these parts. But relying on Jake is a rare risk. "Could you take it to the dealership for me?"

"I'm gonna pretend you didn't just suggest that." A joint leaps in his clenched jaw.

Shock lowers mine to hang slack. "That's where I get the maintenance done."

"Until now. They've clearly failed you, and you're insulting me." Yet he exudes nothing but confidence.

"I didn't realize your ego is so sensitive."

"You can stroke it later to make up for this offense. Don't deny me this simple pleasure, Pitch."

A soft breeze cools the sting on my cheeks. "Are we still talking about my ruined motor?"

"Only if you are," Jake rasps.

My gaze implores his, seeking the emotions he can't keep hidden there. I haven't agreed to anything when it comes to him. Sydney is simple and effortless. Jake is the one to make our situation complicated, which is ironic since he originally claimed that honor as mine.

"You're willing to do the repairs?"

"I'm the only one who can." His insistence is almost charming.

"And why's that?"

He tucks my uplifted chin between two bent knuckles, then traces my bottom lip with his thumb. "It's my job."

"Does that make you my hero?" I flutter my lashes at him.

His mulish snort disagrees. "I think we both know I have a long ways to go before earning that title."

"But you're trying." It's not a question.

"Get in the truck." He nods toward his Ford that's idling in welcome.

Arguing seems futile, not to mention foolish. "And then what?"

"Syd and I will take you to dinner while Penn tows your car to the shop. I already texted him."

"How can I refuse an offer like that?"

"Real simple." Jake allows a dashing smirk to slip beyond his mask. "You don't."

chapter nineteen

Jake

Harper taps her fingers on the polished table while surveying our surroundings. "Are we cheating on Roosters? It feels a bit unfaithful."

I glance over my shoulder to follow her scandalous perusal. It's been a while since I've stepped foot inside Bent Pedal. As the only other decent place to eat in Knox Creek, it couldn't be more different from the rowdy cock den down the street. This sleek establishment caters to a more upscale crowd with its fancy cocktail menu, food items I can't pronounce, and repurposed whiskey barrels that just look expensive. But variety keeps the good folks satisfied and loyal.

"There's nothing wrong with spreading our patronage. We're still supporting our town and community." I hitch a thumb at the black and white photographs hanging on the wall behind me. The collection captures our local traditions and festivities.

Harper rests her chin on a closed fist, leaning forward to scrutinize me. "That sounds like an excuse to absolve your guilt."

My scoff is richer than the overpriced booze stocked in this bar. "I'm not guilty."

Harper wrinkles her nose as if my response reeks. "You sure about that?"

"Still mad at me, huh?"

Her shoulder lifts in a lopsided confirmation. "It's hard for me to trust you."

Air whistles between my teeth. "I should've known taking you to a fancy restaurant would raise suspicion."

She tries to frown, but a smile cracks the droopy edges. "You're such a shit."

"It's one of my most reliable attributes. Twice a day without fail."

"Gross," she giggles.

The pitchy melody heats my blood. "Ah, there's my girl. You can't ignore a solid poop joke. It's too gassy to resist."

Her laugh grows louder. "Stop being funny. You're too irresistible as it is."

"Is that so?" I recline in my seat, ready to take a load off. "And here I thought this would be difficult."

"Don't let it go to your big head."

"Hey." My tone loses every ounce of humor. I steal a liberty and thread my fingers through hers, tugging until our hands are clasped. "I fucked up once and it cost me years of anguish. Hell, I'm still suffering. Please believe me when I say that I'll never take your kindness for granted again. You're it for me, Pitchy. I'm gonna prove it."

Harper stares at me while holding her breath, like any small movement will ruin the moment. Then her gaze drops to where my palm engulfs hers in a protective hold. "Okay."

I lift our linked fingers and press a gentle kiss to her inner wrist. "I'll be so good to you, baby. Just give me a chance."

Her breath hitches as she watches me inhale her scent. "Why now?"

My nose and lips drift across her skin. "Better late than never?"

"Even you can do better than that," she quips.

"I plan on it." Conviction settles in my marrow, a part of me at the core. "I'll do whatever it takes. Leave me out in the cold and I'll build a shelter until your heart warms up to me again."

Harper sighs, the fight deflating from her posture. "You're quite swoony."

"Never been accused of that before." I scrub over the scruff along my jaw. "But I suppose it makes sense."

"Why's that?"

"Been saving it all for you." I squeeze her hand.

"Oh, boy." She releases me to fan her eyes. "I need something strong to wash that down with."

"Guess we came to the right spot."

"Yeah, yeah. They have an impressive selection. You did well." Harper scans the list of mixed drinks, tapping each option with her finger. "I'll try this one."

"Sex with a Bartender?" My stiff tone borders on a growl.

"Delicious." She smacks her lips.

"Yeah, for me. Especially if it's a twirling bartender. That won't pleasure your acquired tastes, though." I whip the menu from under her nail. "This one is more to your liking."

"Grease Monkey?"

"I'll toss in a free lube job."

She chokes on nothing but air. "What has gotten—"

"I'm backkkkkk," Sydney yells before reaching her seat.

Harper and I startle in unison at the interruption. My gaze whips to Syd. Amusement quickly replaces the shock. "Did you clean out the entire kiddie corner, Boop?"

"Huh?"

"How long were you over there?" I check my watch.

"Like seventeen hours." She plops onto her chair with an exaggerated sigh. "I was super busy. There's lotsa crafts to do."

"I can see that."

It looks like she just returned from a birthday party. Stickers cover her shirt, she's clutching a completed coloring sheet, and there's a macaroni creation dangling around her neck. The sight isn't surprising. There's a large sectioned-off area dedicated to children's entertainment.

Her joy grants this place my approval and allows me to forgive the ostentatious atmosphere. As an added bonus, the owners have two kids near Syd's age. They become the best of friends whenever we stop in.

"Can I see Glitzy?" Sydney wiggles her fingers for my phone.

I grunt while waking the screen. If somebody told

me I'd have a Pomeranian who frequents a doggie day-care called Pampered Pooch, well… I'd call that person a liar. Yet here I sit, opening the app with a live stream that allows owners to watch their pets play.

Syd squeals once the video lands on her beloved companion. "Glitzy is soooooo cute."

"Sure is," I mumble.

Harper rolls her lips together to smother a laugh. "You're wrapped around her tiny pinky."

"Well aware, thanks for noticing."

Sydney babbles something unintelligible at the phone. "Did you see that? Glitzy just climbed a ramp. Awwwweeee, now she's curled up on a fluffy pillow. I bet it's super soft. We should get one for her to use at home."

I glance at the grainy feed. "Not sure that'll match with the rest of our furniture."

Although, if I'm being honest, I'm not the master in charge. That dog and my daughter rule the roost. I'm just their property manager who puts food on the table. It's a responsibility I take very seriously.

"What're you thinking about?" Harper's smooth voice drags me from the random thoughts.

I trail my fingers along her arm. "Adding another to the household."

She shivers as goosebumps follow my touch. "Dog?"

"Female," I correct. "A certain blonde that reminds me of sunshine would brighten our dynamic."

Her lips part. "You'd be severely outnumbered."

"Already am, and I don't mind."

My daughter whimpers, putting those unbalanced plans on further delay. "I wanna get Glitzy. She misses me."

"After we eat. That's why she's at Pampered Pooch."

"Can we order? I'm starving." She flops against her chair with the dramatics of a paid actress.

As if hearing Sydney's complaints from across the bar, Rylee Walsh—formerly Creed—appears at our table. "Hey, friends. I didn't realize Becky wasn't covering this section. Were you waiting long?"

"Yes." I offer the owner a blank stare—my specialty.

Harper nudges me. "Be nice."

"That term clashes with my personality." I narrow my eyes at her.

"Maybe you need an attitude adjustment."

"Only if you're handling the repair."

A breathy exhale bursts our intimate moment. "I didn't realize you two finally got back together. Rhodes better pay up."

Harper laughs, swatting at the other woman's arm. "Oh, don't encourage him. We're not a couple."

"Yet," I counter.

She rolls her eyes but doesn't argue further. "He's fixing my car."

The redhead grins. "Gotcha."

I might be an asshole, but even I can appreciate that Rylee is able to smile again. The tragedy of her older brother's death was a huge blow to the whole town. It still cuts deep six months later. Rumor has it that this bar was Trevor's dream. Thanks to the combined efforts of his sister and best friend, Bent Pedal continues to thrive in his absence.

"What can I get for you?" Rylee's gaze roams over our trio.

Sydney thrusts her arms toward the ceiling. "Pizza!"

"You're gonna turn into pizza," I tease.

"It's yummy for my tummy."

Harper glances at the menu that holds far more creative choices. "Works for me."

Rylee nods. "Got it. Just cheese or…?"

"Sausage and green peppers," I reply.

Harper's brows wing upward. "You don't like green peppers."

"But you and Syd do."

Rylee winks at the speechless blonde. "How about drinks?"

"Chocolate milk please," Syd requests.

"I'll just have a Coke." My focus turns to Harper after I order.

There's an expectant pause before she says, "Grease Monkey for me."

"Great choice. I'll put sugar on the rim so he's extra sweet."

Harper clucks her tongue to deny the suggestion. "Nah, I think he's better with bitters and salt."

"The sour edge does keep things more interesting," the bar owner notes.

A pleased rumble rolls off my chest. "That sounds promising."

While distracted by Harper's specified preferences, I fail to notice Sydney's eyes locked onto Rylee's midsection. "Are you having a baby?"

I cough over her comment. At least she's adorable and can get away with it. But still. "Sydney Grace, we've talked about this. That's not a question you're supposed to ask. Remember the incident with Miss Tiffany?"

My daughter gives a sheepish shrug. "That wasn't my fault. She said there was a food baby in her belly."

"That just means she's full."

Syd's attention returns to Rylee who's busy trying not to laugh. "Did you eat too much?"

The redhead nods. "I did, but I'm also pregnant."

"Told you so." Sydney's sass is aimed pointedly at me.

"Lucky guess, Boop. Please don't make it a habit." Or a disgruntled mob of women will be pounding down our door. My gut clenches at the visual.

"Congratulations," Harper croons at the expectant mother.

"Thanks." Rylee rests a palm over the small swell. "We're having twins."

Syd's expression pinches. "What're twins?"

"There are two babies in here," Rylee explains while pointing at her stomach.

"Two babies?" Her awe shouts to the opposite end of the restaurant. "How did that happen?"

"Gage and Payton have a theory." She points to her kids in the designated play area. The pair appears to be in the middle of an imaginary sword fight.

Sydney gasps and leaps from her seat. "I'm gonna find out where babies come from."

"I apologize in advance," Rylee rushes to say.

Before I can question why, she scurries off like trouble is chasing her. "What the fuck was that about?"

"Should we be worried?" Harper's focus is zeroed in on the trio huddled in a tight formation.

"They're just kids. What harm can come from them exchanging a few stories?"

Alarm blares at me from her wide eyes. "You should never say that."

"Just like how your precious Camry is dependable."

"It is."

"Tell that to the blown gaskets and leaky fuel injectors."

"You already know what's wrong?" Suspicion laces her voice.

"For starters."

She waits for me to add more. "Do you have a loaner for me? The dealership always provides one."

A disrespected grunt spews from me. I'm still steaming over her earlier audacity. As if I'd haul that hunk of junk to another garage to be serviced. Get fucking real. "Nah, Pitch. You'll just have to rely on me for transportation."

"That's not realistic."

"Why not? You can even stay in our spare bedroom to make things more convenient."

"And never leave?" Her perceptive gaze can see exactly where I want this situation to lead.

"Well, now that you've mentioned it…"

"No." Harper slashes a hand across the space between us.

"I don't even get a maybe?" I drag my bottom lip between my teeth. If I try hard enough, I can pretend her flavor still lingers there. Feigned disappointment tempts me to groan.

Her throat bobs as she tracks the purposeful action. "You know that maybe will have me tucked under your covers before midnight."

Arousal spears into me, straining my cock against unforgiving denim. "Fuuuuck—"

"Daddy!" Syd yells from the corner. "Miss Rylee is gonna have two babies 'cause she swallowed lotsa sperm!"

Harper's face bursts into red splotches. She buries the evidence of her embarrassment behind a flat palm. "Oh. My. Gosh."

Meanwhile, Rylee is mouthing silent apologies to us from behind the bar.

"Well, shit. Forget the loaner," I chuckle. "We're gonna need a getaway vehicle."

chapter twenty

Harper

"That's it for announcements," I conclude. My bare feet glide across polished wood on a direct path to the door. "Great job tonight, twirlers. You learned the new steps very fast. See you Thursday."

The tiny dancers are quick to form a line. Each gives me a hug before floating off in a cloud of tulle to find their parent or trusted adult. Sydney trails behind the group, more than happy to be saved for last.

"Love you," she murmurs into our embrace.

My proverbial cup overflows, putting my exhausted tear ducts to work. I smooth a palm along her back. "Love you too."

Once she disappears in search of her dad, I spend longer than necessary cleaning the space that's already spotless. My delay is methodical and therapeutic. It allows me to relax and decompress after several hours on display. There's no reason to rush through the motions. All that awaits me is a lonely apartment.

I switch off the lights, dousing the mirrored room in complete darkness. A passing glance confirms that Ginger took care of the other studio. Only the lobby remains illuminated. My stride skids to a halt when the bright area comes into full view.

Jake and Sydney are practicing the partner choreography for their performance. She beams at him while he guides her in a flawless spin. They turn toward each other, shimmying their shoulders while leaning in and bending out. Next, he picks her up for a simple turnaround lift. Their coordination is worthy of applause. I almost clap on instinct. Instead, I feel like a spy intruding on a special moment.

He notices me while returning Syd to her feet. Jake's gaze feasts on me, as if he didn't just see me an hour ago. I'm beginning to think he has a thing for spandex. With a long blink, it seems our surroundings return to focus for him. He scrubs at the back of his neck while scuffing his shoe against the carpet. If history didn't dictate otherwise, I'd think the broody grump is blushing. My brows reach for the sky when he dips his chin to hide the evidence. Well, damn. That proves anything is possible.

I walk toward them, a bit dazed. "Um, hi."

Sydney bounces in place. "Did you see us, Harper?"

"I sure did. Excellent routine. Bravo!" I give them the applause they deserve.

She bows. "Thank you, thank you."

"We can't take too much credit. Our teacher is the best," Jake boasts while sporting a broad grin.

The compliment paired with a smile from him nearly

topples me sideways. "Slow down, JJ. I can't handle the sudden influx of sweetness from you."

His temporary glee tightens into a scowl. The loss earns him a pout from me. "Who's JJ?"

I use a hand to block my mouth from innocent eyes, yet my stage whisper will be purposely audible. "Jerky Jacob."

Syd giggles. "It's 'cause you're grouchy."

"She gets it." I jab a thumb at my fellow instigator. "But maybe you're due for an upgrade. How about Jolly Jacob?"

The frown that remains firmly planted on his filthy mouth is an answer in itself.

Then his adorable little girl cackles loud enough to shake the front windows. "No way! That's toooooo cutesy tootsie for my daddy."

Jake grunts. "Boop is right. I'm not at that level yet."

"Yet? Someone is being optimistic for a change."

"I'm here, aren't I?" He spreads his arms wide. "Better get used to it, Pitch."

That's when it dawns on me that these two are lingering far past expectations. My head tilts at the optimal angle to study his motives. "Why haven't you left yet?"

"Didn't want anyone to break in while you spent twenty extra minutes doing who knows what back there." He points to the hallway that leads to the studio spaces.

"Ginger has it handled." I turn to address my friend, only to find the chair behind the desk is empty. "Where'd she go?"

"You're just noticing she's gone?"

I press my lips into a terse line. "Excuse me for being distracted by your sneak preview."

"We're super good," Syd agrees.

"You've been practicing a lot, huh?"

"Yep. Daddy dances with me whenever I ask." She cups her palms around her mouth to imitate the whisper-shout like I did earlier. "I ask like a bazillion times a day."

The man just shrugs, further whittling down my restraint to a toothpick. "We want to win."

I blink at him. "It isn't a contest. There's no prize."

"Your heart," Jake amends. "And bragging rights."

The traitorous organ that he wants to claim lurches in my chest, desperate to land in his clutches. I slap a palm over the inflicted area to keep myself in one piece. "Okay, we're getting sidetracked. What happened to Ginger?"

"She left early."

A huff buzzes my lips. "Yes, I can see that. But why?"

"I told her we'd hold down the fort." He swings an arched gesture from Sydney to himself.

"Ginger was my ride," I mumble.

Smug satisfaction brightens his expression. "Guess you're stuck with us."

Syd rushes forward to grab my hands in hers, shaking with wild enthusiasm. "We should have a slumber party!"

"Umm."

"Pleeeeeeease," she begs.

An ice cube over an open flame stands a better chance of survival than I do against this captivating duo. Once I agree to spend the night, there's a high probability I'll stay indefinitely. The potential of such a major move requires more consideration. "Are you allowed to have sleepovers on weekdays? You have school tomorrow."

She releases me to seek permission from her dad.

He nods at her, as if they reach a silent agreement. "We can make an exception, but no pressure. I insist on taking you home, though."

Not like I have much choice. "How's my car doing?"

"Still broken."

I suppose that's fair. It's only been two days, but I'm grasping at straws. "Any idea when it will be fixed?"

"Not until the parts arrive," Jake explains.

"And when might that be?"

"Still don't trust me?"

"It's not that…" At least not entirely.

"Your lack of faith wounds me, Pitch." The tease in his tone suggests otherwise.

I'm about to throw in the towel when a convenient interruption tries to unlock the door. Joy is standing outside, fogging up the glass. She waves her keys frantically while trying to juggle a wide-awake Baby Belle. The newborn is along for the bumpy ride, pleased as poop to be snuggled in her detached car seat. Maybe her diaper blowout is finally manifesting itself. My legs are in motion before I can fully comprehend what her unexpected visit means.

"Hey, bestie!" I greet once the door is unlocked.

Joy shoves her way inside, nearly clobbering me with Belle's carrier. She's across the room and dropping onto the couch within moments. "Why are you still here?"

The situation might be more serious than I put into the universe. I join her on the sofa, blowing kisses at Belle perched on the middle cushion between us. "Hello to you too."

"Sorry. Hi," she relents. Her frazzled gaze swings to Jake and Sydney. "Am I intruding?"

"Yes." He doesn't hesitate or beat around the bush. Go figure.

I shoot a glare in his direction a few paces away. Then my focus returns to my friend. Upon further inspection, she looks two seconds away from succumbing to a deep slumber. "What's wrong?"

Her sigh suggests the list is long. "Nothing. Belle won't sleep for more than five minutes. I thought a drive might soothe her. When I saw the studio lights on, I figured we could stop in and see whoever's burning the midnight oil."

"Worried we're having fun without you?" My smile is lopsided as I gesture at our mellow gathering.

"Yeah, pretty much. I miss adulting and being social."

"You've only been mommying for two weeks." As if I have any concept of the impact.

She tugs at her crooked ponytail. "It takes a toll real quick."

"I second that." Jake snorts while moving to stand behind me.

If I recline the slightest bit, my head will brush his crotch. I get the sense that's intentional. "You're tarnishing my assumption that motherhood is constant bliss and merriment."

Joy hums thoughtfully. "Consider me a bubble burster. Cole and I are one sleepless night away from using clothespins to keep our eyeballs open."

When I offer my finger, Belle latches on like we're already best friends. Instinct has me leaning forward to nuzzle her soft cheek. "Do you need help? I can watch her whenever I'm not working if you need more rest."

Most of my experience is with children who talk and

use the potty, but diapers can't be that difficult to master. A few test trials with Belle might come in handy for the future.

She waves away my offer. "No, no. Thanks, though. It's just an adjustment. This first month with Belle is very important for our bond. Besides, there are two of us. We take shifts to divide and conquer."

"Always wondered what it felt like to equally share parenting responsibilities. Must be nice," Jake mutters.

"Better luck next time." She stretches to give him a consoling pat on the arm.

I wince and capture Sydney in my peripheral. It's only then I realize that she's been abnormally quiet. The little girl appears frozen in place while mesmerized by Belle.

"Why don't you come sit next to me, Syd?" I point to the available space that separates the carrier and my thigh.

She breaks free from the trance and leaps onto the sofa. Her face is immediately pressed into the infant's personal space. "Hello, Belle. I'm Sydney Grace Evans. It's super nice to meet you."

I laugh. "You're so polite, superstar. Don't be upset if she doesn't answer you for a year or two."

"M'kay. She's sooooo teeny tiny. Can I hold her?" Her skinny fingers tap at the harness buckles.

Joy cracks an eyelid open that I didn't see her close. "Maybe next time, twinkle toes. We should probably get going before I pass out sitting upright."

"Already?" Syd's whine is the definition of devastated. "You just got here."

"It's late. You need to get your beauty sleep," she counters.

"Then I'll be extra pretty like you and Harper," the little girl states proudly.

Joy's gaze questions mine at the obvious change in how Sydney addresses me. Rather than veer off on that tangent, she stands with an exaggerated yawn. "You're well on your way, kiddo. Soon enough, you'll have us beat."

Syd squeaks. "No way!"

"Try and find out." She winks.

I peek at the clock to see it's almost nine o'clock. We've stayed an hour later than normal. "Would you mind dropping me off on the way, mama bear?"

Strong hands settle on my shoulders, kneading at the sore muscles. "Let me take you, Pitch. Depend on me."

I groan as Jake's thumb digs at a knot. "It's the opposite direction for you. Why are you going through so much trouble?"

"It's not trouble. I wanna be there for whatever you need." He stoops forward until our eyes meet. "Going out of my way for you doesn't bother me."

"I'm not trying to uproot your routine."

The smolder he pins on me threatens to incinerate my resistance. He lowers his guard completely, exposing the blatant hunger and yearning in his gaze. "I'm finding that I'd like you to uproot a lot more than that."

Joy exhales a pleased noise. "And that's how babies are made."

Sydney gasps. "Really?"

"In a nutshell."

The little girl pauses for a beat. "What do nuts have to do with babies?"

"More than you know," Joy replies.

Syd bounces on the couch. "Daddy, you gotta kiss her."

"I do?" The question is for his daughter, yet he's still staring at me.

"Uh-huh. Like a king kisses his queen." She hops off the cushions to twirl in rapid succession. "And I'm the princess who wants a brother or sister."

"We shouldn't mess with the fairy tale," Jake rasps.

My face heats under the attention from our captivated audience. I study him from this slightly upside-down angle, looking way too sexy with his stubbled jaw and backward hat. His descent is slow to allow me a chance to escape. But I don't. My stomach flips and twists to sync with the feverish thrum in my veins. Each breath is torture until his lips press against mine.

I allow my lashes to flutter shut. The kiss is a chaste peck to appease any lingering doubts. When he pulls away, I get lost in the commitment his eyes promise me. The honesty in those blue depths begs me to leap.

"Welp, that'll do it." Amusement laces Joy's tone as she hoists Belle's carrier off the sofa. "I better get outta here before I try to convince Cole to knock me up on purpose."

"Like on a door?" Sydney giggles.

"That might do the trick," she muses.

I snap from my lusty Jake daze. "Who's knocking on the door?"

Joy wears a smug grin. "That'd be love, babes. It's about time you answer."

chapter twenty-one

Jake

ROOSTERS IS SUPPOSED TO CLOSE IN TWENTY MINUTES BY the time I stride through the door. Only a few stragglers remain at the rail. None of them bother to turn while I settle onto an empty stool in my preferred corner. The spot just so happens to be directly in front of where Harper is wiping down the counter, singing in my favorite off-key pitch. That unique melody gets me hard before my ass is fully planted on the seat.

She appraises my awkward shifting while finishing the task. Her eyes haven't left me since I walked in. I should know, seeing as mine haven't strayed far from hers either. There's a gleam in those green depths that reflects an unfulfilled hunger. Or maybe it's my own cravings trying to trigger hers into manifesting. Both could lead to mutual satisfaction.

A grin curls her glossy lips as if my wishful thinking

is amusing. The bright red color draws me in, urging my bent elbow onto the bar while the other arm rests flat on the wood. Harper quirks a brow while watching my desperate measures to reach her. That flippant reaction makes me want to hop over the barrier separating us and kiss her until she's senseless. Then we'd be equal in lack of logic.

"Why are you staring at me?" Harper tucks her hair behind her ear.

"You're smiling."

"I smile all the time."

"But not because I caused it. This is a special smile."

"Maybe that makes it yours." She startles, as if shocked by her own words. Her posture straightens and she flings the rag into a nearby sink. "I already did last call, JJ."

The nickname almost gets a grin from me. "Not here for a beer."

She studies me through a narrow squint. "Just some company then?"

My nod is a single jerk. "And once we're done, I'll drive you home."

Her blink is slow. "You're still planning to act as my personal chauffeur?"

"Didn't we settle this debate yesterday?" It took a heroic amount of control that I normally don't possess to refrain from tossing her over my shoulder at the dance studio. The same uncharacteristic patience gnaws at me in this moment. "In case there's still confusion, my answer is yes."

"Where's Sydney? It's Wednesday, and really late."

"My dad is staying at the house until morning."

"Your dad?" She stutters over the words as her jaw goes slack. "As in the only man more surly than you?"

"That's the one."

"And he came from three towns over just so you could pick me up?" Disbelief clangs in her reply, and rightly so.

I shrug. "Syd invited him over for dinner. She knew you were working and would need a ride home. He's fairly worthless, but the guy is actually fond of his granddaughter."

Harper uses several beats to compile a response. "That's very considerate of her."

"She cares about you a lot, and so do I." With that admission, I lean forward to stroke a finger down her arm. "Mine is just a very different type of love."

Her body stills. "Love?"

My pulse thunders loud enough to quake the room. "Yeah, Pitch. You must see it by now, or do you still doubt me?"

She stares at me, locking our gazes in an unbreakable trance that leaves me exposed and dangling in her clutches. Whatever she sees has moisture pooling in her eyes. "I should finish cleaning."

Garrett appears behind her with impeccable timing. "Nah, you can get going. I'll finish what's left to do behind the bar."

She peeks at him, and I bristle at the loss of her attention. "Are you sure?"

"Absolutely. You busted ass all night." That's the instant he decides it's a smart choice to massage her neck. He must have a desire to meet my fist.

"Hands to yourself, Foster." The threat in my voice has him raising his palms.

He chuckles, but the sound is tense. "You don't gotta worry about me, Evans. Harps is like a sister to me."

"I won't worry about you so long as you don't touch my girl."

That gets a disgruntled squeak from Harper. "I'm not your girl, JJ."

My grunt strongly disagrees. "Does that stand for Jealous Jacob?"

"It does now," she returns.

"Good. I'll own that shit. You're mine, Pitch. The faster you realize it, the fewer black eyes I'll have to deliver."

Her eyes roll skyward. "And for a second I thought you were being sweet."

"We were interrupted." The gift in my pocket burns with renewed purpose. "C'mere."

She remains firmly rooted. "Why?"

"I need you closer. Please," I tack on in an effort to be decent for once.

Harper shuffles to the gap and rounds the counter, although hesitation measures her gait. I flip my hat backward in preparation. Once she's within reach, I tug on her belt loop to drag her between my splayed legs. Then I cradle her jaw in a gentle embrace fit for the precious treasure she is.

My sole focus doesn't waver from hers. "Forgive me?"

Her chest rises and falls with a heavy delay. "Are you actually sorry?"

"For telling Garrett to fuck off? Not even a little bit."

Her mouth forms a firm line. "Then why are you

apologizing? If that's even what you're doing." She flails her arms between us.

My fingers dig into her hips to anchor our bodies together. "I don't want you to be upset with me."

"Maybe you haven't noticed, but your offenses are already stacked to the ceiling." Harper points upward for emphasis.

"Can I make it up to you?"

"Aren't you supposed to be doing that already?"

Regret expels from my lungs in a weighted sigh. "I'm an incurable asshole, but I'm trying to be better. Only for you and Syd, though. Everyone else can kick rocks."

Harper fights a smile, pulling her bottom lip between her teeth. "I don't mind you being rough around the edges. It's kinda sexy when you defend my honor, even against Garrett's harmless flirtations."

A rumble builds in my chest. "Probably shouldn't have told me that, Pitch."

"Why not?"

"You just gave me permission to be an unreasonable brute. I'll be relentless in my efforts to protect you." The insistence to be territorial whenever she's concerned already surges in my veins.

"Okay," she breathes a few inches short of my lips. "That pairs well with how openly affectionate you are. I'm a fan of that too."

Two knuckles drift along the blush heating her cheek on my trek to tuck some stray hair behind her ear. "You like when I touch you?"

She nuzzles against my palm. "Very much so, especially when it seems like you can't stop yourself from doing it."

"Probably because I can't. It's a force I'm done fighting against," I confess freely.

Her shiver has me pressing our upper halves flush. "Much easier to surrender. Your impulse to do so makes me feel cherished."

"That reminds me, I have something for you." My fingers blindly dig for the box. "I was waiting for you to get off."

She giggles. "That sounds dirty."

I grab her ass with my free hand. "You hear what you want. Put those filthy ideas on pause for a few, okay?"

Harper's eyes widen when the small package comes into view. "What is it?

"That's for you to find out." I raise my flattened palm higher to give her better access to the proffered item.

She removes the lid, only to immediately drop it once her present is revealed. "No, you didn't."

It's suddenly hard to swallow. "Yes, I did."

Her watery gaze searches mine. "Is this *the locket* from Memory Lane?"

The mention of her beloved antique store spreads warmth through my chest. She used to drag me there at every available opportunity just to browse the shelves. I was all too willing to watch unfiltered glee brighten her expression at whatever random trinket she'd deem worthy. We shared several unforgettable moments between the dusty aisles.

"It is," I confirm after pulling myself from the reverie.

"But why? How?" She shakes off the fumbled questions. "I mean, when did you buy it?"

"The same day you spotted it in that case. It was the easiest decision I'd ever made."

Her bottom lip trembles. "That was way back when."

My head bobs to a sullen tempo. "I was planning on giving it to you for your nineteenth birthday, but I fucked that up."

"Um, wow." A mixture of gratitude and old wounds strain her unsteady voice. "Wasn't it expensive?"

"Doesn't matter. I wanted you to have it." Even a shmuck like me could recognize that the heart-shaped pendant was meant to be hers. The gold necklace and I have that in common.

"I can't believe you did this, and kept it even after we broke up."

Prickles attack the back of my neck and I rub at the sting. "Guess I was holding onto the assumption that I'd be able to give it to you someday."

"More optimism? Maybe I've been selling you short."

Which bodes very well for me. "Open it and see what's inside."

Harper unclasps the tiny closure. Fastened on the left is a faded picture of us. Shock hitches her inhale as she gets swept into the past. "Oh, I remember when you took this."

The captured memory is from a sunny afternoon during Knox Creek's summer festival. I was giving her a piggyback ride as we wandered the grounds. She clutched on tight with her cheek pressed against mine. Our matching smiles were untroubled and dedicated to young love. We had the entire future sprawling ahead of us. There wasn't anything to block our happily ever after. At least not yet.

I clear the bitter reminder from my throat before

it can spoil our reminiscing. "We were really good together, huh?"

Harper sniffs, her focus still on our unblemished history. "We really were."

"Do you think we can be again?" I allow vulnerable honesty to plead from my stare while grasping for her fingers, locking our palms together. "The space on the right is blank, just waiting for an updated photo. If you're willing to create more memories with me. There's a pint-sized addition to consider too. I hear she's pretty irresistible, though."

"She must get that from her daddy."

Hope blooms in my chest. "Yeah?"

Her nod is fast. "My resistance never stood a chance against you. I'm not sure how I held out this long, especially when Syd is at your side. You two are a compelling team."

The laugh I release is loose, free of the jaded bumps the notes usually carry. "Does that mean you believe we can be good together again?"

Harper flutters her lashes. "Maybe."

My gut threatens to plunge until I recall a piece of our conversation from Bent Pedal. "You're giving me a maybe?"

"Do you know where that will lead me?"

A jerky nod is all I can manage at first. "I do."

Lust builds at a speed that makes me dizzy. My palm smacks the edge of the bar to maintain balance. The visual of this woman tucked under my covers by midnight is more erotic than the lewdest fantasy my crude mind can conjure.

"Well then." She plucks the locket from the velvet pillow. "Will you help me put this on?"

"Fuck, Pitch. You don't even need to ask. It would be my honor." The gruff edge in my tone is desperate to make a claim on her, even in the form of antique jewelry.

A blush stains her skin as she admires me for several silent beats. Then she turns and swipes her hair to the side. "You're full of surprises."

"And your response guarantees that there are many more to come," I rasp.

My thick fingers fumble with the delicate chain, but I manage to secure the clasp at the base of her neck. The sight of her finally wearing the gift I've kept hidden for years does something indescribable to me. It's a miracle my ass stays on the seat. In order to stay grounded, I dust kisses along her nape while cinching an arm around her waist.

"I look forward to it," she says while swaying into me. Harper whirls to face me as her fingers drift across the gold pendant with reverence. "I'm not sure how you'll top this. It's very special, not to mention beautiful."

"Only because it's yours."

Desire pools in her gaze. "Good grief, Juicy Jacob. Keep talking like that and I'll be tempted to take a big bite."

My throat tightens along with my jeans. "Wanna get outta here?"

Harper loops her arms around my shoulders and bends forward until our mouths almost touch. "I thought you'd never ask."

chapter twenty-two

Jake

THE EXPLICIT CONSENT IS A BETTER INDICATOR TO GO ahead than every traffic light on Main Street flipping to green in unison. I stand in a hurry, which sends my stool toppling to the floor. The loud crash barely registers as I plot my next move. Meanwhile, Harper startles from the noise and stumbles backward. There isn't a chance for her to recover before I'm scooping her into my arms and rushing for the exit.

"What're you doing?" Her humorous tone bounces with my choppy stride.

I dip my face to brush our noses together. "Sweeping you off your feet like I should've done years ago."

"Oh, my." She presses the back of a palm to her forehead. "My panties are gonna melt right off at this rate."

"Keep it together, woman."

"Then stop being romantic. Your growly beast mode

is hot enough without adding swoon. I'm about to spontaneously combust from the intoxicating blend." She fans her face in warning.

"You better wait until we're alone." I toss a glare over my shoulder at Garrett and the two stragglers still slumped on the rail.

The bar's owner whistles at our retreating forms. "It's about damn time, in case you haven't already heard it."

I adjust Harper's weight onto one arm for the sole purpose of flipping him off. "Go fuck your fist, Foster."

His chuckle meets my rude gesture. "Screw a smile on his face for all our sakes, Harps."

"I'll do my best," she hollers from my clutches.

"Don't encourage him," I grumble.

"Me?" She scoffs, pretending to be affronted. "You're the one being unnecessarily crass."

"Can you blame me?" I gulp at the fire blazing under my skin. "The woman of my dreams just agreed to be mine. I'm barely clinging to reality, Pitch."

The challenge in her gaze snuffs out and she sags in my grip. "Gosh, you make it impossible to stay mad at you."

"It's a secret talent."

Harper laughs, then glances at the doors we're rapidly approaching. "I can walk."

"And I can carry you. It's a slushy mess out there and I don't want your shoes to get ruined."

"You don't want my shoes to get ruined," she reiterates.

"That's right." I drop a kiss to her parted lips. "But don't worry, I have plans to wreck you later. The slightest movement will be a struggle once I'm done with you. Then you'll beg me to carry you."

Harper snorts as I stomp onto the sloppy sidewalk. "Someone is confident."

The cool breeze is a welcome relief against the feverish arousal wreaking havoc on my sanity. "When it comes to pleasuring you, I'm a fucking expert. I look forward to hearing you sing my praises soon. It's long overdue."

"You always liked it when I sang," she murmurs.

"Feel free to serenade me on the way." I juggle better than an overpriced clown while depositing her on the passenger seat in a fluid maneuver.

Her mouth pops open when I take the liberty of buckling her safety belt. She stares at my towering form in the glow of the overhead light. Liquid desire rushes over me as her gaze roams downward in a seductive path I can feel fondling my shaft.

I cough to yank myself from the illicit grasp. "Hold that thought, Pitch. I gotta drive."

Harper is already turned toward me when I settle behind the wheel. Her floral scent wafts over me, luring me into a trap. And I'm a willing captive. "Your truck is really cozy."

"Thanks." I blindly stab the key into the ignition, nearly slicing my finger in the process. "Your place or mine?"

"Why not both?" Her purr harmonizes with the engine's rumble.

"Gonna need you to explain how that's possible," I mutter while shifting the pickup into drive.

"We can start at mine to do the dirty, then go to

yours for the sleeping portion. Fully clothed," she tacks on with a chastising wag of her finger.

"Do the dirty?" My chuckle fills the gap between us. "Fuck, you're incredible."

"Does that mean my plan suits your needs?" The suggestion in her voice sobers my humor faster than a cold shower.

"My needs revolve around you. Whatever you want, Pitch." If she asks, I'll pull over after being on the road for only ten seconds.

"You're giving me a lot of control," she whispers in the dark.

As if there's an alternative. I'm weak when it comes to her, but that's not entirely true. Allowing myself to love isn't a weakness. Love isn't foolish. It's strength and belief and courage. Harper makes me feel like I deserve her, and that confidence is beyond powerful. I'll gladly surrender to her will since she always has our best intentions at heart.

"Use it wisely," I say to break the silence.

The lull that follows is electric. Static swarms in the divide separating us, trying to pull us together like magnets. A buzz hums under my skin as I wait for her response. An untamed energy thrashes in my pulse. I force my focus to glare at the windshield.

She must miss the drool that's collecting to dribble off my chin. As if refuting my assumption, her palm wanders along my arm that's responsible for steering. My knuckles turn white as I tighten my grip around the leather. This woman is determined to make me pass out from blood loss to my brain.

I switch hands in an effort to remain conscious. It also

grants me the privilege of linking our fingers together. The connection sends a calm wave across the furious lust I can't escape.

"Can I suck your dick?"

"Holy shit." I damn near swerve into the opposite lane. Thanks to the late hour, there isn't any incoming traffic. "Care to repeat that?"

Harper leans across the center console to touch my thigh. In a purposeful motion, she traces the inner seam of my jeans. "Will you let me suck your dick?"

A fantasy I never gave much promise to suddenly bursts across my vision. "Now?"

"That'd be ideal."

I pull some much-needed oxygen into my lungs, but the breath does little for my revved composure. "Why the sudden urgency? Not that I'm complaining."

In fact, I should staple my lips shut.

Harper releases an agreeable noise. "I'm done denying what I want, and I'm ready to take it."

"Which includes offering me road head?" Even just saying it earns a twitch from my cock.

She blinks wide eyes at me. "It doesn't have to mean anything."

I grunt and turn onto another deserted street. "The fuck it doesn't. Once you wrap those lips around me, I'm a goner. More than I already am."

She walks her fingers up and down my leg at a teasing pace. "Should we find out?"

The sound that chokes from me is meant to be an agreeable one. "Why did I ever mistake you as timid in this department?"

"Because I couldn't say pussy without blushing."

"And now?"

"You can't see the color of my cheeks."

"My good girl is brazen." And ready to prove it.

Harper slinks out from under the confines of her seat belt like an erotic contortionist. The buckle stays latched as she kneels on the seat and props an elbow on the console. My heart hammers while her hand begins drifting along my thigh again. It's a struggle to see straight. When she almost touches my balls, white spots break apart the black landscape filling my vision.

I turn my hat around and tug at the brim just to give my fingers a task. What I really want is to devour her, but that requires a different scenario. The reminder of our long night ahead calms the desperation clawing at me.

Instinct has me slouching lower to offer better access in the cramped space. She hums in approval when I stretch my left leg and spread wider for her. The adjustment grants me a slight reprieve from the tension in my muscles. The hunger won't be satisfied with a simple shift in position, though.

As if hearing my impatience, Harper cups me through the fabric pulled taut over my lap. Sparks sizzle in my bloodstream as I cruise toward a secluded stretch of town. There are miles of nothing but unplanted fields on both sides. No one will be near these parts at this point in the season and we can circle the country block in uninterrupted peace.

Her fingers grip my cock that's straining the material, giving a sluggish pump that only mocks the ache. "It seems you're rubbing off on me. I've been waiting for an opportunity to try your bold methods."

"You've been planning this?" The words grind out from between clenched teeth.

She continues toying with me while I squint to see beyond the limits of my headlights. "Well, claiming you as mine in general. Your dick in my mouth is a bonus."

"Jesus, Pitch. If you mention my cock and your lips in the same sentence again, I'm gonna bust in my pants." The damn thing is already hard enough to chisel concrete.

"That would spoil the fun." There's an audible pout in her voice.

"We wouldn't want that."

"Definitely not." Her playful touch wanders along the steely length of me.

I fight the urge to reach for her and rush this process along. A blowjob from Harper Wilson has been top-tier spank bank material since she first smiled at me. Acting on those depraved wishes back then would've landed me in hot fucking water. But there's nothing stopping me now.

"Do you need help?" I lift my hips in invitation.

"No," she chides. "But I have a rule."

"And what's that?"

"You have to keep driving until I make you come. If you stop, so do I." Harper's terms wrap around my cock and stroke to make me leak prematurely.

"Fucking hell," I spit. I've never been more grateful for planning ahead. We're already on a private route to nowhere.

Her laugh is throaty. "I'll try to make it really good. Then you won't suffer long."

"That won't be a problem." I'm about to spill my load just thinking about her mouth sinking down on me.

Whatever restraint had been constricting her actions suddenly vanishes. Deft fingers hook into the waistband of my jeans. Harper yanks at the button and zipper like a rabid carnivore in the presence of meat after years of eating only vegetables. I sag into the leather when my dick escapes the restrictive cage.

"You're freaking huge," Harper blurts.

I chuckle, but the noise is pure gravel. "Second thoughts?"

"Um, no. But my jaw might have a few regrets."

"Just use your fist." Three pumps would send me over the edge at this point.

"Do you take me for a quitter? Puh-lease. "You're gonna melt in my mouth. Not in my hand."

I spew a colorful array of expletives when she fists my girth. The strength of her grip on me threatens mine to loosen on the wheel. This is already too much, yet not nearly enough. Her skin is velvet against the abrasive lust thrashing in my veins. Abrupt movement on the speedometer alerts me that I'm slowing to a crawl. It takes direct instructions from every brain cell for my foot to stay on the accelerator.

She kisses her locket, then tucks the pendant under her shirt for safekeeping. Anticipation crackles in the air as she bends over my lap. The unfastened denim barely offers any slack. That doesn't seem to bother her. She holds me at the root while licking several laps around my flared tip. The slick warmth sends a ragged shudder through me.

My filter drops with a groan. "Fuuuuuuuck."

Her lips smile against me. "Do you think I spit or swallow?"

"I think you're a figment of my imagination." A haze blurs my vision when she exhales across my cock.

"That's where you're wrong, Jake. I'm very real, and I'm about to blow your mind." Little does she know that mission is seconds away from being accomplished.

My dick jerks in her clutches. "Please do."

The simple nudge latches her mouth around me. That single motion has me veering off the road. I wrench on the wheel to set us straight. Meanwhile, Harper becomes intimately acquainted with my cock. She isn't shy in the initial introduction phase. Quite the opposite as she swirls her tongue and sucks me deeper. Each move is meant to discover what incites the loudest reaction from me. When her nails tickle a sensitive patch, I nearly leap to the roof. I suck in several shallow breaths and instantly get lightheaded.

"Don't forget the rule," she whispers along my shaft.

The steady thump from the truck's tires keeps me grounded. "Couldn't if I tried."

It would take a blizzard to stop my forward track. She must agree and resumes her seductive progress. The slippery glide along my rigid desire is addictive. Harper is a confident goddess to be worshiped. Silent praises chant in my mind. I'll never recover from this. Her motions are rhythmic as she bobs on my length. I thread my fingers into her hair just to prove that this is actually happening.

She rolls her wrist to meet her mouth, working the two vises in tandem. I gnash my teeth as a prickling sensation bathes me. Just as predicted, a noticeable tightness already cradles my balls. The thrum of release builds under my flesh with each downward stroke. As if sensing the end fast approaching, Harper suckles me like a drought desperate for a drop of rain.

The thrill that balances a fulfilled fantasy and the challenge of driving through it reaches its peak. An unrelenting pressure builds, gaining momentum in a desperate act to break free. "Gonna come, Pitch."

She moans around my length, making no move to heed my warning. My good girl is thirsty, and the fact that she wants to guzzle me opens the floodgates. She pushes me into her throat, and the release valve bursts open. Tingles spread in pleasurable ripples as I surrender to the best climax of my life. Euphoric numbness crashes down in waves, then I'm submerged in comfort. The relief floods out of me until I'm depleted and wrung dry. I blink against the blinding splotches while trying to calm my labored breaths.

She sits upright, wiping the corners of her puffy lips. The lingering evidence of what she just did rebounds my arousal with dizzying speed. I grip the wheel with both hands to anchor myself.

"You followed the rules," she purrs in a tone that could seduce me all over again.

"Did you expect me not to?" I lacked faith in my control, but she doesn't need to hear that.

"No, you're very dedicated."

"I won't disappoint you."

Her eyes gleam in the shadows. "I'm counting on it. Take me to bed, JJ. You're gonna do me real dirty."

After that performance, she deserves nothing less than hours of simultaneous orgasms. "Do you realize what you're asking for?"

Harper blesses me with a sultry grin. "Whatever you're willing to give me."

chapter twenty-three

Harper

JAKE PAUSES IN THE HALLWAY JUST OUTSIDE MY BEDROOM. His white t-shirt rides up when he grips the door frame overhead. The casual pose puts his tattoos and biceps on tantalizing display. Approval dominates his steely expression, but he doesn't move.

I dig my toes into the plush carpet to stop myself from humping his leg. "Are you going to come in?"

He drags his teeth along his bottom lip, biting the flesh until white blooms over pink. The smolder in his gaze is a match ready to strike a blaze. I feel the heat curling over me like a lover's caress. My body yearns for his, swaying toward him without conscious permission. His molten focus doesn't relent as I begin to quiver. Anticipation is a pest whispering in my ear, urging me to shove him onto the bed. But a louder insistence demands patience.

The silence expands to encircle us while our gazes devour one another. It's a visual feast that leaves me ravenous. That gnawing hunger syncs with the empty pang in my core.

When Jake has eaten his fill, he shifts positions. Muscular arms cross over an equally brawny chest. Drool puddles in my mouth again and I almost slurp to avoid spillage.

"Strip for me, Pitchy. Ditch everything but the locket." The gravel in his gruff timbre is a sensual tease down my spine.

I shiver from the heat. There's an urgent fever rushing through my veins. The urge to follow his command sets flames to my clothes. I'm suddenly too hot, but the quiet is distracting.

"Can I turn on music?"

Jake leans against the door at a sexy slant that weakens my knees. "Whatever makes you comfortable."

Nerves lump in my throat. "And you're just going to watch me?"

"For as long as my patience allows. I might rip my clothes to shreds once you're bare for me." His hands are already curling into tight fists. The sight of him holding back nudges me into action.

This is just like dancing, which is my passion. There's no reason for jitters to be somersaulting in my stomach. I can pretend to be on stage for a captivated audience. A pointed glance ahead claims the latter part of my imaginary scene as true. He's not taking his eyes off me, and I'm not going to give him a reason to.

"Alexa," I call. "Play Jake and Harper."

The gentle opening notes of "Can't Help Falling in

Love" begin crooning from the speaker on my dresser. Samantha Harvey's version hits different. There's a yearning in her voice that resonates with me. That's why several of her unique renditions are included.

"You have a playlist named after us?"

My pulse thunders at the pained edge in his question. "I do."

"Fuuuuuck," his guttural tone bellows to the ceiling. He whips off his hat to rake through his hair. When his gaze falls on me again, desperation swims in the blue depths. "Please hurry. I can't wait much longer to make love to you."

A fresh wave of need rushes to my lower belly. "Me either."

With the soothing melody to guide me, I drift a finger down the center of my torso. Cotton fabric lifts to expose my stomach at a pace meant to tempt. My nipples harden into stiff peaks from the slinky motion. I stifle a whimper when those sensitive tips rub against my bra. These confining layers need to go before I combust.

While removing my shirt, I let my eyes slide shut to embrace the gentle beat. A chill pebbles my freshly bared skin and I shudder. The fiery lust in my lower belly is quick to smother the prickly sensation.

"Look at me," Jake rumbles.

A gasp tightens my lungs when our gazes connect. Desire burns in his eyes as he straddles the threshold. His wide stance does little to hide the rigid length bulging alongside his zipper. Shadows dance across his chiseled jaw that's clenched tight.

"Keep going." He juts his chin at my pants.

I undo the button fly with a practiced yank. After a

sultry wiggle, the denim pools around my ankles. Jake's unwavering stare on my mostly naked form encourages me to do a lazy twirl. When I'm facing him again, erotic fantasies are playing across his strained features. Carnal passion practically wafts from him. His fraying control is illuminated by the soft glow in my room, contrasting with the darkness behind him. He looks unhinged, and ready to pounce. My inner muscles clench, weeping at the emptiness that begs to be filled. I debate between prolonging the striptease or slicing through the flimsy silk that remains.

Jake makes the decision for me. "Get rid of the rest of it. Now."

His voice is sandpaper across a rusty surface. The abrasive demand suggests he's in charge, but I've never felt more powerful. I unclasp my bra and let the straps slide down my arms. Once my breasts are free, I hook my fingers into the elastic waistband of my panties. The last item concealing my modesty slips down and off. Cool air kisses my nude flesh. The locket nestled in my cleavage is warm like a brand I wear with honor.

Rather than cower behind my hands, the blatant arousal in Jake's eyes makes me bold. I toe the discarded lace, kicking the scrap toward him. He catches the thong in midair. My breath stalls when he brings the material to his nose. A starved grumble accompanies his inhale. His eyelids grow heavy as he savors another whiff. The primal act is an unexpected turn-on. I stumble backward until my ass lands on the mattress.

Jake's predatory stare latches onto mine. "Are you wet for me?"

I nod automatically. The slick heat between my legs

can't be ignored. My thighs rub together in a weak attempt to ease the ache.

"Show me, Pitch." He still hasn't abandoned his post in my doorway. His knuckles are white where he grips the frame.

While my cheeks burn, I spread to show him the slippery evidence hidden within my slit. "See?"

His head shakes in outright refusal. "Touch yourself. I want to see your fingers drip for me."

I gulp at the dryness sticking to my throat. The naughty request dangles in the space separating us. This smutty territory is uncharted for me, but I'm realizing my kinks align with his. That doesn't mean nerves don't tremble my hand as I swipe through my center. Air stutters from me when Jake bites his fist. When I pause to reveal the proof, my digits glisten in the dim lighting.

That's what it takes to set him into motion. He stalks across the room, shucking his clothes along the way. I'm caught in a trance as he reaches over his shoulder to rip off his shirt in a fluid motion. A feral noise wrenches from him as he drops his pants and boxers in one downward sweep. Before I can admire Jake's impressive cock, he crashes to his knees between my splayed thighs.

He holds my wrist with a tenderness that contradicts his savage appearance. I watch in stunned fascination as he brings my wet fingers to his mouth. My unblinking gaze doesn't stray from his while he licks me clean. But the dedicated man doesn't quit there. Jake sucks my two digits between his lips to complete the task. His tongue swirls around my knuckles with the utmost care. I squirm when the heatwave becomes too humid to remain upright. It's difficult to inhale through the haze. If a girl can expire from sexual excitement, I might be approaching the end of my line.

After a more thorough job than a power washer, he pops me free from his mouth. "Damn, I've missed you."

Before I can question him, he has my knees bent over his shoulders and his tongue buried in my pussy. A squeak of shock escapes me as I collapse flat onto the bed. Jake takes advantage of the change in position and shoves his face deeper into my center. His stubble scratches my inner thighs and the friction is electric.

I'm rendered immobile under his determined feasting. Static buzzes in my ears when he growls like I'm his first decent meal in weeks. Any fool who dares to interrupt him is likely to be maimed. Pleasure floods me under the relentless onslaught. The knowledge that he gets this untamed while eating me is a heady experience, especially when he lashes at my clit.

My fingers blindly search for purchase and thread into his hair. I use the grip as an anchor to grind myself closer. Tingles begin to spread and stars speckle my vision. The crest appears in the distance like a taunt. One or two accurate swipes and I'll detonate.

Jake's eyes are a bit crazed when he rips himself away from me. "I want you to come on my cock."

"Okay," I readily agree while propping myself on a wobbly arm. The promise of an orgasm still quivers below the belt.

"Do you wanna know what's kept me awake at night these past several weeks?" He sounds breathless and exhilarated while moving to hover above me.

My fuzzy brain struggles to process his meaning. The challenge of that task triples with his woodsy scent and domineering presence looming inches from my face. "Um, sure."

Jake crashes our lips together. A pungent tang assaults me, but it's not totally unpleasant. His urgency doesn't allow me to focus on tasting myself for more than two seconds. Before I can swallow, his tongue is plundering my mouth. Our individual flavors blend into a unique concoction that makes me dizzy with want. I grip his shoulders, digging my nails deep enough to bruise. He tucks an arm under me to press our naked flesh together. The hum between our bodies is like a contented sigh. It's only when my head rests on a mountain of pillows that I realize Jake shifted us.

I break apart from our kiss to find us sprawled in the center of the bed. "Wow, you've got skills."

His thumb drifts across my cheekbone. "You haven't seen anything yet."

My thighs part to cradle his. Our lower halves lock into place, two separate pieces finally finding the missing link to join them as one. His cock slides along my pussy with a measured roll of his hips. My arousal makes the motion seamless, a slippery glide that awakens my rebuffed climax from moments ago.

"Okay," I breathe. "Let's have the sex. Do me dirty, JJ."

Jake's smirk is cocky, which is especially appropriate in this instance. "You're not quite ready, Pitch."

"I'm not quite ready," I deadpan. "How do you figure? I'm naked and spread underneath you."

"It's more than that for us."

My palm drifts along his back. "Well, yeah. We already established that."

"Did we?"

"I thought so?"

"There's still doubt," he insists. "Once I get inside you, I'm never gonna wanna leave. That's a future you need to be fully committed to."

My gaze searches his for the truth he can't hide there. "I'm in if you are."

"As if I'm not already sunk." His longing bores into mine, delving beneath the surface. "It's always been you for me."

"Why did you push me away for so long?" It's a question I've already asked, but it's the last thread of uncertainty that's still clinging on.

"I'm a coward." His sigh is steeped in remorse. "My greatest fear is failing Sydney, but I've been using that as an excuse to shut everyone out. If nobody could get to me, they couldn't see the broken man I've become. But you've never shamed me, Harper. Even when I deserved it."

My pause is drawn out to give me a second to recover. I shift to cradle his scruffy jaw. "You're an incredible father. It's a natural role for you. I don't think it's possible for you to fail."

Moisture collects in his gaze while he chokes down an audible gulp. "I'll never regret having that little girl. Not for a second. But you know what I do regret?"

"What's that?"

"Not fighting for you."

I sniff, blinking against the sudden burn in my eyes. "Is there room in here for me?" My palm covers his left pec.

Jake rests his hand over mine where I can feel his

heart beating an erratic rhythm. "It's yours, but you have to share with Syd. And any other babies we're blessed with."

My lungs seize and I barely manage to wheeze an exhale. "What?"

His chuckle cracks into the heavy context we're treading in. "Keep pretending you haven't thought about us having kids. It's endearing as fuck."

"I'm just shocked to hear you admit it," I counter.

He dips to brush our lips together in a chaste kiss. "I'll admit a lot more than that."

My breath catches at the devotion shining from his eyes. He could never hide his true feelings from reflecting there. More than ever, I see how much he genuinely cares about me. "Make love to me. Please."

"Are you sure?" The fire in his eyes could blister my skin.

"Positive."

"Do you understand what you're agreeing to?"

"Um, yeah. Even if you hadn't clarified the fine print, it's kinda hard not to. Pun intended." I buck my hips, sliding his dick against me.

Jake grunts while repeating the motion. "Once we cross this line, you're mine. There's no going back."

"Gonna ruin me for all others?"

He snorts. "I did that years ago."

"How Jerky Jacob of you." But my smile betrays any false upset.

"And serious. Especially about you, and us doing this." He buries his face into my neck, his breath hot and hungry on the sensitive flesh there. "I need you."

"You have me, for always." I roll my pelvis upward,

shivering when his cock brushes my clit. "Make me yours."

Jake shifts to align his dick with my center. Just when his tip nudges my entrance, he stills. "I won't wear a condom."

"You won't?" To be honest, I hadn't considered the topic of protection until he mentioned it.

He clenches his jaw. "I really don't want to. No, fuck that. I won't."

His brash demand might come across as an ultimatum, but I choose to hear it as the opposite. There shouldn't be anything separating us. Not now or ever. We have to experience our love without barriers. Our souls will be stripped bare while our bodies finally join.

He mistakes my silence for concern. "I've waited too damn long to get in this pussy. Once I finally do, there won't be a rubber cock-blocking me. Nothing will sheathe me other than you. If you're not ready for that, we can hold off until my pullout method rivals the Duke's. Unless you're on the pill or we figure out an alternative contraceptive. It'll drive me mad to stop right now, but this is important to me."

I snag onto a specific piece of his speech. "Did you really include a Bridgerton reference?"

"That man deserves mention."

"Um, okay. Anyways," I sing. "You don't have to do the Duke. We're good to go without."

"You're sure?"

"Yes, but I'm beginning to think you're not. It's giving me a complex." I lightly spank his ass.

"Can't have that," Jake laughs.

The gritty note brushes our chests together. I moan

when my pebbled nipples rub along his sculpted pecs. My locket seems to vibrate from our shared attachment. It's a signal that he must feel too.

He presses closer while pushing into me. His entry is gentle, allowing me to feel the stretch of his cock against my inner muscles. I'm slick and ready for him, but he's extremely blessed in the penis department. A whimper trips from my parted lips as I wiggle to adjust.

Jake inhales my gasp with a kiss. "You're gonna take all of me like a good girl, aren't you?"

"Yes," I moan.

His choice in phrasing makes me want to please him. The very center of my being accepts him like the perfect fit he is. All of our shared pain and suffering and grief vanish with each stroke. He retreats an inch or two before sinking in further. The shallow motions are a tender exchange as our bodies unite completely. Once he's fully seated inside of me, we exhale in harmony.

That's when "H.O.L.Y." by Florida Georgia Line begins playing. I'd almost forgotten that the music was still on, too consumed by the man above me. The moment to notice couldn't have been timed better.

"I remember this song," Jake rasps against my throat. "Sing for me, Pitch."

And I do. The emotional lyrics spill from my mouth as he thrusts into me. My mouth brushes his ear as I serenade him about our love that never fled or faded. His pace is synced with the heavy beat. Our joining might be slow, but pleasure is fast to ignite between us. My body reacts to his, a thirsty flower soaking in the stormy shower. The significance of us being together after years apart crashes over me. Heat pricks my gaze, but I don't look away from the unwavering adoration shining down on me.

Jake's eyes search mine with a frenzied intensity. He stops moving, but his dick is buried deep. "Am I hurting you?"

I'm quick to soothe his worry, sealing our lips together for a brief kiss. "Not anymore."

My meaning registers and the strain melts from his flexed composure. He swoops down to press his forehead against mine. "I'm so damn sorry, baby."

"You're forgiven," I whisper.

"I fucking miss you. When you're gone for a day or an hour—or shit, even a minute. It wrecks me, but I never want it to stop. Wanna know why?"

"Tell me."

"It means I love you. And you've made a believer outta me again." The spark in his voice strikes flint and erupts into flames over my flesh.

A spasm clenches my core to reveal what that confession does to me. "I love you too."

"Thank fuck for that, Pitch." Jake accentuates the sentiment with a sensual thrust. The forward glide drives him in from tip to hilt.

I arch into his steady rhythm. "Now deliver us to the stars."

"As you wish upon one."

"For our happily ever after," I finish.

With that encouragement, Jake's tempo increases. He searches for my hands and stretches our arms flat overhead. My fingers weave through his in a tight grip. Comfort surrounds us while the peak approaches. His hips surge into me with a need I sense thrashing throughout every molecule.

His passion rivals mine and we move as a combined unit to reach relief. I wrap my legs around his waist to grant us a deeper angle. Jake doesn't hesitate to stroke harder at the change in position. My eyes set a flame to spread within his. Tingles erupt as I quake in release. Our smooth movements become disjointed before he spills into me.

Labored breaths float in the humid air cocooning our afterglow. Music still plays in the background, but the blissful thrum in my ears drowns out the noise. Jake's damp skin sticks to mine as we struggle to recover. I'd be more than satisfied to stay like this until forced to move. That reminds me of his conviction while he insisted on carrying me. My weak laughter shakes us, disrupting the post-coital cuddle.

"What's funny?" He mumbles the curiosity into my hair.

"Not sure I can walk," I admit.

Jake perks up, propping himself above me. "Does that mean I did you dirty enough, Pitch?"

I squish my lips to one side, pretending to evaluate his performance. "Maybe, but we should do it again just to be sure I'm thoroughly done for."

chapter twenty-four

Jake

AN UNFAMILIAR COMFORT ROUSES ME. THE PRESSURE against my cock is next to register through the groggy clutches. That cushioned friction stimulates me to shake off the remaining disorientation. I drape an arm over the warm body tucked tight against mine.

My face uses the delicate slope between Harper's neck and shoulder as a pillow. I drift my nose along the sensitive flesh. The unmistakable scent of ripe fantasies lingers there, eager to be plucked. A long inhale pulls our mutual desire deep inside to take root. We're together in this, which is the purest dream come true.

Harper hums in approval while snuggling closer. A sideways glance suggests that she's still mostly asleep. Her relaxed pose doesn't stiffen as awareness trickles in. The same goes for her slack features. It's as if she's drawn to me even when unconscious. The natural instinct clenches my heart.

I nuzzle against her like the whipped sap she makes me. This woman doesn't have a damn clue of how much I love her. That gives me pause. After last night, she could probably guess. But soon there won't be a tiny shred left for doubt.

"You're toasty," Harper mumbles. She stretches, effectively grinding my dick into her ass crack. "Oh, and very alert."

"If you haven't noticed, I'm constantly hard for you. Feel free to put me out of my misery." I grind into her, begging for mercy.

Her moan is a stroke to my insistent arousal. "I can't believe you're spooning me."

"Get used to it, Pitchy. I plan to wake up this way from this morning forward." My palm snakes under her shirt, trailing upward until I'm cupping a naked breast. "Especially if you don't wear a bra to bed."

She shivers against me and burrows into my embrace. "Are you for real?"

"Fuck yes. That was the most peaceful sleep I've had since childhood."

"Ah, you just want to use me for rest and relaxation."

"Don't forget wreckage and leisure." I thrust against her again.

Harper giggles. The throaty tune fondles my balls. "That's not quite right."

"I said what I meant to say."

"Well, someone is very clever before the sun even

rises. What time is it?" Drowsiness still clings to her voice.

"Early, but Syd—"

On cue, the door flies open and crashes into the wall. Harper shrieks in alarm, as if an armed robber is breaking in. Her fingers yank the blankets to her chin in a white-knuckle grip. She's visibly trembling while I don't so much as flinch from the expected intrusion.

"Rookie," I chuckle.

Her chest rises and falls with labored breaths. "What—?"

Sydney pops up at the foot of my bed, her eyes like saucers as she processes the very obvious addition to our normal routine. Nobody moves for several seconds. The silence is so dense that a mouse fart would be deafening. Then Glitzy leaps onto the mattress and shatters the momentary freeze.

"O. M. G." My daughter pauses for several seconds between each letter to add emphasis to her shock. "Daddy, did you marry Harper?"

That sneaky intuition earns a reaction from me. I choke on visions of the blonde beside me in a white gown. The snug rein I've kept on my imagination to avoid obsessing over Harper as my bride goes slack, allowing those fantasies to run wild. "No, Boop. We didn't get married."

Yet.

"Oh." Her shoulders slump. "You only had a sleepover?"

"Yep, we're still wearing our pajamas. Totally innocent." Harper's chirpy tune might as well point a guilty finger at our dirty deeds.

Sydney's expression brightens. "I'm in jammies too! Mine are Gabby's Dollhouse."

The theme song pops into my brain like a genius marketing scheme targeting the wrong audience. Or maybe that's on purpose, since I'm the one with a bank account. Regardless, it's embarrassing as fuck that I can recall every single episode.

I'm wrenched from the nonsensical deliberation when my reliable meddler twirls like the ballerina princess she is. We applaud her performance, and she rewards us with a cheeky grin. After a flawless launch, she dives into the tiny gap that Harper wedged between us during her startled maneuver.

My girls hug and cuddle as if this is a typical start to our day. Glitzy curls up beside them, refusing to be forgotten. When Syd taps Harper's nose, my heart soars straight to the ceiling. The significance and ease and completeness of this moment crashes over me. This is how we're meant to be, at long last. There have been more bumps in the road than I prefer to count, but that riddled path led us here. Together. I wouldn't change a damn thing.

Pressure builds behind my eyes when Sydney releases an expanded sigh. Through my blurry vision, it appears that her collection of troubles and worries just melted away. Harper notices, of course. Her gaze turns glassy as she embraces my daughter. I scrub at the moisture and mutter about dust under my breath.

Syd breaks their tightly knit contact to peer up at Harper. "Are you gonna be my mommy for real?"

"Oh, ummm..." Her unblinking stare shifts to plead with mine.

"Maybe." I wink at the woman who's stuck with us, knowing full well where that answer will land her. Seems fitting, seeing as she's already between my sheets.

My daughter squeaks in pure delight. "Does that mean you're gonna get married?"

An immediate confirmation burns on the tip of my tongue. I've pictured Harper as my wife since we first started dating. Probably even before that, when I was nothing more than a punk ass kid crushing on a girl way out of my league. She was smart to steer clear of me until I could appreciate her. Although, I still managed to fuck up. That didn't change the fact that I've only ever seen her as the one to walk down the aisle toward me. Nobody else would get me to bend on one knee.

"Someday soon," I offer as a compromise.

"Huh? Did you just…? How can you…? I mean, what?" Harper goes pale while struggling to form a sentence. "Are you really ready for that?"

"Heck yes. Where else do you see us going?"

She stammers on her disbelief. "I'm not sure."

"You are," I correct her.

Her gaze searches mine. "This is serious."

"Too fast?" It would hurt, but I could pump the brakes.

Relief fills my chest when she shakes her head. "No."

"Then we're on the same page. I'm ready to make you a permanent part of this family, but I won't rush you. Unless you want me to." I trail a bent knuckle down her arm. "Forget the one who got away. Nah,

Pitch. You're the one I let get away. I've been regretting it every single day since. There's not a chance you're straying from my side again."

"Wow, you're very…" Her statement tapers off on a breathy exhale.

"Impressive?"

Harper laughs. "Yes, that's a perfect fit."

"Like us," I rasp. "It just took a while to convince you to love me again."

She clasps her locket in a gentle grip. "That's what you think."

"What was that?"

"You heard me," she quips.

"It deserves to be repeated whether I did or not."

Her pupils dilate. "Domineering man."

"Always have been when it comes to you. The only difference is that I'm no longer afraid to claim what I want, Pitchy."

Syd silently digests our mutual conviction while gazing at her second favorite person. "I need a nickname for you."

Harper's focus lingers on me for another beat before lowering to her pint-size admirer. She smiles like a mega-million lotto winner. "I would love that."

My daughter gets lost in thought for a few seconds. "How about Harpy?"

"Harpy and Pitch," I muse. "Another perfect fit."

"Yep, I love it." Harper boops my daughter on the nose.

Syd lifts her bare feet in the air. "Harpy can help you find matching socks when the washing machine eats them."

A dry chuckle gets aimed at the tiny taskmaster. "I thought you didn't care if they match?"

She shrugs. "Whatever."

The flippant remark terrifies me for the teenage years to come. "Laundry has to wait, Boop. You have to get ready for school."

Her wobbly pout weakens my resolve. "Are you gonna have a tea party without me?"

"We'd never." Harper gasps as if the thought alone is offensive.

The dramatics appease Sydney, her grin rebounding broader than before. "But we can have one when I get home, m'kay?"

"I'll be at the studio waiting for you," Harper reminds.

"Yay! I get to dance tonight!" She springs to her feet and spins in erratic circles. Her twirls come to an unsteady halt. "Whoa-ahhhh. I'm dizzy."

I snort. "And full of energy. Good thing Spring Break starts tomorrow."

Harper lifts her brows. "On a Friday?"

"End of the trimester or something. I just follow the calendar."

"Uh-huh. I get like a thousand days off to play. It's awesome!" Syd bounces on the bed. "I'm gonna get dressed. Don't move a muscular."

Laughter spews from me in an unfiltered stream. "It's muscle."

"That's what I said!" She dashes from the room before I can try to correct her again.

Glitzy is quick to follow, the jingle on her collar signaling her retreat. Harper and I rest in the quiet lull the duo left behind. We have approximately three minutes alone—and not a second to waste.

I drift a palm along the space separating us, roaming until my hand is clutching the heat between her thighs. "Can you still feel me here?"

She yelps and arches into my touch. "What're you doing?"

"I can't stop thinking about my cum in your pussy." My insatiable appetite groans along the column of her throat. "There was so much that it spilled out."

"How did you see that?" Her voice trembles to match my hunger.

"Couldn't look away. Are you still sticky from me?"

"That's so dirty," she mumbles.

"Tell me."

"Yes."

"Fuuuuuck," I rumble. "Do you know what it does to me?"

Harper squirms. "The eight or nine inches against my hip are a hard hint to miss."

"Yeah, that's all yours. The thought of you covered in me satisfies a primal urge I didn't realize existed."

Her cheeks are flushed. "How do you switch roles that fast?"

My nose skates a path along her rosy skin, inhaling secret desires she desperately craves. "It's a gift."

"Makes my head spin." She slumps into me.

"You'll get better with practice," I inform before sucking on her bottom lip. "Tell me when I can fill you to the brim again."

Her gaze is unfocused. "Um, later?"

"That's not very specific." My fingers tease the lace concealing her arousal.

"I could come by on your lunch break."

"Yeah, you'll come all right." I tap above her clit. When her jaw unhinges to hang slack, I bump her chin. "Close your mouth or I'll give you something to gag on, good girl."

She snaps her lips shut with a smothered moan. "Good grief, you're addictive. My body gets a buzz off you. I'd ride you straight to Pound Town right now if—"

"I'm baaaaaack!" Syd reappears as if she never left.

I lurch upright against the headboard, forcing images of Blippi and Baby Shark into my lust-clouded brain. That strategy deflates my cock faster than an ice bath. Just thinking of the latter snuffs out any lingering heat. A shudder racks my limbs at the imaginary torture.

Meanwhile, Harper still appears under the influence. She's palming her forehead as if that will erase the visual I stamped there. It's a wasted effort, if I have any stakes in the game.

My daughter studies her dazed expression. "What's wrong, Harpy?"

"Uh, nothing. Just warm." She fans her face.

Syd races to her side of the bed. "Get out from under the covers."

Harper gasps when my little girl rips the blankets away. "Thanks, superstar. That's much better."

She beams under the praise. "I'm a super good helper."

"And very stylish. I love your outfit." Harper

appraises the clashing patterns as if mixing stripes, polka dots, and leopard is the latest trend.

"I'm really colorful." Sydney spins to give us the full picture.

"Just like your personality," Harper croons.

"Daddy just needs to fix my hair and I'll be ready." She produces an elastic band from thin air.

I stand and stretch, joints popping with the motions. My stride is lazy while I step into the adjoining bathroom. Sydney is hot on my heels, getting into position at the mirror.

"What would you like today, Boop?" My mind skitters through the limited options in preparation.

"A bun," she instructs.

"Excellent choice." I begin gathering her dark strands into my fist.

Harper hovers in the doorway. "Is it wacky hair day at school?"

Syd's nose wrinkles. "No, that was last week."

The teasing critic giggles. "Do you want a brush or comb?"

I rake over the bumps in a weak attempt to smooth my progress. "Nah, that just prolongs the inevitable."

"It's true," Syd agrees. "Daddy has a system."

"I can see that," Harper laughs again.

"My gracious child accepts my faults. Pigtails and twists are hard to grasp. Don't even get me started on braids." I struggle to tighten the tie while maintaining my grip. "Darn fingers are too big."

"You try your best. That's what matters." Her grin stretches wider with pride.

I didn't think my spirits could lift much higher

this morning, but she just proved me wrong. Warmth spreads through me at a rate that's almost staggering. A favorable sigh from our rapt audience pulls my attention to the right. Harper is using the wall for moral support. Her unwavering focus demands attention as I finish the task at hand. If she's not careful, neither of us will arrive at work on time.

"What's that look for?" My voice is gruff.

"You're just... daddying."

"Daddying?" I mull that explanation over. "Is that a verb?"

Her shoulder rises in a noncommittal shrug. "If it wasn't before, it is now."

"Can you use it in a sentence?"

Harper taps her lips. "Daddying was made for you."

I chuckle and scrub over my mouth. "You better remember this when I'm done daddying in about twenty minutes."

Sydney claps, yanking our concentration back where it belongs. She tugs on the lopsided bun to straighten it somewhat. "See? I look ah-mazing!"

Harper and I nod in unison as my daughter inspects her reflection. She's the one to speak. "Couldn't have done better if I tried."

I grunt. "No need to blow smoke up my rear."

Syd's features crease in a confused grimace. "Why would Harpy blow in your... where?"

"Never mind." I swat at the phrase better left unexplained. "Just adult talk."

She sticks out her tongue. "Boooooooring."

Harper is busy smothering a smile. "And you thought this would be complicated."

"Only if you hadn't agreed to be ours." Not just mine. I'm in a package deal with my daughter.

"Uh-huh." Her snarky brow calls me on my shit, as usual.

"I've learned from my mistakes."

Something sparkles in her gaze. "That reminds me, the three of us need to take a selfie."

That piques my little girl's interest. She's a huge fan of seeing herself on the screen. "For what?"

"An update." Harper opens her locket and taps on the empty side.

"Oh, oh!" Syd bounces on her toes. "We can take lotsa pictures at the resort. Right, Daddy?"

"Absolutely."

Harper glances between us. "The resort?"

"With the water slides by the Mall of America," Sydney explains.

"How fun. When are you going there?"

"We're going," I correct her. "Consider this your invitation to all events and activities from this point forward."

"Noted," she murmurs. "Did you already choose a date? I'll check my schedule."

"It's flexible, but sometime this week during Syd's break."

Her head bobs in acknowledgment. "I can be there."

"Yippppeeeee!" Sydney bolts toward her, crashing into her legs for a hug. "You're totally gonna be my real mom. I can feel it in my feelings."

My gaze sears this moment to memory. "Can't argue with that, huh?"

Harper sinks to her knees to return the embrace, not appearing bothered by the claim in the least. "Nope, I sure can't."

chapter twenty-five

Harper

S YDNEY TUGS ON MY ARM THE MOMENT WE ENTER THE hallway for the main entrance to the waterpark. "We gotta hurry, Harpy!"

I laugh but allow her to hustle me along. "It's not even ten o'clock yet. They won't let us in for another three minutes."

"But there might be a line. If we wanna get a table, we need to arrive early. You heard the lady." This girl is a stickler for instructions. She clung to every word the lobby clerk had to say.

"Your teachers at school must love you," I gush.

"Uh-huh, but you love me more." Syd pauses our brisk pace to wrap me in a quick hug.

I bend to rest my cheek on the top of her head. "That's right. You're my favorite, superstar."

"The other tiny dancers will be pleased to hear that," Jake mutters.

His daughter whirls to confront him, squishing a finger to her lips. "It's our secret, Daddy."

"Oh," he chuckles. "My mistake."

"You're forgiven." I toss him a saucy wink.

Jake wrenches open the glass door that separates the pool area from the hotel. "Ladies first."

A humid cloud billows out, smacking me with a sticky heat that immediately makes my skin clammy. I purposely brush against him while strutting inside. "Such a gentleman."

Sydney giggles next to me. "You fixed him, Harpy."

My flip-flops smack against the tile as we pass the concession stand. "I did?"

"Yep! He hasn't been grumpy or grouchy since you became his girlfriend. You make him super happy. Like super-duper."

The compliment makes me smile, but my title is what dominates her statement. It's the first time I've been referred to as Jake's girlfriend in an official sense. And I like it. A lot.

"Wow, that's really sweet." I peer at the imposing guy who's steering us toward the fun that lies ahead.

His gaze is hot on mine, cranking the steam setting to sweltering. "And very true."

Syd blows rapid-fire kisses at us. "Your love is my most favorite fairy tale. Even better than Beauty and the Beast. I can't wait for you to get married and have babies. Can I have a little sister right away? Maybe you'll have twins like Miss Rylee. That would be awesome."

"Oh, jeez." But my shock shifts in the next second.

I stumble to a stop as the massive spread of thrill and entertainment comes into full view. After researching the resort, I was curious as to how ten splash attractions could fit under one roof. One glance solves the mystery.

It's a challenge to take in the immensity of the place through my stupor. Sectioned pools spread across almost the entire room. Only a narrow path forms a perimeter around the edge. There's a surf simulator in the far corner. Four tube slides twist and carve through the wide space to demand attention. The wonder stretching before me is definitely worth the lofty ticket price. A soaked adventure awaits. We just need to dive in.

"Holy moly," I breathe.

"Look at all the stuff!" Sydney's excitement blasts over the noise echoing off the domed ceilings. "Wowww, that tower thingy is super huge!"

A knot lodges in my throat just glancing at the frightening height. "Um, yeah. That's definitely a sight to see."

Jake suddenly appears at my side to act as a sturdy presence. His fingers curl around my nape and he uses the gentle grip to pull me against him. "Don't panic, Pitch. I'll take her up there. Keep your feet on the ground where you feel safe."

"Thank you." I appreciate his consideration more than he probably realizes. My fear has gotten worse, bordering on a phobia.

His gaze shifts to Syd for a blink, finding her mesmerized by kids leaping across floating platforms. "But don't tell her you're scared, okay? I don't want her to adopt the behavior. She pretended to be allergic to cats for months after Polly said she was. It was a strange ordeal I'd prefer to avoid."

"I actually remember that. She asked if I had cats and seemed really concerned about my answer." My lips quirk at the memory.

"Yeah, exactly. She idolizes you. If you tell her you're scared of something, she's bound to copy the fear just to create a connection."

My heart warms at the magnitude of her adoration. "You think so?"

His bottomless gaze sears into mine. "She's more attached to you than the woman who birthed her."

"No," I deny.

"Yes."

"Why would she be?"

"You're here for her. Simple as that," he says.

"Is that okay?" I search his eyes for honesty.

Our surroundings fade momentarily as we get lost in each other. His timbre is pure gravel when he asks, "What do you think?"

A nod is the extent of my communication abilities for several seconds. "And I'd hate for Syd to mimic my weakness. It's nearly paralyzing if I reach a certain height. If necessary, I'll give her an excuse that doesn't involve being afraid."

He kisses my forehead. "You're incredible."

"And why is that?" I flutter my lashes at him. "Feel free to list the ways."

"Well, most importantly, you didn't put up much of a fight before saddling yourself to a bitter single father and a rowdy kid."

"Why would I? Syd is the best. You're not so bad either." A coy grin curves my lips, and I snuggle against him.

He tightens his hold on me. "Plenty would, not that I care about them. A child comes with a lot of responsibilities. You're making a sacrifice for us."

"I've never considered our relationship as such, and don't plan to. My life has new meaning and purpose thanks to you two." Gratitude blurs my vision and I blink against the sting.

"Fuuuu… *udge.*" He cuts off the end of the word after a quick glance confirms Syd is still within earshot. Jake stoops until his mouth brushes my ear. "I'm gonna worship you, Pitch."

"Only if I get to return the favor," I murmur into his stubbled jaw.

Sydney crashes into us, expanding our private embrace into a familial one. "What're we waiting for? I wanna swim!"

"Then let's go." He ushers her forward. "I spy an open table."

"Oh, oh! We better go get it." She looks one timely leap away from racing across the slick floor.

"Remember no running," I recite from the posted rules.

"I knowwww. It's slippery. The lady told me to walk super slow."

And that's what we do. Syd takes extra precaution and tiptoes. Chlorine wafts in pungent waves as we cover the distance to the table. Our careful steps bounce off the tiles and concrete but are quickly drowned out. People are piling in fast for a Monday morning.

"Can I play right there?" Sydney points to three fountains that spew in the shallow entry near us. "You're taking foreverrrrrrr."

Her father nods. "Go ahead, Boop. Just don't go too far."

"I won't," she calls while skipping in the low tide.

"Does she need a floatie?" Alarm is shrill in my tone.

Jake chuckles. "Nah, she's part mermaid. I enrolled her in swim lessons starting at eighteen months."

"Impressive," I muse.

A low rumble ripples from him. "Keep stroking my ego and I'll need to plunge straight into the deep end."

My belly swoops at the visual of him dripping. As a distraction, I whip off the plain cotton dress covering my suit. A choked grunt from the hulking temptation has me peeking over. His rapt focus is feasting on me and my exposed curves. That heated stare is a serious boost to my confidence. I roll my shoulders back, which thrusts my breasts out.

"What're you wearing?" The question is a barely restrained growl.

I glance down. "A bikini."

"It's more string than fabric," he complains.

"This is the—"

But my justification falls flat when he strips off his shirt. Lava floods my veins at the sculpted muscles he just casually tossed on display. His tattoos seem to glow under the sunlight streaming through the windows. Drool puddles in my mouth while I take my fill.

"See something you like?" His smug grin is far too satisfied with my slack-jaw ogling.

"We better cool off." I ditch my sandals in preparation.

Jake takes the hint a little too far. Before I can move, he has me hoisted over his shoulder and saunters into the pool. My squeak of outrage is swallowed by his splashing stride. Meanwhile, Syd is cheering him on while swimming laps around us. The water reaches me at mid-thigh when he sinks lower, slipping my body down the front of his. A moan nearly trips from my parted lips at the wet friction. I manage to slam my mouth shut to muffle the lusty sounds.

The cool temperature is a welcome relief. I plunge under the surface, relishing the chilly sensation sweeping over me. Tiny fingers pull at mine and I break from the depths with a sputter.

"Harpy, you gotta come up for air." Syd's chastising is too adorable to ignore.

A laugh tumbles from me while I wipe the moisture from my eyes. "I wasn't down there for long."

"It was like three hundred seconds," she insists.

"Did you count for me?"

Her expression scrunches. "No. Why would I do that?"

"To see how long I can hold my breath."

"I have a different method we could try later," Jake mumbles too quietly for his daughter to hear.

My throat tightens at the dizzying thought. A feverish spike in temperature encourages me to submerge myself again. Instead, I make the error of meeting his stare.

He has his arms crossed, drawing attention to his flexed biceps. This man consumes my concentration by just standing still. Movement in my peripheral confirms that I'm not alone in this trance. I realize my oversight in believing this would be a relaxing day at the pool. At least six women in our direct vicinity are openly giving him thorough thrice-overs.

One is bolder, swinging her slender hips to make

waves as she inches closer. She reminds me of a shark after catching the scent of fresh meat. I'm going to dunk her head underwater if she keeps staring at my man. That aggressive thought gives me pause. Damn, when did I get so possessive? Jake must be rubbing off on me again.

"Someone is in the mood to snack on a daddy," I mutter.

"Huh?" He's oblivious, his gaze shifting from me to Syd at regular intervals.

His daughter doesn't share that trait. The intuitive kiddo studies Jake's horny admirers with a knowing squint. She points directly at a lurking trio. "Daddy, do you know those girls?"

He doesn't spare them a glance. "No."

Before we could attempt to silence her, she turns to confront the harlots. "Why're you looking at my daddy? You're strangers."

The women recoil, but their shock is quickly replaced by matching sneers. Mama bear mode surges through my veins. I glare at them, just waiting for so much as a peep against her. Turns out my protective instincts aren't required in this instance.

Syd isn't satisfied with their silence. "Stop staring at him. It's rude. My daddy is gonna marry Harpy. Then she's gonna be my new mom."

I roll my lips between my teeth to stifle a giggle. It probably isn't wise to encourage her, but Jake's smirk shines with fatherly pride. On the sly, I sneak a palm out toward her. She slaps hers down and the resulting splash feels like an achievement.

Once the hussies slink off to trap their next prey,

Sydney's mood instantly brightens. "Can we take our selfie now? Those ladies won't bother us again."

I'm still trying to smother my amusement, but the effort is futile. Laughter bubbles out in a loud stream. "After that territorial performance, we can do whatever you want."

chapter twenty-six

Jake

HARPER FLINGS OPEN THE FRONT DOOR BEFORE I CAN slip the key into the deadbolt. "Welcome home!"

Sydney gasps before rushing at her. "O. M. G. Harpy! You're at our house to greet us. This is the best surprise ever!"

My girlfriend—who will be upgraded to a more significant title soon—squats to accept her hug. "Where else would I be?"

Glitzy darts out to leap at them, never one to be excluded. Her beloved master gives her a scratch behind microscopic ears buried in fluff. The three of them paint a portrait meant to hang above the mantle. It's a scene I'd stare at with gratitude every single night.

The fluff puff yips and barks before disappearing the way she came. With her gone, Sydney refocuses on the woman crouched beside her.

"Daddy said you'd be working until waaaaay after I went to bed and I wouldn't get to see you again until morning. I was super sad. But you're here. Yay!" Syd skips inside, twirling circles across the entryway.

Harper straightens and graces me with a shy grin. "Hey, JJ."

I cinch an arm around her waist and yank until she's flush against me. My mouth crashes onto hers in the next breath. The obsessive infatuation I'm forced to smother while we're apart pours from me. Her fist clings to my shirt, hungry for more. When I pull away, her expression is dazed.

"Missed you," I exhale against her lips.

She trembles in my hold. "Missed you too."

My nose drifts along the bridge of hers. "What's JJ stand for tonight?"

Her palm rests over the spot where my heart thumps a feverish rhythm. "Just Jake. The best version, and the one who claimed me again."

"Good answer." I kiss her cheek. "Why aren't you at Roosters? I was going to come get you."

"Garrett let me leave early. It was pretty slow. Ginger gave me a ride."

"And you chose to be dropped off here?"

"I did." She munches on her bottom lip. "Is that okay?"

My thumb tugs the abused flesh from between her teeth, soothing the bite with a gentle caress. "I always want you at our house. Consider it yours."

"Not sure I'm quite there yet, but…"

"But?" I prod after her pause drags through miles of mud.

Harper stares at me from under heavy-lidded eyes. "Maybe soon."

"Maybe will lead you right where I want you to go."

A giddy squeal interrupts us. "What. Is. This?"

Harper's features light up when Syd's exclamation hits us. She pulls me down the hallway at a fast clip. "Come on. I'm shocked it took her this long to notice."

We arrive at the living room to find my daughter frozen in front of a crooked structure that's featured in every child's dream. I stare at the draped blankets purposefully arranged in the center of the room. Love for this woman spreads over me like warm honey, sticking us together for eternity. A dry chuckle rasps from me. I'm fucking sappy in this gooey state.

My astonishment whirls on Harper. "You made this?"

She nods. "I did. Thought it might be fun to snuggle in for a movie night. Do you like it, superstar?"

Syd and Glitzy run laps around the fabric exterior. "Is this a palace 'cause I'm a princess? I don't have a castle of my own yet. Does it come with a crown or throne or fire-breathing dragon? But maybe that's for the king and queen to figure out. Where do I sit?"

I can only laugh at her energetic ramblings. "Harper built you a fort."

"A fort?" Syd slaps an open palm to her cheek as stunned silence whistles from her gaping lips. "I've always wanted a fort!"

That has me reviewing years of memories, only to find nothing relevant. "You have?"

"Uh-huh."

I remove my hat, only to flip it backward. "Why didn't you tell me?"

"Didn't know I wanted one until right now in this very moment." Spoken like the true princess she claims to be.

I grunt without an ounce of malice. "Oh, I see."

Her head begins to bob rapidly. "I was wrong about Harpy at the front door being the best surprise ever. This"—she thrusts her arms forward—"is the bestest surprise ever."

"Really?" Harper is clutching her hands to her chest.

Sydney doesn't hesitate to run toward her. "Thank you, thank you, thank you!"

The brilliant blonde sways from the enthusiastic onslaught. "You're very welcome. I'm glad you're excited."

"Like sooooo super-duper! Does this mean you're gonna move in forever? I don't ever want you to leave."

"If your daddy gets his way," she replies with a lifted brow at me. "How's my car doing, JJ?"

I rock on my heels at the sudden change of topic. "Fine."

"Is it fixed yet?"

"No."

She scoffs, but there's no masking her smile. "Why not?"

I rack my brain for a plausible excuse that won't make me sound like a deplorable asshole. "Do you know how to check the oil?"

Harper squints at my diversion. "It has something to do with a dipstick."

"Let me teach you how." There isn't a request in my statement.

"Then my car will be done?"

"Not even close."

She groans at the ceiling. "You're doing this on purpose."

"And if I am?"

"There's little I can do other than continue being dependent on you."

"Whatever keeps you in my bed until I get a ring on your finger."

Her eyes widen, but our audience is captivated elsewhere. "Relentless man."

"And you love me," I brag.

"I do." She doesn't sound the least bit upset about that fact.

"Yeah, Pitch. That wouldn't be too rough, huh? We're about to have a cozy evening." I jut my chin at the accommodations she created for us.

"Can I go in yet?" Syd points at the only visible point of entry.

Harper nods eagerly. "Of course. What movie should we—"

"Beauty and the Beast!" she blurts while diving into a pile of pillows.

"I assume that's an option?" My girlfriend raises a brow at me in question.

"As if there's another choice. I'll grab the remote. After you," I motion for Harper to join Syd in the fort.

After getting the television set to play, I switch off the lights and duck inside the draped blankets. Sydney had been staring adoringly at the new picture in Harper's locket. At my crawling entrance, they make space for me to get situated between them. Their warmth flanking me is a blessing I never knew I'd receive. It's one I don't deserve. That's precisely why I won't take a second for granted.

It takes about ten minutes for Syd to nod off. Harper follows soon after. Their deep breathing lulls me into an unfamiliar calm. Soon my arms are tingling from lack of circulation. A cramp begins to spasm in my lower back. There's an unsexy kink in my neck. But fuck, I've never been more comfortable.

After planting a kiss on each of their foreheads, I allow myself to doze off.

chapter twenty-seven

Jake

"And that sealed cap"—I bend Harper lower over the engine—"is where you add more washer fluid."

She shivers against me. "How much longer are you going to insist that this is an innocent lesson?"

My lips skate along the column of her throat until my teeth nibble on her earlobe. "What do you mean?"

"Puh-lease." She grinds into my cock that's hard as an exhaust pipe against her ass. "You're not fooling anyone."

I brace my hands on the header panel, caging her between the car and my insatiable thirst for her arousal. "Neither are you, Pitch."

"This was your idea."

And my restraint never stood a chance against her outfit. "Who wears a dress to learn about automotive mechanics?"

"Me, and let's be honest." Pride sings in Harper's voice as she spins in my boxed hold. "If you were serious about teaching me, we wouldn't be doing this in the middle of the night."

My palms drift along her bare legs. "I didn't want anyone to interrupt us."

"Ah, right. Fine-tuning a motor is very intimate."

"I love it when you talk shop to me," I rumble into the crook of her neck. "Do you want to know what I've been wondering?"

Her head tips back, granting me permission to explore. "Other than if I grasp the concept of proper fluid levels? I'd hate for the valves to burst."

My teeth nip at her sensitive skin. "What color are your panties, dirty girl?"

She trembles when my fingers skim along her inner thighs. "Who said I'm wearing any?"

Desire plunges into my bloodstream in a feverish rush. "Fuuuuuuck."

"Why don't you find out?"

"Thought you'd never ask," I groan.

My mouth descends onto hers in a feral swoop. Harper opens for me, allowing my tongue to clash with hers. My hands roam along smooth flesh until I'm cupping her naked ass. With a solid jerk, I have her hoisted into my unrelenting grasp. She cinches her legs tight around my waist while I blindly stride to the far corner. My lips swallow her moans as she rocks against me. Her wandering fingers knock the hat off my head, then sharp nails rake across my scalp. That bite of pain spurs the furious demands gnawing at me.

When my knees bump into a metal edge, I lower

Harper onto the flat surface. I'd prepared for this thanks to my newfound optimism and spread a clean cloth over the abrasive rubber mat. Her mouth slips from mine as she inspects the wide platform.

"Just keep that pretty ass parked right here, Pitch." I tap the space between her splayed thighs.

She glances down to study the scissor mechanism of the portable lift, and taps the top, testing its strength. "What does this... device do?"

"Think of it as a very expensive jack."

Her gaze gives the equipment another skeptical once-over. "And if I stay on it...?"

"I'm gonna raise you to my mouth. Once I'm done with my meal, I'll lower you to service this part of me." I nod at my cock that's already straining for release.

"Seems I'm already in the optimal position for that." And she's not wrong. Her face is currently aligned with my dick.

I swat at her reaching hands. "That's not on the menu."

Her lips pop open to form a small circle. "No?"

My head jerks in a sharp refusal. "You have your tools, and I have mine. Let me use this how I wish."

"I can't argue with that." Harper wiggles and shifts to test her seat. "Is it sturdy?"

"Damn well better be. Do you trust me?"

"Yes, but this thing is a stranger to me."

I massage her calves to ease any nerves. "The brake lock setting is meant to hold a vehicle steady while aloft. If the gears were to fail, I'd be crushed under the weight. It's safe to say I trust this bad boy with my life."

"That earns a seal of approval from me," she murmurs.

"You're ready?"

Her fingers grip the frame, and she nods. I crank the lever to engage the hydraulic pump. A low hum cracks into the silence as the lift raises her to my desired height. The ascent is smooth without a hitch. Harper's calm expression doesn't waver as the platform stills again.

"Relax for me." With a gentle nudge to her cleavage, I encourage her to lie down.

She flops flat onto the makeshift bed and stretches out like a starfish. "Eat me for a midnight snack, JJ."

"I plan to." In a seamless maneuver, I flip the skirt of her dress up to expose her naked pussy. The fact that I'll devour her on a platter meant for my other passion is intoxicating. "But first, I want to tease your limits."

She props herself onto an unstable elbow. "How do you plan to do that?"

My stare implores hers, sharing the fantasy that's been playing on repeat since the pool. "Hold your breath."

Her chest heaves with a quiet gasp. A seductive flush races along her skin in a burst of scarlet. The blatant desire collects into a fierce bloom on her cheeks. "Why?"

"I'll lick your clit until you exhale." My terms waft along her needy slit.

"A rule of your own? This feels like payback." Yet her squirming hips suggest she doesn't mind.

"Call it whatever you want. I control the guidelines. Will you comply?"

"Yes."

I lean forward until her sweet aroma floods my nostrils. "Tell me when you're prepared."

"Now."

When she sucks in a deep breath, I stiffen my tongue to taste her. A single swipe through her slick center coats my mouth in tangy honey. I groan while burying my lips in her arousal. The flavor of my addiction nearly staggers me.

Harper quakes, but is shockingly still otherwise. My pace is sluggish on purpose. I give her twenty seconds at the maximum. The pulse from her swollen clit matches the beat against my temples. Her hands begin to pound on the metal to keep count.

After longer than I predicted, Harper sputters for oxygen. "Holy shit, Jake."

"Yes?" I groan into her pussy, not quite ready to be done.

"That was intense," she sighs.

It takes every ounce of willpower I possess to pull myself away before she gushes down my throat. "In a good way?"

She's nodding fast. "I've never been so turned on, but couldn't concentrate on my orgasm while trying not to breathe."

My thumbs trace circles on her inner thighs. "Damn, baby. I didn't mean to torture you."

"Then lower this bitch down and feed me your dick." Her feet shove at my shoulders, as if sending me to my knees will satisfy her.

"My girl is hungry," I utter while grasping the lever.

"Starving," she corrects while bucking against nothing but empty space.

Within moments, the lift delivers her straight to my filthy intentions. I free my cock, giving the length a languid stroke. Harper whimpers as I make her wait.

One step has my tip aligned at her entrance. Her warmth commands me to push inside. The slick friction stimulates my arousal with a jolt. I clench my teeth while stroking in and out. My thrusts are shallow as I coax her snug resistance to greet me properly. Harper sighs when I'm fully sheathed in her depths. Pleasure surges into my veins and makes my head spin.

I begin a measured tempo, latching my fingers onto her bent legs for stability. "Have I told you that I'm obsessed with sliding into your pussy bare?"

"Yes, but tell me again." Her voice is wanton, a fierce appetite to be sated.

"Fuck, baby. I can't even describe the comfort that fills me."

"Try," she urges.

"This"—I plunge into her with a savage entry—"tells me you're really mine. That claims we belong to each other. It's like I'm home after too many hours away."

Her whine is laced with approval. "Ohhhh, that's romantic."

A snarl escapes from my clamped jaw. "The beast can only be soothed when you're wrapped around me."

Harper smiles, the expression dreamy. It still rattles me that this woman deems me worthy of such a gift. "There's my savage lover."

That reaction prods at my primal instincts that only she awakens. I use my grip on her thighs to slam forward at a punishing force. She squeals, immediately rolling her hips for more. The silent demand lashes at my spine to chase our mutual relief. My movements are hers to steer. Through parted lips, she begs for me to get us there quicker. Harper's muttered nonsense is a siren song that only I can decipher.

"Yeah, Pitch. Let me hear you." I thrust faster while she continues babbling.

My muscles bunch while I work us into a frenzy. The furious motions don't so much as rattle a hinge beneath her. I couldn't have chosen a better platform for fucking. Her tits bounce to the erratic rhythm. That's when I realize she's still hidden from view.

"Are you attached to this dress?" I toy with the hem bunched around her waist.

"Not really, but—"

Before she can finish the sentence, I wrench the fastened material apart. Buttons scatter across the concrete floor. Then I'm able to feast on the vision spread in front of me. Raw arousal rushes through me and I grunt at the heated assault.

"No bra either?" My fingers tweak her pebbled nipples.

She gasps and arches into my rough treatment. "I wanted to make this easy for you."

"You knew I wouldn't be able to control myself." It isn't a question.

"Yes, yes, yes," she chants.

"And you can't get enough of me either."

Harper thrashes on the covered surface. "No, never."

Harsh bellows shout in my ears. The deafening noise demands that I finish us off. On cue, her inner muscles become an unforgiving vise around me. I surge to fulfill her body's desperation. My dick swells, demanding a reprieve that will be granted once she receives hers.

"Drench me with your desire, baby."

She shatters in the next instant, and her spasms trigger my release. Prickles creep along my flesh as I surrender. With a final thrust, I spill inside of her. We crash together as blinding pleasure rewards our efforts. My cock is still nestled in her warmth as ripples race through me.

I blink to clear my distorted vision. "How was that?"

"Better than ever," she mumbles.

"We take customer satisfaction very seriously at Evans Auto Body."

"I believe you," she exhales to the rafters.

"Just one more question, Pitch."

Harper's head lolls on the lift. "Mhmm?"

"Would you like a complimentary donut to go with your orgasmic bliss?"

chapter twenty-eight

Harper

SUSAN LINGERS IN THE ENTRYWAY WHILE ASSESSING Polly's hair. "That style is quite… unique."

"Sydney's daddy did it all by himself. He didn't ask for help." The little girl dips her head to proudly show off Jake's efforts.

The woman shifts her gaze to the guy responsible for her daughter's quad ponytail mess. "You got creative with the design."

He smirks at the slanted compliment. "Do what I can."

She offers a gentle smile in return. "Thanks again for letting Polly spend the night."

I brush off her seventh scoop of gratitude. "Don't mention it. Syd has stayed at your place every other weekend for years, right?"

"Something like that," she agrees with a laugh.

"Jake was long overdue to take a turn. I was available to run interference. We were more than happy to finally return the favor."

Susan's grin spreads. "And I'm very glad you two are dating again."

"A bit more serious than that," Jake rumbles while edging closer to me.

"Ah, I see." The town gossip gets a twinkle in her eye. Maybe that was the purpose of my boyfriend's clarification. "Either way, our suspicions are confirmed."

Bingo.

"I had the superest-duperest time!" Syd exclaims and wraps her friend in a hug. "Will you come over again really soon?"

"Uh-huh. Like tomorrow?" Polly pulls from the embrace to clasp her palms in a pleading gesture.

"Yay! My daddy always says that's right around the corner. It's not far away!" Sydney squeals. The girls join hands and begin spinning in a premature celebration.

"We'll talk about it," Susan deflects. "For now, it's time to go."

After a final round of waves, she steers her daughter outside to end our long-winded Minnesota goodbye.

"Can I go play with Glitzy?" Syd's blink is slow. She looks ready for a nap and it's only nine o'clock.

"Go right ahead. Looks like a fun activity you can do together." Jake nods at the pampered pooch snoozing on the couch.

"Welp." I brush off my palms. "Our first official kiddo sleepover was a success."

He loops an arm around my shoulder, pulling me in until his lips land on my forehead. "Thanks to you."

"Pssssh." I swat his chest. "Don't give me too much credit. Your tea party and wacky salon were the true scene stealers."

"We make an excellent team," he says in response.

"The bestest," I gush.

Just as we're striding to the hall, a timid knock stalls our progress and calls us back. Jake peers at the door with a furrow creasing his brow. "Maybe they forgot something."

He turns the knob, a grumpy comment already parting his lips. But whatever he planned to say manifests as a foul curse. I'm not left to wonder why for long.

The breath whisks from my lungs at the sight of the visitor on the porch. Jake attempts to block the doorway, hiding her from view, but it's too late. Time sputters to a stop as I stare at the woman who has the power to rip my fairytale to shreds. It feels like my legs buckle, but I'm frozen solid.

Morgan.

"So," she clips. "It's true."

"That you haven't been by to see your daughter in over four months?" Jake's glare is nothing short of menacing as he prepares to face off against her. His wide stance and crossed arms aren't meant to be trifled with.

"Yikes." I wince at the restrained anger rippling off his flexed muscles.

Her huff is misplaced. "It hasn't been that long."

He flips his hat backward to give her the full force of his frustration. "Not sure on the exact amount, seeing as I quit keeping track. Didn't find it necessary."

She flinches but recovers quickly. "I've been busy."

"Same here." He makes a circular gesture to indicate

his house before hitching a thumb in my general direction. "You're causing a disruption."

With a heavy heart, I recognize that honor belongs to me. My expression falls as they continue flinging snide remarks. An unmistakable presence clings to my legs and shakes me from the sorrow.

Syd has tucked herself behind me. She peeks at her mother with what resembles fear. But that can't be right.

I spin and sink to my knees. Our eyes meet, a silent understanding passing between us. The pressure in my chest is crushing. "Why don't you say hello to your mom?"

She shakes her head. "I don't wanna."

"But she's here to see you," I insist.

Sydney glances between her mother and me. The conflict pinches her brows together. My stomach plummets at the sight. I had every intention of standing my ground until this moment. But the last thing I'd ever want is to put her in a difficult position where she might suffer. I'll make the decision easier, especially since it isn't a choice at all.

"There's plenty you need to tell your mommy. You two can chat while I get some work done."

"But it's the weekend." Her intuitive nature and clever wit don't fail to notice my slip.

"That just means I'll be extra prepared." My mood takes a nosedive when her bottom lip wobbles.

She sniffles. "You're not gonna leave forever, right?"

I cup her cheek. My resolve weakens when she leans into my touch. "Of course not, superstar. You'll see me soon."

"Like when?" Her firm tone demands that I stay put.

It's becoming more challenging to hold back my upset. The pain urges me to curl inward—cold and empty. "When you're done hanging out with your mom."

"But I don't wanna go with her," Syd wails.

"You don't have to," Jake assures her from his unrelenting post guarding the door.

Morgan makes no attempt to argue. The silence that follows is tense, crackling against my skin. This situation is suddenly too familiar, stitching past and present in harsh clarity. It's enough to prick my eyes with unshed tears.

I stand, tapping Sydney's nose. "Don't forget that I love you, okay?"

She flings her arms around my waist. "Love you, Harpy."

My retreat forces her to release me. The hurt spears down to my marrow as she starts to cry, but makes no move to seek comfort from her parents. I don't trust my voice while shuffling toward Jake. His grip snags my elbow before I can cross the threshold.

"Pitch—"

I gulp at the sharp lump in my throat. "No, it's okay. I should go to avoid more complications."

"Damn that word to hell." He clenches his eyes shut.

"You need to be alone with your family right now. I'm sure there's stuff you need to discuss."

His hand clasps mine, threading our fingers together. "That involves you."

"Later," I murmur.

"This isn't right," he grinds out.

I squeeze his palm that's pressed to mine, then drop

the connection. "Maybe we're better off as wrong after all."

"Fuck that," he spits under his breath.

But Jake relents and gives me the space to leave that I'm practically begging for. I don't spare Morgan a glance while brushing past her. The battle against my tears fails, sending hot streaks pouring down my face. A hiccupped sob escapes. I slap a palm over my mouth to muffle the noise. The fact that I don't have a car to drive off in a blaze of misery somehow makes this scene more pitiful.

Footsteps approach as I kick gravel across the shop's lot. My stride doesn't falter at the unknown interloper. If they want to speak, maybe I'll listen. The voice that carries along the breeze calls me a liar when I slam to an abrupt halt.

"Harper, can we talk?"

chapter twenty-nine

Harper

I STARE AT MORGAN FROM ACROSS THE TABLE AT BEAN ME UP. The usual comfort that surrounds me in my favorite coffee shop is noticeably absent. As my focus bounces between her and my neglected latte, I wonder who will speak first.

She clears her throat, satisfying my curiosity. "I'm relieved to see the rumors are true."

A sour gurgle turns in my stomach. My experience with this woman and reliable gossip has a terrible track record. I can only imagine what the town blabbers will spread just from seeing the two of us together. "And why is that?"

"Several reasons." Morgan drums her nails on the wooden ledge. "First, I'm tired of playing the villain in this story."

I bristle at the accusation. "Who said you were?"

"Me," she states simply.

"Okay…?"

Her exhale is thick. "Each day I fail my daughter makes me feel like a horrible person. Considering that's been the vast majority of the past six years, I've been pretty low most of the time."

It would seem there are several solutions to that problem, but I'm sure she's aware of that. The responses rattling in my brain fall short. Rather than offer hollow platitudes, I settle lower into my chair as a sign that I'm listening.

Morgan smiles, but the expression is brittle. "I'm riddled with guilt, but maybe I don't have to be anymore."

My mind whirls as I try to calculate the equation she's scribbling. Her meaning could veer off in several different directions. Whatever challenges lie ahead, we can find a solution.

At my extended silence, she rolls our stilted exchange onward. "I was young when Sydney was born."

"So was Jake," I counter.

"It's not a surprise that you'd come to his rescue. I've caught the way you stare at him." Her smile is too coy for my preference.

I flatten my lips into a hard line as defenses rise with a clatter. "What does that have to do with Sydney?"

"How you care about both of them is important to me, for the sake of my sanity."

A dull throb pulses at my temples. "Please don't tell me you used my history with Jake as an excuse to leave Syd."

Morgan scoffs. "Hardly, but I thought he'd be eager to fill the gap. Not that we had a romantic relationship for him to rebound from. It just seemed that he would realize his mistake in letting you go to begin with. Why did it take you this long to get back together?"

I drag in a slow breath while deciding how much to reveal. The scent of rich coffee calms my jitters. "Jake wasn't interested until recently."

She pins me with a flat stare. "I find that hard to believe. He never got over you, Harper."

"Well, that's reassuring. I've been pining for him just the same."

"But you only recently started dating again." There's no question in her tone. Even while living two states away, she's connected to the latest Knox Creek updates.

"It was more like he didn't want Sydney to feel neglected," I amend.

"By giving her a real mother she can rely on," Morgan deadpans.

That response makes me pause. My heartbeat launches off at a gallop. "Is that how you see me?"

She averts her gaze, finding a random spot to stare at over my shoulder. "Jake took to his fatherly role without hesitation. I didn't accept parenthood like that. Maybe it makes me a shitty human, but being a mother wasn't a natural instinct for me."

"I've heard that's fairly common. Don't be too hard on yourself."

"That's what I originally told myself too. If only those impulses kicked in eventually. I can't explain this... defect in my system, but I'm not sure that's necessary anymore. Some people just aren't cut out to be parents." Morgan gestures to herself.

Fear of saying the wrong thing clamps a vise around

my vocal cords. This is another slippery slope I'll more than likely tumble down. But maybe she just needs me to hear her side and remove some weight off her chest in the process. That appears to be the correct course of action based on her relieved sigh.

"It's physically painful to feel detached while holding your baby. I talked to a slew of doctors and therapists. Their answers didn't fix the void. It didn't take much for me to acknowledge that this isn't a temporary illness with a cure. When a mother is away from her child, she should miss them." Morgan sucks in an uneven breath. "Don't assume the worst of me. I do miss Sydney. I think about her often and hope she's doing well. But my concern is fleeting. It's not the vital extreme an absent parent should harbor. A big part of me believes that I've been able to separate myself because she's in very capable hands."

I probably resemble a statue, but the mention of Jake yanks a response from me. "Have you talked to him about this?"

She sucks air between her teeth. "That's a negative. He's not very… supportive when it comes to me."

"But this explains your lack of involvement," I reason.

"Would it matter? Jake is fully capable of parenting Sydney on his own."

"But your daughter…" I trail off before causing offense.

"Is fine without me," Morgan finishes.

"He's an incredible father," I choose as a safe reply. This entire discussion is very foreign territory.

She exhales while moisture gleams in her eyes. "I'm so relieved, Harper."

"So am I," I admit.

Her eyebrow quirks. "Did you see this conversation going differently?"

"Um, yeah. To be honest, I figured you hated me."

Morgan's laughter eases the tension needling me. "That's hilarious. If anything, I admire you."

I nearly topple off my chair. "How is that possible?"

Her hand rests on top of mine. "I'm also grateful for you."

Heat springs to my eyes faster than I can blink. "Why?"

"You're doing what I can't. I'll never be mother material, but you proved to be exactly what she needs in the five minutes I witnessed. It comes naturally to you, just like it's meant to be."

I sniff at the burn in my nose. "Do you really mean that?"

She nods, resolute. "That's why I feel justified in my decision."

"Which is?"

Morgan's posture straightens. "To step away. Permanently."

I gape at her, not certain the message came across correctly. "Is this something you've really—"

"Yes," she confirms before I can finish. "If I stayed, I would only cause more damage. Sydney doesn't deserve that."

My flinch can't be contained. "You're sure that's what you want?"

Her frustration at my disbelief bleeds through when she tosses her hands up. "It doesn't matter if it's what I want. What's best for Sydney is the priority."

"That's very selfless," I commend.

She swipes at a stray tear. "Maybe, or I'm finally getting an out that I can accept. I never deserved her, and I've been such a disappointment."

"But you're still her mother."

"Am I?" Her pause is brief. "I might've given birth to Sydney, but it's obvious you're meant to raise her."

I glance at the ceiling to keep my own tears from leaking. "Wow, that's... just wow. I'm not trying to be insensitive, but this is hard for me to digest."

"You're good." Morgan's grin is calm, but resigned. "I'm not meant to be a mother, but you are. Will you take care of her for me?"

My lips tuck between my teeth to stop trembling. "I could never replace you."

"I'm not asking you to. Just be there for Sydney like I can't." Her stare is a plea I'm not capable of refusing. "It shouldn't be hard. She's already claimed you as hers, which makes me happier than you probably realize."

"You're just planning to vanish without letting Syd know?" My tone is stricken even to my own ears.

"If I tell her I'm leaving for good, she'll just be more confused. It's better if I just disappear. Then it's on you to love her the way I'm unable to."

"No pressure," I blubber.

"None whatsoever, but could you do me a favor?" Morgan passes me an envelope across the table. "Give this to her once she's old enough to understand."

I accept the task without hesitation. "Of course."

"Maybe she'll have a few fond memories of me. Or maybe not. Either way, she's going to have you always." She slides another envelope across the space between us.

"This one is for Jake. I've signed the required documents to relinquish my parental rights."

"Oh, gosh. This is official." A strangled noise rips from me while I nod repeatedly. "I'll do everything in my power to honor you and your wishes."

"That's all I ask." She stands, the motion steeped in finality.

I leap to my feet. "Can I hug you?"

Morgan collapses against me, the fight draining from her limbs. "Thank you, Harper. Please take care of them."

"I promise."

And then she's gone, never to return again.

My knees buckle and I fold onto the chair. Sensations overwhelm me. All that's left to do is hang my head, bury my face in a cupped palm, and let the tears spill over.

chapter thirty

Jake

FORCE MY GAZE FROM THE BRICK BUILDING AS SOUNDLESS expletives demand progress. In response, my boots pummel the concrete in a valiant attempt to carve a path. We've been camped across the street, waiting for… what exactly remains a mystery. The important factor is that Harper is inside talking to Morgan. It's the unknown that's taking a sledgehammer to my composure.

"What's taking so long?" Syd's impatience mirrors mine. "We've been stomping on the sidewalk foreverrrrr."

"They're probably almost—" My assumption cuts in half when I spot Morgan fleeing Bean Me Up.

"There goes my old mommy." Syd's whisper is swept away by a gust.

I hold steady to let my daughter decide our next

move. She grabs my hand, looks both ways, and yanks me into action. My extended stride covers the ground, but I'm no match for her haste. There's still a choice to be made when we reach the opposite curb. For a brief moment, I'm not certain what direction she'll choose. But I should've learned by now not to doubt her authority.

Sydney tugs at the heavy door. "C'mon, Daddy!"

We storm into the coffee shop, leaving the past to eat our dust. My daughter doesn't appear concerned about Morgan in the least. Her only worry revolves around the woman currently racked with sobs, hunched over a table across the room.

Upon hearing the chaotic whirlwind that accompanies our approach, Harper lifts her tear-streaked face. The sight of her swollen eyes guts me. I'm not alone in that sucker punch either.

Sydney gasps and rushes into her open arms. "Why're you crying, Harpy?"

She nuzzles her wet cheek into my daughter's shoulder. "I'm just... draining my pain and doubt."

"Do you mean in a sink?" Syd's features twist as she tries to comprehend the explanation. "Your nose and eyeballs are dripping. I guess you could be a faucet."

Harper laughs, but the sound is a pitiful rasp. "You're very clever, superstar. It's just..." She draws in a shallow breath. "I can't believe this is real."

My tolerance for the guessing game snaps along with my clenched jaw. "What did she say to upset you?"

"Nothing—"

"Baloney," I spit. "There's no reason to protect her, Pitch."

Harper wobbles to her feet. I reach out to grip her elbow for support. Shock slaps me when she rips herself from my grasp.

"Don't speak ill of her." She stabs a finger into my chest with a brute force that doesn't belong in her arsenal while in such a mournful state. "Morgan isn't our enemy."

I recoil at her defensive actions. My mouth works silently, chewing on this unexpected turn. Confusion swirls even if I redact my personal bias from the record. "Countless empty promises and years of witnessing my daughter's disappointment suggest otherwise."

"Be that as it may, she isn't a villain. She's a mother, but never truly felt like one. Morgan is the bravest woman I've ever met." Harper's chin quivers and fresh tears pool in her eyes.

I'm stunned still again. "You've lost me."

"Her selflessness is"—she flails a hand while searching for a proper term—"courageous and inspiring and wonderful."

My pulse thumps faster as the ground seems to shift. "What the heck did I miss?"

"There's something you need to see." Harper lifts an envelope from the table. "She left this for you."

I rip open the sealed tab without further instructions. My eyes scan over the fine print, not digesting much more than our names and personal information, until the bold purpose of the document finally registers. "What…?"

Harper is already nodding. "She granted full custody to you."

"To us," I correct.

Her lips tremble. "That's another process entirely."

I drift a palm down her arm to interlock our fingers. "Which we'll begin when you're ready."

"Okay, but that's not all." Harper points at a single piece in the stack.

Behind the legal paperwork, there's a letter. I read the words with the respect they deserve. Morgan outlines her decision, telling me to ask Harper if I need more details. "Why didn't she tell me sooner?"

"That's a question to ask yourself," she murmurs.

"I never gave her a chance." Which hurts more than I'd prefer to admit.

Harper leans into me, rubbing the ache spreading through my chest. "We'll do right by her."

My head rests against hers as I absorb our fresh outlook. A broken edge that's kept me jaded and bitter suddenly crumbles into nonexistence. What remains is free to move forward without restraint.

"I owe her an apology." The crack in my voice echoes the sentiment.

"She might appreciate that." Her grin is warm, an encouragement I'll have at my side from this day forward.

Sydney tugs on Harper's shirt, done watching plans unfold beyond her knowledge. "What're you guys talking about?"

She crouches to my daughter's level. Her hand trembles as she cups Syd's cheek. "Your mommy loves you very much, superstar. That's why she had to leave.

Her love is so big that she chose to share it with me and your dad. Then we can love you even more since she can't be here with you."

"My old mommy isn't ever gonna visit again?" Her tone is soft and unsure.

"That's right, Syd. I'm sure it's hard to understand, but I'll do my best to explain whenever you have questions. Your daddy will too." Harper looping us as a cohesive unit soothes any lingering scars.

Sydney crumples against her. "You're never gonna leave me, right?"

"Never." Conviction clangs in her voice.

Which pumps relief into me that's so profound I feel my legs shake. I sink to the floor and gather my girls in a hug. Heat burns my eyes, but I don't hide the joy from leaking down my face. Our bond solidifies without uttering another sound. We huddle together for several minutes before Syd pulls away.

Her gaze shifts between us. "Does this mean Harpy is part of our family, like for real?"

"For real," I confirm.

She stares at Harper with sheer wonder glittering in her eyes. "Are you gonna move in with us?"

The woman responsible for expanding our duo into a trio offers a playful grin. "Maybe."

My mouth brushes her temple. "I like that answer."

She winks. "Maybe you'll show me how much later."

"By saving the corner pieces for you?" Syd chirps.

Harper's brow furrows. "What corner pieces?"

"The super cute little triangles in the corners on a pizza." Exasperation huffs from the little diva.

"He does?" Her request for clarification is aimed at Sydney, but Harper's focus is solely on me.

My chuckle is smoother than I've ever heard. "I know they're your favorite part. Guess you haven't noticed."

"Must've been too busy dreaming of this." Harper makes a circular gesture around our linked embrace.

Warmth thrums through me at the perfect response. "You're forgiven."

She tightens her hold while swaying us. The rocking motion flows naturally from her, like many other comforting instincts. "Should we go home?"

A rumble rolls off my chest. "Yeah, Pitch. That's music to my ears."

Her hum is the melody that my fantasies feed on. "Been waiting for me to ask?"

"Mostly to accept our house as yours."

Harper sighs. The sound can only be described as content. "Well, as it turns out, my heart and soul already live there."

chapter thirty-one

Harper

JOY GLANCES FROM ONE WALL TO THE OTHER. THE VISUAL sweep is slow, as if she can't believe her eyes. Her skeptical behavior isn't misplaced. Roosters has been transformed into a pastel paradise fit for the occasion.

"Let me get this straight." My friend peeks at Baby Belle cradled in my arms. "We're having an Easter celebration in the bar?"

I nod, all too eager to provide confirmation. "It was my idea. The egg hunt starts in an hour."

She snorts. "Of that, I have no doubt."

"We have to compete with Bent Pedal somehow." The upscale establishment has been making us look like slackers for long enough. Their nonstop festivities are about to get competition.

"Uh-huh, right. And you managed to convince Jerky Jacob to make an appearance as the Easter Bunny."

"Yes, that's correct. Although, to be fair, he isn't that jerky these days." Not to me at least. Except when I place a special request between the sheets.

Joy whistles. "Wow, your hoo-hoo-ca-choo must have Coors Light on tap. I bet you're a sex kitten in the sack. Maybe you can give me some pointers on improving my blowjob form. Then we can get Cole to be Santa Claus this Christmas."

I nudge her with a soft bump, trying not to disrupt the snoozing infant in my hold. "Will you hush? There are children present."

"Which is entirely your fault."

"It would be a very different event if kids weren't involved." Which could be an interesting concept to explore for our adult patrons once the youngsters are tucked into bed.

She gives me a sideways squint. "Aren't you worried that Syd will recognize her father pretending to be a beloved holiday figure? That could traumatize and scar her for life."

I huff off the concern, beginning a bouncy rhythm when Belle fusses. "Already took care of that. We told her the real Easter Bunny can't be in multiple places at once. Her dad has the honor of filling in for him. Also, the headpiece thingy included with the costume conceals the person's identity."

"Ah, not just a dynamite lay." Joy taps my temple. "You've got big brains in there."

"The whole package right here." With some clever maneuvering, I gesture down the length of my body.

"Oh, my stars. This child is brilliant." My mother appears beside me with Sydney flanking her.

"Hi, Mommy." Syd freezes after delivering the greeting, waiting for my reaction to the title.

It's difficult to breathe for a moment, but I attempt to act nonchalant for her benefit. This is only the second time she's referred to me as Mommy and I don't want to discourage her progression. There's no hiding the mist gathering in my eyes, though.

I blink against the hot sting. "Hey, superstar. Are you having fun?"

She beams at me while snuggling into my mother. "Uh-huh. Lots and lots. Grandma is gonna take me to a super huge toy store."

"Spoiling her already?" I tease my mom.

"This little cutie is quite a smooth talker," she breathes.

"Just like her daddy." I lift my chin at the large bunny who just entered the scene.

"O. M. G." Sydney enunciates each letter with extra pizzazz. "It's the Easter Bunny!" She takes off in his direction as if she believes he's the real deal.

"Great actress," Joy muses.

"Runs in the family." My tone is laced with humor while I watch the shenanigans begin.

Kids quickly swarm him. Jake appeases the crowd like a professional entertainer, pausing for photos and high-fives. The noise level escalates as he weaves through the room. His basket is full of themed goodies to pass out, which he manages to do with the fuzzy gloves on.

"He's never going to live this down," Joy cackles.

I join in her amusement. "Absolutely not."

"We should probably make this an annual tradition."

"You better hope my hoo-hoo-ca-choo pours Coors Light for that tall order."

"Check those tap lines, Harps. Give the man what he wants."

"In that case, I better buy more leggings and leotards." Heat crawls through me just thinking about peeling the tight fabric off while he watches.

"Oh, gosh. Please don't tell me you've done the deed at the studio." Joy hangs her head when my lips remain sealed. "Too much information."

A laugh spews from me. "I didn't say anything."

"Precisely." She shudders. "Anywho, are you ready for the recital?"

"Nice transition," I quip.

"You can thank me later for ditching my maternity leave to assist." She blows me a kiss.

"Have I told you lately that you're the bestest business partner ever?" I snuggle against her, smooching Belle in the process. "Pee-yew, somebody has a stinky butt."

"It isn't me." Syd reappears out of thin air. I've come to realize it's one of her many talents. As is decorating herself from head to toe in the span of two minutes.

"Did you get enough stuff?" My gaze moves in a downward sweep beginning at her bunny headband, a bubble wand necklace, several snap bracelets, window clings stuck to her legs, and ending at the cupcake toppers she's tucked into her shoelaces.

She shrugs. "I didn't wanna take too much."

Meanwhile, Joy hefts a diaper bag over her shoulder and scoops Belle from my grip. "Fingers crossed she didn't blow out."

"Where are you going?" I call as she heads toward the hallway alcove.

"To the changing station."

"What changing station?"

"You've got to be kidding me." Joy whirls to seek out her brother in the throng. "Garrett, I need to speak with you about a poopy situation."

He jogs over, his face covered in egg stickers. "What's up?"

Syd's jaw drops with a gasp. "Where'd you get the stickers?"

"From the Easter Bunny," he replies.

"No fair! He didn't give me any." Her voice is shrill in outrage as she darts back in Jake's direction.

Joy taps her brother on the shoulder. "Excuse me. What's this about you not having a diaper changing station in the bathroom?"

Garrett looks like a lifelong bachelor caught in a positive paternity test nightmare. "Uh, we don't get many babies in here."

"Never hurts to be prepared," she snips.

"That's true," he hedges.

"Should I change your niece on the dirty floor?"

He winces. "I guess so."

"Unbelievable," Joy mutters. "If we weren't related, I'd leave the poopy diaper in your office."

Garrett gags. "Please don't."

After they've wandered off, I catch a white figure approaching in my peripheral. I turn to greet the good sport with a wide grin. My stomach flips into giddy cartwheels at the fact he agreed to play the part for us.

"I don't believe we've been properly introduced." Jake's voice is muffled inside the headpiece.

"Well, hello." I walk my fingers up his fluffy chest. "Has anyone told you that you're a very attractive bunny?"

"If they did, I wasn't listening. I'm a very happily attached bunny." He slaps a sticker over the area covering my left breast, patting several times for good measure.

When I glance down to read the bold text, a giggle escapes me. "Some bunny loves me. How original."

"And don't you forget it." He sticks one on the other boob to match.

"Branded by the Easter Bunny. That sounds like the opening lines of a very inappropriate story." I bite my thumbnail while giving his costume a thorough once-over.

"Careful, Pitch. It's almost impossible to see in this thing, but I'm not blind." The growly edge in his voice unfurls heat in my lower belly. "Have I mentioned what the sight of you holding a baby does to me?"

My lashes flutter with mock innocence. "No."

"It fills me with a barbaric urge to get you round with my child."

"That's quite a development." I get dizzy as the visual flips an instinctual switch inside of me.

"Only a matter of time until you let me."

I rise onto the balls of my feet to reach the mesh window near his mouth. "Make sure to find me when you're done bunnying and daddying and you're ready to do me dirty."

"The way you tease me, woman." Jake bumps me

with his hips. "And for the record, that's not a carrot in my pocket."

"Should I take a bite just to be sure?"

"If you lick me long enough, you'll get to the cream filling."

"Oh, my." I flutter a palm to my chest, feigning a scandal. "Is there a certain amount that it takes?"

"Mommy!"

"Holy shiitake mushrooms!" I leap straight into the air, yelping when Sydney suctions herself to my hip. "Didn't see you there, superstar."

"Do you want a sucker?" She produces a lollipop from seemingly nowhere.

"Uh, thanks." I accept the proffered treat.

"You can find out how many licks it takes to reach the center."

My face flames. "Why would I need to know that?"

Syd rolls her eyes. "You asked Daddy how many it takes."

I slap a palm to my roasting cheek. "Oh, no."

Jake's chuckle rumbles from under the protection that masks his humiliation. "Rookie move, Pitch. You'll get better with practice."

chapter thirty-two

Harper

STRONG ARMS CINCH AROUND ME FROM BEHIND. I LEAN against the comforting wall of muscle, a sigh wheezing from me. "Where have you been?"

"In the audience. You're the one who assigned my seat," Jake murmurs into the crook of my neck.

I roll my eyes. "Before that."

"Had something I've been meaning to finish." He shifts his hold to show me the bandage on his forearm.

"A tattoo?" I can't recall what design is underneath. Come to think of it, he often distracts me whenever I've wanted to get a closer look at that section.

Jake peels the protective layer away. Even cast in shadows, the fresh ink is clearly visible. My jaw slowly unhinges as the significance settles in.

"Is that a harp?" I grab him by the wrist and yank the skin closer.

He chuckles. "We both know it's not just a harp."

"And it says…" Shock steals the rest of my response.

His lips brush my ear. "Pluck my strings and sing for me, Pitchy."

"You did this for me?" My tone is a whisper-shout, still aware of the tiny dancers performing mere feet away.

"I did."

"But this part looks older." My nail traces the first half of the phrase.

"It is."

"From when?" I hover my fingers over the entire area, wise enough not to actually touch him.

He blows out a heavy exhale. "What was meant to be our one-year anniversary. It's always been you for me, baby."

I sway into his warmth. "Oh, JJ. You swoon me so very good."

Jake presses a kiss on my cheek. "I already have the next design planned."

"Oh?" My stare is still locked on the tattoo.

With a bent knuckle, he lifts my chin until our eyes connect. "The day you exchange your last name for mine. I can't fucking wait to have you officially join the Evans tribe."

My knees wobble and I slump against him. "Oh."

"Yeah, you're with me now." He rubs his thumb along my bottom lip.

"Hey, heyyyy! We're done practicing." Sydney twirls onto the scene in her frilly costume. Her spin moves come to a stop at her father's side. "It's almost time."

Jake bobs his head, lowering a flat palm for her to smack. "We've got this."

That's when Joy struts on stage to make the next announcement. "Excellent job, Daffodils. And our final performance for the Barre Twirl spring recital is our partner dance featuring the Dandelion and Peony squads."

"That's our cue." Jake holds his bent arm out for Sydney to accept while rowdy cheers welcome them.

"We're totally gonna win." She bends into a plie, then grips his elbow.

"It's not a competition," I remind as they skip off to their designated spot.

"That'll just encourage them." Joy laughs as she takes her position beside me in the shadowed wing.

Music streams from the speakers, setting the group in motion. Every duo demands attention, but it's difficult to force my gaze away from a certain pair. I watch them with unshed tears blurring my vision.

The routine is flawless, just as planned. These kids and their trusted adults worked hard to nail the steps. Their dedication radiates under the spotlights. It's over all too soon, the last chords fading into silence. The auditorium bursts with deafening applause. I'm clapping while mentally preparing my closing speech. This has been a night to remember for always.

My thoughts are interrupted when Jake saunters to the front of the stage. There's a microphone in his grip, which instantly sets off internal alarm bells. He flips his hat backward with purpose. The captivating action is almost comical considering he's wearing it at the recital to begin with. A hush follows as we wait for him to speak.

"He's going rogue," I mumble.

"Good luck with that." Joy checks me with her hip.

"Would the lovely Harper Wilson please join us out here?" Jake turns toward me, crooking his finger to hurry my stunned progress along.

Before I can move, every dancer from our studio rushes to fill the illuminated space. My pulse hammers an unsteady beat as I erase the distance separating us. Once I'm in reach, he laces our fingers together and lifts our clasped hands. "Let's hear it for this woman and her company for putting on quite a show."

The crowd goes wild, matching the erratic possibilities my mind is conjuring. I silently mouth my appreciation to everyone in attendance. Jake cuts into the celebration by clearing his throat.

"There's a question I need to ask."

The crowd gasps as he lowers to one knee. He digs in his jacket pocket, producing a small box that shreds any lingering doubt. When he flips open the lid, I almost tip over. Sparkles flood my vision in a blinding streak. Once the splotches clear, the sight waiting for me steals my breath.

Nestled in the crushed velvet is the most beautiful ring I've ever seen—cliché as that might be. Dark and light gems blend into a swirling pattern along the band. The visual impact is mesmerizing. A large diamond is perched in the center, connecting the opposing colors.

"I got creative with the design," Jake murmurs. His words are just for me now, the mic off and discarded.

My eyes burn, a lone tear escaping to cascade down my cheek. "It's gorgeous."

"Fit to make a statement for the woman who I hope will wear it." The grin he wears threatens to derail my focus.

"And what might that be?" I hiccup a breath while more happiness leaks down my face.

"The clash symbolizes us." He inhales until his broad chest expands from the force. "I'm the storm to your sunshine. You're the smile to my scowl. We balance each other, baby."

Sniffles meet his romantic explanation. "We do."

"Love can creep under the radar undetected. That's not the case for me with you. I've loved you since I had the temporary privilege of calling you mine. That might be hard to believe, but this broody grump has always been yours."

"At least you're finally able to admit it," I tease.

"I'm a changed man thanks to you. And now, I hope you'll be willing to permanently tie yourself to me." He takes my left hand in his, gently kissing the bare skin on my third finger. "Would you do me the honor of becoming my wife?"

My watery stare anchors on him, seeing our future bright in his gaze. Tears stream down my face in hot rivulets. I'm nodding, my throat too tight to squeak out a peep.

"Sing it for me, Pitch."

"Yes! Yes, yes yes," I chant.

Jake manages to slide the platinum band over my

knuckle before I collapse in his arms. I smother his face in kisses, landing one on his lips. The crowd goes wild with whistles and applause, but I pay no attention to them. I'm perfectly suspended in this moment. It's just me and the man I've loved for so long.

And then Sydney dives into our tangle of limbs. It's a shock she waited this long. We loop together as a tight-knit unit, never to be broken.

"Mommy, I have one for you too." She breaks from our hold to show me her gift. In her grip is a thin silver band, decorated with our names and ballet slippers. "It matches mine!"

"It's perfect, superstar." I'm a blubbering mess as she puts the symbolic token on my right ring finger.

"In case you couldn't tell, she said yes to us," Jake yells into the microphone.

Syd immediately snatches it from his grip. "They're gonna get married and give me like seven little sisters."

I might be crying, but the biggest smile recorded in history is stretched across my mouth. "What would've happened if I said no?"

Jake scoffs. "You couldn't deny us if you tried, Pitchy. We might be wrong every now and then, but in the end, we'll always be right."

epilogue

Jake

BLINDLY SEARCH FOR THE DISCARDED BOTTLE WHILE TONGUING Harper's clit. She squeals when I latch on, clamping her swollen nub between my teeth. The suction I add only heightens her screams.

When I find purchase on the hot fudge, my solid grip squirts a generous amount down her slit. Harper gasps at the slick sensation. I smile into the slippery topping that coats her arousal. That shocked reaction she gives me is the same with each pour. My feasting doesn't waver either as I begin my third serving.

The sweet sauce floods my mouth, momentarily drowning the addictive flavor I truly crave. Her tangy spice quickly overpowers the artificial sugar, much to my pleasure. A groan rips from me as I devour the taste of her need for me. I grind into the sheets in a desperate attempt to relieve the strain in my cock. Just one more and I'll sink deep into her.

I lick her with fast strokes, pulling away just enough to speak. "Your pussy is a delicacy on its own, but this combination is fucking exquisite."

Harper's grip on my hair tightens to shove my face tighter against her wanton core. "Keep eating. I'm close."

"Shit, my wife is hungry for me tonight." More than normal, not that I'm complaining.

She rocks her hips in silent prodding. "Ravenous. I need to come. Do it for me."

I slow my pace on purpose, earning a whimper for the tease. "Ask nicely."

"Please make me come. Please, please, please." The chant sounds like it was wrenched from her heaving chest.

And I'm a man determined to please his woman. My tongue lashes at her clit as I slide two fingers deep into her warmth. A clench from her inner muscles is quick to greet me, spurring my motions to begin pumping. I curl my digits to reach that hidden spot. Harper trembles when I find it, begging me for more.

Pure instinct drives me to comply. My lust is fueled by hers. The connection thrums in my veins until I can feel the moment she's teetering. With a final swipe, she shatters in my mouth. Her release replaces any trace of chocolate. I rumble in gratitude while slurping every drop she gives me. Once the last quake flees her system, I rise to kneel on the mattress. A demanding ache spreads from my dick at the sight of her legs spread for me.

Harper props herself upright, although her elbow is unsteady. Her fingers open and shut in a beckoning gesture for the bottle. When I don't immediately pass the sauce over, she swipes it from my grip.

"Damn, Pitch. If you want to slob my knob, you could've just told me. He's all yours." I thrust my hips forward in permission.

She rolls her eyes but doesn't bother smoldering a wide grin. "It's my turn to do a big reveal."

Without further explanation, she uncaps the hot fudge and starts painting her stomach. I stare while she makes a plus sign followed by a diagonal dash and finishing with a minus symbol. She peeks at me to make sure I'm following along. When I nod, Harper draws a circle around the plus marking.

I blink at the sloppy doodle for several seconds before a wishful thought pops into my brain. "Whoa, wait. Are you...?"

"Am I what?" She rolls her wrist, urging me to answer.

My throat is suddenly dry. "Pregnant?"

"Yes!"

What happens next is a blur. While heat brims in my eyes, I collapse on top of her. I pepper Harper with kisses, collect her tears, and the sugary mess sticks our bodies together. She giggles and lifts her thighs to cradle mine. My palm wedges between us to rest against her flat belly.

"You're gonna have my baby?"

"Yeah, you knocked me up real good. The test couldn't have been more clear."

"But we barely started trying," I murmur against her wet cheek.

She loops her arms around me for a hug. "Once can do the trick."

I rest my forehead against hers, nuzzling our noses like the sap I've become. *"How did I get this lucky?"*

Harper cups my jaw in a shaky palm. The love shining in her gaze reflects my own. *"We didn't let the struggles defeat us."*

"And we never will."

That's technically the end, but I have a bit more from Jake and Harper that you can read free! Get the additional scenes here.

Rhodes and Rylee—the owners of Bent Pedal—have their own book. *Mine For Yours* is a total standalone and available now. Enjoy this snippet from the first chapter.

Air whistles from between my clenched teeth. "I'm interested in hearing your plans."

She sputters out a sigh. "I honestly planned to just stop by and say hello. That's why I let him tag along."

I follow her meaningful glance to the corner, where Gage has moved on from the puzzle and is now building a tower of blocks. "And yet, you're ready to show me the door."

Her lips twitch. "Only after recent developments."

"This phase is temporary." Not sure who I'm trying to convince.

Rylee's bottomless stare renders me immobile. "His dreams don't have to die with him."

The sucker punch lands a direct hit to my gut. I narrow my eyes while wrestling with the accusations ready to be flung at her. "That's a shitty thing to say. I'm allowed to grieve in my own way."

She glares at the ceiling, her mouth forming silent words. Maybe to ask forgiveness—or for patience. "You are. I would never claim otherwise."

"Sure about that?"

"Yes," she snaps. "I didn't come here to strike low blows. Besides, this shouldn't be a battle."

"Something we can agree on."

"I'm not trying to cause problems for you," she continues.

"Try harder," I grunt.

It looks like she's biting her tongue. "Shutting the bar down isn't fair to his memory."

"Good thing that's not what I'm doing."

"Fine, whatever." She blows out a loud exhale. "Just let me share this burden with you."

I'd be more willing to cooperate if she quit jabbing at me. "Why did I think this would be a pleasant negotiation?"

Rylee presses her mouth into a firm line. "There's nothing to negotiate. Just let me take the lead. You can return to other investments that I'm sure take greater priority. We both win."

Stubborn pride flexes my muscles. "That's not happening. I'll maintain my role in this business."

"And that is…?"

"Owner, and a very involved one at that. I don't just sit back and let others decide how my money should be spent."

The slight curl in her upper lip suggests she wants to argue. "These principles extend to every pot your hand is dipped in?"

"Yes," I clip.

"Great. Glad to have you on the team." She wipes fake sweat from her brow. "But if it's all right with you, I'd like to fulfill Trevor's wishes."

"Which are?"

Her smile wobbles at the edges. "To keep this place running in his absence."

I yank at the loosened tie that's suddenly too tight around my neck. "Dammit, I can't fault you for that."

"Exactly." She sounds far too smug under the circumstances. But any positive boost in our situation is a win.

I recall a minor detail Trevor once told me. "Don't you live on the east coast? Minnesota is a long way from home."

"We actually moved to this 'tiny town beyond the 'burbs' a few weeks ago." Her brows lift as she recites my description from earlier. "I'm from this area originally, and always planned to return at some point. This is just sooner and far more tragic than anticipated."

Not to mention barely the beginning.

"Well, I guess this makes us partners." I extend my hand in a peace offering.

She nods while sliding her palm into mine for a quick shake. "Afraid you're stuck with me, honey."

Unlike her implication, I allow the endearment to bounce right off. "Should we seal the deal with a toast?"

"Looks like you started celebrating without me." Her gaze flicks to behind me where two glasses rest on the wood bar. "Were you expecting company?"

Both are neglected, untouched, and sweating into the coasters. Why I bothered making them on the rocks is beyond me. I didn't have the nerve to take a sip.

An odd tightness cinches around my lungs. The tradition has become second nature and I'd completely forgotten about it. Just one more pitfall this bar has carved into me. "Nah, I pour an extra for Trevor."

"Oh." Her eyes shimmer, reflecting the emotion I cough to hide. She lifts a trembling palm to her lips as a single tear trickles down her cheek. "That's very sweet."

"Or pathetic." I scoff at my own coping mechanisms that have formed lately. "His death has taken a toll on me. Not sure why."

But deep down, underneath the denial, I could find the truth. I'm just not at that stage yet.

Rylee shuffles forward until we're close enough to touch. "You guys were friends."

I cross my arms. "So what? I have plenty of those."

"Don't do the detached macho act. Not after that." She lifts her chin to the sentimental whiskey beside mine.

Discomfort churns in my stomach. This isn't an easy topic. Trevor might be gone, but I haven't forgotten. I'm suddenly trapped under the weight of it all. This is too strange.

"Maybe I should go. These walls are too damn loud." Which is the main reason I've kept others out.

"Do you mind if we stay?" She motions from Gage to herself.

"Knock yourself out." I lean over the counter for a spare set of keys stashed by the register. "It's your place now, right? Just lock up when you're done."

Continue reading *Mine For Yours* now

Want more single parent romances from me? I have several for you to fall for.

Here's a piece from **Ask Me Why**—a single (extra broody) dad, enemies-to-lovers romance.

I check the clock again. Thirty minutes until close. I can survive that long. If only a customer or two would come in and take my mind off food.

As if hearing my silent plea, the door swings open. The bell calls out, and a familiar little figure zooms inside. I peer around the display case that's obstructing my view. Ollie sends me a beaming smile and my hunger pains are instantly forgotten.

Oh, this kid is going to break so many hearts when he's older.

"Hi, Miss Braelyn." Ollie strides up to me like we're the best of pals. Maybe we already are.

My depleted energy seems to spring back. I give him a wave. "Hey, Ollie. Glad to see you again."

"Sorry I'm late."

I shake my head. "Nonsense. You're right on time. Is Mary with you?"

His forehead creases. "Uh, no. She went home. We would've been here sooner, but my dad was working." Ollie hitches a small thumb over his shoulder.

That's when the door opens with a bang. A tall man stomps in with the power of a hurricane. Is the ground shaking? If it is, I barely notice.

Holy. Hotness.

Who ordered the sex in a suit?

The guy's laser focus is on the boy beside me so he doesn't notice my slack jaw. He's tall, but not overly bulky. His thick hair is styled in a messy sort of way, and I want to smooth the unruly flyaways. A five-o'clock shadow dusts his jaw, the first signs of stubble barely visible. The contrast between his light eyes and dark features is hypnotic. An impeccable suit covers his broad frame, cut to fit his wide shoulders and trim waist perfectly. He could easily sell this look. Hell, after one glance I'm ready to buy it off him.

He's fucking lickable.

"Ollie, I told you to wait. Selective listening isn't cute anymore. Why do you insist on running ahead of me?" The stranger's boom ricochets around us.

I blink, and the haze evaporates. What the actual eff was that? I look down at the child in question and wait for him to answer. He's squirming all about. Ollie barely gives his father a second glance, too busy studying the assortment of candy on display. But no worries. I'm giving this man more attention than he needs anyway. I can hardly take my peepers off him.

Ollie lingers for another beat, then quickly dashes to the taffy bins. I see him move from one to the next in my peripheral vision.

"Need a camera?"

I startle at the harsh growl. "Huh?"

"Then you can take a picture." His frosty blue eyes narrow on me, and I'm frozen in place.

"Excuse me?" Why is my voice so breathy?

"It'll last longer." He raises a dark brow.

Clarity seeps into my stupor, and the urge to tuck tail streaks through me. But I don't. I raise my chin and openly appraise him. "I like your suit."

"It's custom fit."

"Looks that way."

He crosses his arms and stands straighter. "You're not my type, taffy girl."

I fight the urge to scratch my temple, being stumped again. "Okay?"

"Stare all you want. It'll get you nowhere." He points between us. "Never gonna happen."

For a moment, all I can do is gape at him. I feel my face go up in flames. Is he for freaking real?

"I w-wasn't… no, I didn't mean," I sputter. "I'm not hitting on you."

His smirk is devilish. "Save it for the judge, sugar. I get it."

Before I can defend myself, Ollie zips toward us and smiles at me. "Do you like my dad?"

Everything inside of me skids to a stop. I pop my mouth open, but nothing comes out. My throat is a tight fist, and swallowing is a challenge. How the hell do I respond to that?

I tug at the collar of my shirt. "Uh, well, we haven't really met. I don't even know his name."

Ollie's gaze bounces between us. "He didn't tell you?"

"Nope." There's no hesitation. Throwing this cocky dick under the bus is an easy decision.

The ass glares at me. "We didn't get that far."

Ollie shakes a finger at his dad. "That's not polite. You're supposed to do introductions first. That's what you taught me."

He remains silent, thoroughly scolded by a child. Ollie huffs loudly. I lift a hand to cover my growing smile. Something tells me this imposing man wouldn't appreciate my humor.

"Brance Stone," he finally offers. A weaker woman might wither under that icy stare. Too bad for him, I'm all out of shits to give.

"It's a pleasure to meet you. I'm Braelyn Miller." I plaster on an extra wide grin for good measure.

A muscle jumps in his jaw. "Likewise."

Continue reading *Ask Me Why* now!

How about a single mama romance? **Loner** is definitely one you should take a peek at.

"Everyone deserves a chance to be rescued."

That's the mantra I'm repeating when a well-equipped biker pulls over to save me. One glance at the scowl Crawford Doxe is wearing proves he isn't impressed with the task. My efforts to change his mind deflate faster than the shredded tire at our feet. But disgruntled or not, my so-called hero still agrees to fix my flat.

I don't expect to see Crawford again, but he's suddenly very visible in our small town. Avoiding him would be my preference. That's not how this story goes. For whatever reason, my daughter finds an ally in the broody mechanic. Denying her is something I do my best to avoid. I can only hope Crawford's shine wears off before he tarnishes what little trust still exists.

As if the odds are ever on my side.

Commitments are a foreign concept to him. He doesn't make any promises to try. That should've been enough for me to steer clear. It most certainly isn't.

What follows can only be described as a disastrous clash of epic proportions.

But one indisputable fact remains. That lone soul has no plans of opening his heart.

Read Loner today!

And if you're in the mood for another swoony small town romance, check out Leave Him Loved!

"You're not from here."

That's one of the first things Reeve Colton says to me after I bump into him—quite literally.
Our meet-cute deserves a standing ovation, and has the potential to reach romantic proportions.
Heck, we're already causing all sorts of gossip in this small town.

If only our situation could be that simple.

See, I'm a city girl temporarily relocated to the middle of nowhere for a job.
This is an in-and-out gig that doesn't need to get more complicated.
After putting our undeniable chemistry on the shelf, Reeve agrees to help me get a lay of the land.
There's no harm in being friends, right?
Yeah, I've heard that before too. But I'm determined to keep our lines from blurring.

Too bad Reeve makes that task nearly impossible with his thoughtful never-ever outings.
Who knew country guys were so charming? Certainly not me.

One little kiss can't do much harm…

Read *Leave Him Loved* with Kindle Unlimited!

acknowledgements

Well, what did you think of *Wrong for You?* Fingers crossed you love this uplifting story as much as I do. I got heavily invested in this one. There's truly something special about their journey that struck me hard. It was a bumpy ride for Jake and Harper to find love, but the road to happily ever after was an incredible ride. These characters were such a blast to write, and I look forward to the next Knox Creek couple. Get ready for all the fun to come!

I want to start by thanking you—the wonderful person who chose to read Wrong for You. There are endless options when it comes to incredible romance novels, and the fact you picked mine from the bunch means more than I'll ever be able to describe. Please know how much I appreciate you.

Next, I need to give endless gratitude to my family. They push me to be the best version of myself. Thanks to my patient husband, I'm able to bury myself in the writing cave when a deadline creeps too close. My son and daughter provide me with hilarious content that I shameless plug into my books. The children in my stories are always heavily influenced by them, which is why they're the best. Right? I love you three to a galaxy far, far away.

If I seem like I have my ducks in a row, it's thanks to Renee. She's always there when I need her, not just for this author gig but as a friend. I'm truly blessed to have her at my side.

The lover of my life wife—Heather—encourages me to keep going when it would be easier to take a nap. She's my alpha queen. I couldn't do this job without her. She's my other half and I love her like a sister.

Thanks to Kate for always being great. No matter what, I can rely on her for kind words and a positive boost. She's a true friend and that type of dependability can't be replaced.

To K.K. for providing me with unconditional laughs and love and acceptance. She's a solid support that I can't go without. Her friendship never fails to light me up. Cheers to happiness!

A big hug to Shain for being there whenever I need a shove in the right direction. She knows just what to say to get a smile on my face.

Thanks to Kayla for being the captain of my hype squad. She's fantastic and knows how to make a girl feel special.

I'm extremely fortunate to have found so many genuine connections and relationships in this industry. There are many awesome ladies in my corner who I can count on to be there for me, and vice versa. They know who they are, and I hope they also know how grateful I am. That kind of reliable comfort is priceless. Thank you, thank you.

If you're not aware, Harloe's Hotties is the best group ever. I'm extremely biased, but join us and you'll see. These folks shower me with encouragement and love on a daily basis, which is irreplaceable in such a lonely career. They're my people and I appreciate each one of them. Thanks for being part of this crazy journey with me. Another toasty hug goes out to Harloe's Review Crew. The excitement in their posts and messages whenever I have a new release coming overflows my cup. I'm very grateful they love my words enough to stick around.

All the thanks to Candi Kane and her team at Candi Kane PR. Five years later and we'll still at it. She does it all, even when I don't understand how that's physically possible. Thanks for everything!

Thanks to Wander Aguiar and his team for capturing such a smoldering shot of Chris for the cover. I think we all agree that Jake is yummy, yes? And to Kris Duplantier for drawing and designing the special edition version. Her talent knows no bounds. I can't wait to see her soar!

There are so many vital individuals who assist in the writing and publishing process. Renee and Heather read as I write, keeping me on track. Thanks to Erica, Kayla, Patricia, and Keri for beta reading. Sending a huge thanks to Alex with Infinite Well for editing and polishing Wrong for You until the story sparkled. To Lacie and BB for proofing. A massive thanks to Stacey from Champagne Book Design. As always, she once again created the most stunning interior for my book baby. I cannot recommend her formatting services enough!

I need to give another huge round of thanks to all the readers, reviewers, bloggers, Bookstagrammers, BookTokers, and romance lovers out there. Because of you, authors like me get to continue writing and doing what we love. You're who we strive to reach, and aim to be better for. Thank you to infinity for continuing to be there for all of us!

And last but definitely not least, if you enjoyed Wrong for You and want to do me a huge favor, please consider leaving a review. It really helps others find my books. Thank you for reading!

about the author

Harloe Rae is a *USA Today* & Amazon Top 5 best-selling author. Her passion for writing and reading has taken on a whole new meaning. Each day is an unforgettable adventure.

She's a Minnesota gal with a serious addiction to romance. There's nothing quite like an epic happily ever after. When she's not buried in the writing cave, Harloe can be found hanging with her hubby and kiddos. If the weather permits, she loves being lakeside or out in the country with her horses.

Broody heroes are Harloe's favorite to write. Her romances are swoony and emotional with plenty of heat. All of her books are available on Amazon and Kindle Unlimited.

Stay in the know by subscribing to her newsletter at
bit.ly/HarloesList
Join her reader group, Harloe's Hotties, at
www.facebook.com/groups/harloehotties
Check out her site at www.harloerae.com

Follow her on:
BookBub: bit.ly/HarloeBB
Amazon: bit.ly/HarloeOnAmazon
Goodreads: http://bit.ly/HarloeOnGR
Facebook Page: Facebook.com/authorharloerae
Instagram: www.instagram.com/harloerae
TikTok: www.tiktok.com/@harloerae

Printed in Great Britain
by Amazon